MW00719078

Pra
LOVE ON THI

"William Torgerson does for movies what Nick Hornby did for music...

He writes with sincerity, clarity, and, most importantly, an antic sense of humor about the way men use and misuse the conventions of love in popular culture to connect and fail to connect with the women around them. This is a novel about life at a Nazarene college, about the joy and tedium of playing basketball, and about the smothering intimacy of frustrated college roommates, but it is, mostly, about the unbearable, unbelievable, unforgivable foolishness of sensitive boys better at loving the women they see on the big screen than the ones they see in front of them. Underneath the jokes, the nicknames, the ruminations on morality, the lovely descriptions of that love game, basketball, and the lyrical evocation of college campuses, *Love on the Big Screen* is a painful novel about the painful way boys learn to become men by learning to love and not love and to be loved and to not be loved by the women around them. This is a book to laugh with and to ponder and, mostly, to read carefully."

— Greg Downs, author of the collection *Spit Baths*,
winner of the *2006 Flannery O'Connor Award*

"...pursues truths about Hollywood's impact on the way we see the world..."

"Torgerson captures both the sincerity and the satire of everyday life on a Midwestern evangelical college campus. His characters are accessible and true. *Love on the Big Screen* pursues truths about Hollywood's impact on the way we see the world in a hilarious, compelling, and very honest way."

— Matt Litton, author of *The Mockingbird Parables*

Praise for
LOVE ON THE BIG SCREEN

"William Torgerson captures young-male-angst in all its poignancy, stupidity, doubt and ego-driven certainty, confusion, and tenderness."

"In *Love on the Big Screen*, through a relentless lens (read Hi-Def accuracy) William Torgerson captures young-male-angst in all its poignancy, stupidity, doubt and ego-driven certainty, confusion, and (most importantly) tenderness. We get stills and jump cuts. We get panorama and telescoping lens. Soft-focus. Close-ups. In the end we get a group of characters we both love and revile, in a story that demands our attention. Isn't that the human experience?"

— Steven Sherrill, author of *The Locktender's House,*
Visits From the Drowned Girl, and
The Minotaur Takes a Cigarette Break

"In the tradition of *Say Anything* and *High Fidelity.*"

"A wonderful coming of age romantic comedy in the tradition of *Say Anything* and *High Fidelity*. Bravo!"

—Lisa Kline, author of *Take Me*

Praise for
LOVE ON THE BIG SCREEN

"I know of few novels that capture the emotionally complex life of a college student as powerfully...

as William J. Torgerson's *Love on the Big Screen*. Set at a small Christian college in the early 1990s, the book vividly brings to life the confusion, the camaraderie, the awkwardness of relationships, and the moments of exhilaration that everyone who has ever been a student will recognize. I loved this novel."

— Joseph Bentz, author of *A Son Comes Home*

"Hilarious and moving"

"At the conclusion of Reagan's America, Gary Willis asks, 'What happens if, when we look into our historical rearview mirror, all we can see is a movie?' In *Love on the Big Screen*, Bill Torgerson asks, 'What happens when a son of the 1980s looks inward and finds only cheesy, irresistible, teenaged romantic comedies?' In a novel with turns hilarious and moving, Torgerson navigates his hero Zuke through the perils of heart-sickness on a quest to distinguish reality from illusion. With riveting, crisp prose (that's TOTALLY AWESOME!), Torgerson delivers a first of its kind—a soul from 'Me Generation' that was almost lost...at the movies."

— Jeremy Collins, author of "Shadow Boxing,"

a *Pushcart Prize* Selection

Copyright © 2011 by William J. Torgerson

All rights reserved. No part of this publication may be reproduced, transmitted in any form or by any means, electronic or mechanical, including photocopy, recording, or any information storage and retrieval system, without permission in writing from the publisher. This is a work of fiction. Names, characters, places, and incidents either are the product of the author's imagination or are used fictitiously, and any resemblance to actual persons, living or dead, business establishments, or events is entirely coincidental and unintentional. References to actual persons or places are used strictly as setting and imply no involvement in fictional events.

ISBN 978-0-9799694-7-8
0-9799694-7-6

First Edition 2011

Cover photograph by Timothy L. Vacula
Cover design by Braxton McGhee
Author photograph by Peter Baker (www.pbakerphoto.com)

Published by:
Cherokee McGhee, L.L.C.
Williamsburg, Virginia

Find us on the World Wide Web at:
www.CherokeeMcGhee.com

Printed in the United States of America

LOVE
ON THE
BIG SCREEN

WILLIAM J. TORGERSON

Cherokee McGhee

Williamsburg, Virginia

Acknowledgements

I'm grateful to Greg Lilly for being the first person not of my relation to believe in this manuscript and for connecting me with his creative team at Cherokee McGhee. It was a pleasure to work with editor Lisa Kline, and I found that we shared a great reading and writing chemistry. Her editorial feedback certainly enriched this manuscript.

Thanks also to my mother and father for their loyal readings of my drafts, and specifically to my father for the times he reminded me of all those lessons from Warriner's *English Grammar and Composition* that I must have missed the first time around when I was a student of his at Winamac High School in Indiana.

Thank you to Harry Battson and photographer Tim Vacula, who worked along with Dr. Marty Lammon, my former professor and director of the creative writing program at Georgia College and State University, to arrange for the photograph that was used to create the artful and eye-catching cover of this book. I also appreciate all the time my former teachers and professors over the years set aside to talk with me about writing and teaching. These include but are not limited to Dr. Allen Gee, who taught me how to read fiction as a writer; Dr. Dan Bauer, who helped me think through my teaching philosophy; Dr. Lil Brannon and Dr. Samuel Watson, who both encouraged me into the National Writing Project summer institute, and special thanks to Sam who showed me that writing floats on a sea of conversation. One last bit about a former teacher: fifteen years ago, I wrote "The Royal Castle" in a writing course taught by Dr. Joseph Bentz at Olivet Nazarene University. He was the first person I ever met who I knew to be working on a book. Joe pulled me aside after class one day and told me, "This is what you should be writing." A revised version of that essay appears in this novel as the work of the protagonist.

In order to create the world in this book, I placed the following nonfiction texts in conversation with my imagination: Dr. Leslie Parrott's *The Olivet Story*, *The Eighties* edited by Gilbert T. Sewall, and Dr. Timothy Shary's *Generation Multiplex: The Image of Youth in Contemporary American Cinema* and his *Teen Movies: American Youth on Screen*. I should also note that some of the headlines, world events, and last names contained in this novel were discovered either while reading old Olivet yearbooks or through browsing copies of the *Chicago Tribune* newspaper in the microforms reading room at the New York City Public Library on 42nd Street.

I dedicate this book to my wife Megan, who not only carves out time and space with me for writing, but also provides the catalyst of love that makes our family go.

CHAPTER ONE

On his very first day as a student at Pison College, Zuke fell in love with a girl he'd never seen before, a young woman in his composition class named Abby Grant. From Zuke's front-row seat, it was the squeak of a chair sliding on the hardwood floors that caused him to turn his head, casually at first, and then snapping to attention as he caught sight of Abby sitting down late for class. Fresh from volleyball practice, Abby was covered with a salty glaze of dried sweat. Her hair was an unruly shock of red, wild as a strawberry patch, and it seemed to buck against the banana clip which held it in place. Maybe it was the tint of Abby's red hair that had such a lightning-bolt effect on Zuke's heart. He was a fanatic of the movies, mostly romantic comedies, and this was the fall of 1989, three years beyond Molly Ringwald's homerun of blockbuster hits: *Sixteen Candles, The Breakfast Club, Pretty in Pink,* and *The Pick Up Artist.* Zuke had seen them all, especially *Candles,* that one five nights in a row with his buddy Road Dog when they were still in middle school.

It wasn't just the joyful surprise of the nude shower scene that drew Zuke back to *Candles* night after night. For the first time in his young life, Zuke had found a role model who wasn't a basketball player: a character played by Anthony Michael Hall named Farmer Ted, a self proclaimed "King of the Dipshits" whose nerdy go-get-her attitude had caused Zuke to believe that he, too, might one day rise from romantic obscurity. Zuke saw Abby's sparkly green eyes scan the classroom, maybe looking for a familiar face, maybe a friendly one. A kaleidoscope of color erupted into the room, all except for at the core of Zuke's vision, which remained as clear as the lens of a Hollywood camera, Abby at its center. Zuke felt a jolt at the near miss of her laser gaze and desire hurried into his chest for want of a day when she'd look at him and care about his life.

For the rest of class, Zuke stole looks to the back of the room to see what he could learn: printed across the front of Abby's shirt was the phrase *Lady Oracles*, along with a gold number 3, bolded above a volleyball net that stretched across her chest. She was an athlete and so was he, an incoming freshman whose only reason for choosing the conservative college was so that he could play basketball. How in the world could Zuke, a nobody on campus, meet a girl as sparkling as Abby?

In *Say Anything*—Zuke's reigning favorite movie of all time— John Cusack's Lloyd Dobler proclaims that he is looking for a dare-to-be-great situation and now having spotted Abby, Zuke felt his own opportunity rise before him. Greatness—and the great life that surely must belong to anyone who dated a young woman as beautiful as Abby, was hanging right there before him, like a ripe apple in the back of the room.

For the rest of the class, Zuke marveled at Abby's visage and began to dream of plans for how he would meet her. In *Say Anything,* chance had brought Lloyd Dobler a seat by Diane Court at the mall and while Zuke admired Dobler's courage and his chivalrous attitude, he saw no reason to leave meeting the woman of his dreams up to something as random as circumstance. Zuke felt that part of reaching for greatness meant not only seizing opportunities as they arrived, but he also believed that he should shoulder some of the responsibility for creating those opportunities. This was an axiom for finding love that Zuke had previously put to practice when as a middle school student he'd first seen the girl who would eventually become his high school romantic steady.

Five years earlier, in the middle of the Reaganite eighties, Zuke and his family had just moved back to his parents' hometown of Horseshoe, Indiana. It was a little place of less than three thousand residents and so named for where it sat on the bend of the Tippecanoe River. Zuke was sitting on the green and paint-chipped wooden bleachers watching his younger sister play softball. It was here that Zuke first spotted Colleen, the opposing team's pitcher, as she mowed down batters with her lithe and whirling slingshot arm.

Colleen was uncannily strong for her fragile frame, with tanned skin from long summer days spent pedaling around town on her banana-seated Huffy bicycle. She sneered at the batters after she struck them out, a fierce girl for someone with the delicate beauty of a morning glory flower.

Prone to pouting on the bench if her coach removed her from the game, Colleen, who wore a big pink ribbon tied up in her hair, injured the opposing catcher when she bowled her over for the winning run. Colleen looked like one of Barbie's bronzed friends, but she hit with the passion of Mike Singletary, the Super Bowl shuffling middle linebacker for the Chicago Bears.

Zuke had been fourteen that summer day in Horseshoe, and upon seeing Colleen it was as if his soul had been inhabited by an otherworldly spirit of wonder. He began to admire her from afar, actually not that *afar*, since she was only twenty yards away and plainly visible through the silver-diamond spaces of air in the backstop, and it was as if she were a painting at an art museum that he'd decided to steal: perhaps, *The Birth of Venus* by Botticelli, a work which depicts the goddess as pale-skinned and naked. In the painting, Venus is a redhead—there's that tint again—and her hair trails across one of her breasts before it snakes between her legs. Zuke had first discovered Venus in his father's encyclopedias, and then later heard her alluded to in the 1987 film *The Pick Up Artist*, when Robert Downey Jr. hits on a character played by (no surprise) Molly Ringwald. Downey first tosses Ringwald one of his usual pick up lines, something to the effect that she has the face of a Botticelli and the body of a Degas. That particular pick-up line actually curdled a bit of disgust in Zuke's stomach. It was something Lloyd Dobler would never say, a character who had famously—at least famously in Zuke's mind—brushed broken glass out of Diane Court's way while they crossed the street on their first date. Ever since Zuke had seen the movie, he looked for ways to be a gentleman with the same mania he pursued the loose balls that sometimes scooted across the hardwood floors of basketball courts.

At fourteen, at least at Zuke's house, there was no calling girls and asking them out on dates. Even if his parents would have allowed this, what was he supposed to do, swing by Colleen's place on his ten speed? Zuke was just socially savvy enough to realize that he couldn't stand outside Colleen's house and follow her wherever she went. So what Zuke did, was to try for the appearance of coincidence or destiny, to situate himself at opportune places at opportune times. He caught a break one morning at the town pool when he saw Colleen coming in as he exited from his morning swim lessons. Zuke went right home and asked his mother to buy him a summer pass to the pool. Because he was an edgy boy, the sort of kid to ask what he was doing next even when he was still in the throes of whatever his mother had planned for the day, Zuke's mom was happy to oblige him. Armed with the season pass, Zuke spent most of that summer in the town pool submerged under three feet of water breathing through a snorkel and weaving in and out of his peers as if they were branches of coral. Thank God his mother had at least persuaded him to leave his flippers at home. Zuke and Colleen never spoke the summer before his freshman year. As the saying goes, she didn't know he existed.

So it was Zuke's experience with Colleen and the many lessons provided by the romantic comedies he so loved that worked together to inform what Zuke did next when it came to Abby, this collegiate volleyball beauty. There in the front of the classroom, Professor Moore, a scary-skinny woman in her sixties quoted the poet Dickinson: "The butterfly's Numidian gown," she said, adjusting with one hand her large and round spectacles while waving the other around as if to capture an imaginary butterfly, "With spots of Burnish roasted on."

Professor Moore hadn't even noticed that Abby had come into the classroom late because as she stood at the front of the room, seemingly forgetting that she shared it with any students, Moore drew with her talon-like fingers what she described as the world's most beautiful insect.

Zuke had just determined Moore's mind to be as chaotic as an overturned hive of bumblebees when that little screech of Abby's

chair lit the fuse which would eventually ignite the star of emotion in Zuke's mind for Abby. Over the course of the rest of the class, Zuke pretended to stretch his back—well, he wasn't really pretending since his spine crunched loud enough that the young man next to him scooted his chair several inches away—Zuke was able to sneak several peeks at Abby and learn that she was likely dating a basketball player. This he discerned from the lettering on the sweatshirt draped across her desk which commemorated the Pison men's basketball team's four consecutive Lake Michigan Conference championships. Zuke was a member of the team but preseason conditioning hadn't even begun, and so he only knew two of his teammates, fellow freshmen who lived on his floor in Chapman Hall. He thought of Abby's attention as a fat man thinks of the marathon, a not too likely accomplishment, the summit of Everest as reached from the level cornfields of Indiana. Marriage was the flag spiked into the pinnacle of the relationship mountain, located somewhere beyond the first kiss, the place where the movies Zuke watched never seemed to go beyond.

Near the end of the composition class when Zuke first saw Abby, Professor Moore asked for a show of hands to see which students planned to major in what. "Business!" she called out. Zuke reached down to the metal rungs under his chair as if he needed something from his Trapper-Keeper, an action which allowed him to see if Abby had raised her hand. She didn't signal affirmatively until Professor Moore had asked about English. Zuke, having come to college mostly to play basketball, had not decided on a major, but suddenly, at the sight of Abby's raised hand, he felt confident regarding the nature of his studies at Pison Nazarene College. Following class, Zuke went directly to the registrar and filled out the paperwork that made him an English major.

CHAPTER TWO

The movies often teach would-be young lovers to look for that special moment when love either blossoms like a red rose or else strikes with lightning-bolt passion. In *Say Anything,* Lloyd Dobler brushes broken glass out of Diane Court's way. The boys in *Weird Science* vanquish the mutant motorcycle gang invaders who threaten the girls they love while in *Sixteen Candles,* the big football star, Jake Ryan, intercepts a note on which Molly Ringwald's character has written something to the effect that she would entertain sleeping with him.

In high school, Zuke and Colleen grew to be close friends, at first along the one-mile easy jog from Horseshoe High to the town park for cross country practice, and then also during shared long bus rides to and from the meets. All the while, Colleen maintained her two-year relationship with a senior star athlete known to the citizens of Horseshoe as Knucklehead. The nickname came easily enough from the family name—Nuckles—but was certainly enhanced by his legendary history for reckless and stupid acts, the pinnacle of which was probably the night he attended a Def Leopard concert in Indianapolis, got kicked out of Market Square Arena for sneaking in two bottles of Jack Daniels, did 360 degree spins in his Trans Am down Meridian on his way home, and was only arrested when he was found by local police relieving himself on the side of Nancy's Country Diner in Star City. Had his father not been the superintendent of schools, surely Knucklehead's exploits would have carried more severe penalties.

Knucklehead was the sort of guy who left his lady with a lot of free time. He was tragically flirtatious, spent long hours with his buddies playing Nintendo sports games, and on the weekends visited older friends at nearby universities to party. Meanwhile, Colleen and Zuke exchanged notes every day in typing class, again just before lunch at her locker, and then for a third time right before seventh period in the hall just outside the science labs. The two were friends in this way, spending more time together than most of the couples in the school, all the while never even exchanging a single kiss, that is until Zuke's junior year, when he finally became a member of the varsity basketball team.

During the first game of the season, Zuke had only gone into the contest twice, both times just long enough for Knucklehead to come over to the bench to get a quick drink. But with three minutes to play and the hometown team trailing the big city (at least compared to Horseshoe) Logansport Berries by seven, Knucklehead committed a dumbbell foul, reaching in for an unlikely steal at center court. It was his fifth foul, disqualifying him from the game, and Zuke was the best player left on the bench. Before the action even began, Zuke's mouth was dry with fear and his hands shook so badly that he could barely get off his warm up jacket. He hadn't even been in the game five seconds when a teammate's missed shot fell into his hands where he stood directly under the basket. Zuke tossed the ball back up toward the rim as if it were a hot potato, and—holy smokes!—it rattled home for two points.

What happened next was improbable, certainly not expected by Zuke's coach or anyone who knew him. For Zuke's entire adolescent life, he had fantasized about taking over games. He'd recorded his voice on cassette tape counting down the time so that he could have a clock for each quarter. He put a stat sheet on a clipboard and propped it up on a coffee table and then he proceeded to announce the solitary basketball games he played in his living room while scoring basket after basket on a hoop he'd nailed to the wall. In Indiana, where basketball was king and 40,000 fans once attended a high school game, there are far fewer mothers who disallow the bouncing of balls in their homes.

As far as Zuke was concerned, the solo living-room games were just for fun, but through the countless times he had scored baskets just as the clock expired, he'd actually participated in what many a sports psychologist would advise: he had imagined himself time and time again succeeding in moments of pressure, and so when he entered that first varsity basketball game, in front of most of the residents of the town of Horseshoe, with Knucklehead sitting and pouting on the bench, Colleen directly across the floor in the front row, and the reigning homecoming queen—her name was Angel—waving her pom poms along the baseline in the corner of the gym, Zuke did what he'd done a thousand times in all those solitary living room games. He went on to score the last nine points of the contest, including the game winner, an off the dribble running one-legger which he released right before the buzzer and watched swish through the net as he fell into the arms of the cheerleaders.

After the game, following an interview with Logansport radio and several local newspapers, Zuke showered and came out of the locker room to find Queen Angel sitting in the bleachers and waiting for him. It was here that Zuke thought he learned it was basketball that made him attractive. Angel asked him if he might not want to head down to the Pizza King with her to hang out. On the other side of the gym, Knucklehead moped toward the exit, bummed someone else was the hero besides himself. Although Colleen worked halfheartedly to console her boyfriend, Zuke could see that she'd taken notice of his royal company.

Zuke went down to the P.K. and after a couple hours of his first hanging out, he had to tell Angel goodnight, knowing his father would be waiting in his Lazy Boy in front of the television to make sure he made team curfew. Heading out into the parking lot, Zuke's mind wandered to Colleen as he walked to his car. Popping into the seat of his little red Chevette, he was startled to find Colleen sitting there in his front passenger seat. She'd let herself into his car and was waiting for him. They dove right into Zuke's first kiss—it was easier than he'd ever imagined—and a week later the two made their first official appearance as a couple at the Winter Ball. Colleen and Zuke stayed together until the summer after their high school graduation when Zuke choose to play basketball at Pison rather than to follow Colleen to Ball State.

There wasn't much about the way Zuke kicked off his pursuit of Abby that differed from his pursuit of Colleen: his high school choice to run cross country became his collegiate decision to major in English. It didn't take a genius to realize that once most people select a seat in a class, they return to that same spot. The very next time Zuke attended Professor Moore's class, he arrived early, sat in the back by the door, and "reserved" the seat next to him when he tossed his textbook and Trapper Keeper into it. Because there were plenty of empty seats in the room, there was no reason for any of Zuke's classmates to ask him to move his belongings. They sat elsewhere.

When Zuke heard Abby coming down the hall—she had an especially loud and intoxicating laugh—he removed his stuff, Abby entered the room, and without a second thought she plopped down beside him.

Had Professor Moore's classroom been the only place Zuke spent time with Abby, it is unlikely that he would have made much progress with her. True, there was the English Club which put on a Moby Dick whale of a good literary miniature golf outing complete with a burning barn in homage to Faulkner, but Zuke's big breakthrough moment—his swimming pool Horseshoe moment with Colleen come again at Pison—presented itself when Zuke arrived at the third floor of the library, where there was a private restroom, clean and air conditioned, Zuke's very favorite place on campus to take a dump. This was just after dinner, when Zuke needed to take a few moments for himself before a long night of studying.

As Zuke emerged from the stairwell, there on the other side of the library, just visible through the tall stacks of books, Zuke saw Abby sitting by herself at a table. Since that first day in Professor Moore's class, Zuke had learned that Abby's boyfriend was a junior and record-setting teammate of his, a spiky-haired blonde shooting guard who some girls thought looked like Drago from *Rocky IV.* The teammate's name was Brett Chezem, he went by the moniker Cheese, and he was the great grandson of one of the founding members of the college, the pride of the entire Pison community both past and present. Cheese was, to Zuke's way of understanding what women wanted, awe-inspiringly good looking, with a clear complexion, a cartoonish strong chin, and blond hair he parted on the side, kept stiff with a liberal application of White Rain hair gel.

Stealing peeks from around one of the shelves, Zuke thought that perhaps he had discovered the time and place Abby studied. Zuke returned the very next night, his backpack loaded with books and notes, ready to set up camp and see if Abby would show. Upon his arrival, Abby was already there, but Zuke—ever conversationally quick—faked a chance meeting and asked a genuine question about an upcoming paper they had due for Professor Moore's class. When Abby invited him to sit down and talk, their secret routine was born.

When the time came to sign up for spring courses, Abby and Zuke created identical schedules and did the same for the fall semester of their sophomore year. As for Cheese, he was a Physical Education major and not prone to visits to the library. Sure, he knew that Abby and Zuke had some sort of English-based connection, but he thought of Zuke—in his words—as "womanish" and thus no threat to him. In fact, Cheese could often be heard saying laughingly that Abby's friendship with Zuke spared him from all that fancy shmancey Shakespeare talk. Just to make sure that there was no confusion about who was king stud, Cheese physically punished Zuke every day in practice, and afterwards, just outside the showers, he cut Zuke and the rest of the freshman's flesh with rattail snaps of his wet towel.

Four hundred and fifty three days after Zuke's initial sighting of Abby (he kept track of this on a workout calendar hanging near his desk) the lights in the library flipped on and off three times, a signal to the building's inhabitants that it was time to leave. Although usually Abby exited the library first for the sake of secrecy, on this night Zuke told her he had a present for her in his backpack. When they came out of the front doors, they walked around the side of the building, the side closest to Barrett, the women's dormitory where Abby lived. Just twenty or so yards away toward college church was a large oak tree which grew up out of a waist high brick planter. It served as a sort of centerpiece for campus, especially for events where students came together to pray. The oak had a plaque denoting it as the Tree of Knowledge.

Abby was just two inches shorter than Zuke, sinewy, with bulbs of joy for cheekbones, and in her eyes was the nervous excitement that comes from a friendship that teeters on the brink of romance. While Cheese wasn't likely to enter the library, it was entirely possible for him to pass by it on his way to Abby's dormitory, where he was to meet her at 9:30. While Zuke did all he could to emulate Lloyd Dobler's knightly treatment of Diane Court, his code of honor did not extend to his teammates, especially Cheese, who was an eternal hazer of the freshman players.

Zuke regarded any potential physical assault from Cheese as an event which would likely further his cause, an inexpensive price to pay for a few more dollops of Abby's consideration. On this day, it was Thursday, December 6, 1990, getting colder, and a silver-hook moon intermittently became visible between fast-moving clouds. In the lobby of the residence hall where Abby lived, a large projection television was visible through one of the glass walls, and it cast flickering images toward them of Saddam Hussein, a man who not so long ago had been given a pair of golden cowboy spurs, a gift from The Great Communicator. Abby and Zuke stood close, talking softly in the shadows in a spot chosen not only because it might hide them from Cheese, but also from the campus security's golf-cart patrols. As part of Pison's mission to create a Christian atmosphere, the administration separated the men from the women, disallowing any sort of visitation in the residence halls.

Zuke leaned down to where he'd placed his backpack on the frosty grass. In the distance, cars buzzed by on Shermer Boulevard, the road on which Pison's main entrance was located. Abby's birthday was the following day, Friday, and Zuke wasn't likely to see her without Cheese's presence looming. She'd have practice; he'd have practice, and although they'd surely exchange thrilled glances in the hallways of the gym, Zuke certainly wouldn't be able to give her a present there. Zuke's hand trembled just a little as he unzipped the small pocket of the front of his backpack. From it, he pulled out a velvety black box. Zuke was nervous. He and Abby lived in the moments of each day, never talking about what they were, but certainly depending on each other's company. There had been a growing electricity between them and so in the spirit of Lloyd Dobler, trying to seize a moment ripe with the potential for greatness, Zuke decided to take a chance with a gift.

"Happy Birthday," he said, handing over the velvet box while he looked into Abby's eyes, feeling silly, feeling vulnerable, feeling more intensely than he'd ever felt at how difficult it was to believe that he would ever really woo Abby away from Cheese.

Inside the box was a locket, a gift chosen according to what Zuke had been able to observe on campus, that many a Pison Lady Oracle wore a chain on the outside of a turtle-necked sweater or tucked under the collar of a satin or silk shirt. He'd noticed that a few times a week Abby wore a silver cross, an accessory he hoped was from her mother and not Cheese. In Zuke's mind, he could already see the locket hanging at the tip of Abby's breastbone, probably tucked under whatever clothing she wore, a little golden announcement for what was to come.

Abby's green eyes showed surprise at the gift; Zuke knew Cheese wasn't likely to get her anything, especially since her birthday was the day before one of his basketball games. Zuke had been tempted to plagiarize from the note Dobler had written to Diane Court after the first time that they'd made love, but his high school buddy "Road Dog" had tried a similar stunt with his own high school girlfriend, copying Jim Croce's "Time in a Bottle," word for word onto a gray parchment and passing it off as his own on Valentine's Day. "Road Dog" had been caught and for months afterwards, his girlfriend had claimed she couldn't trust him. Because of all that, Zuke wrote his own material for the engraver: "With Hope For Glorious Love."

The word "Glorious" had special meaning between Zuke and Abby. Just as in the wide world of sports, where names such as Sweetness, The Golden Bear, Mr. October, and The Round Mound of Rebound are fairly well known, Zuke and his friends were big into nicknaming: first they'd called themselves the Fab Five, but then later they took to meeting on Sunday nights and using the phrase "Adelphoi en Diogmi." These words, as best as they could discern, were Greek for "Brothers in Pursuit." Each member of the Fab had his own nickname, and they'd also given nicknames to the young women on campus they were interested in as a means to talk about them in front of others without giving away their identities. Abby knew her nickname—"Glory"—and liked it. Zuke's friend Cowboy, a history buff, had come up with it according to the following logic: Abby Grant as in General Grant, as in from the Civil War, as in the Civil War flick starring Matthew Broderick and Denzel Washington, *Glory*.

"I love it," Abby said, having read the locket and now in the act of hanging it around her neck just as Zuke had imagined, tucking it under her shirt against her bare flesh. Zuke felt a shiver of emotion. Behind them and toward Ludwig Hall Cafeteria, the campus opened up into a hedged and elaborately landscaped quadrangle, serene and frozen, where the Tree of Knowledge seemed to shine in the moonlight. Up in the night sky, overseeing all, beyond the cafeteria, was the great steeple of College Church, white as fresh snow, lighted for all of the village of Beau Flueve to see. The town's name was French, a phrase meaning Beautiful Bank and chosen by fur trappers in 1830.

Abby's face was close enough to Zuke's that he could smell the powerful scent of her Obsession perfume. Her lips inched toward his and her head tilted just a little. It was a move, if Zuke had reciprocated, that would have resulted in their first kiss. But he didn't, mostly because he'd developed a theory of sorts that cheating was a bad place to begin a relationship and everything after that first bad event would surely go poorly. This theory of course didn't go so well with the fact that Zuke had for over a year now been trying to woo away the girlfriend of one of his teammates, but this wasn't a paradox that Zuke recognized. In the millisecond of the awkward pause that had begun to grow between Zuke and Abby, the unmistakable voice of Cheese bellowed, "No way!"

Abby, startled, grabbed Zuke's coat, pulling herself to him, while at the same time yanking them both toward the ground, well out of any light from the quad or the residence hall. Zuke thought maybe his faceoff with Cheese had arrived. He'd never entertained any notion that he could win a fight with his upperclassman teammate, but he thought that if he were pummeled, eventually Abby and Cheese would have to get around to confronting the issues that littered their relationship. A fight, Zuke reasoned, might cause something to happen.

But it was not to be. Cheese hadn't seen them. He was still far from Abby's residence hall, coming from the off-campus apartments where only the boys were allowed to live. His "No way" had only been in response to something one of the women he was walking with had said.

"That felt like a moment for a kiss," Zuke whispered, the moisture in his mouth drying up, an oral-desert condition, the result of excited energy for Abby, and the adrenaline that had just pumped through his body at the possibility Cheese could come tramping through the shrubs for him. Abby's hand rested on the place where Zuke's neck and shoulders met and her thumb and forefinger twirled one of the half curls of Zuke's hair, which except for the back, he kept *Hoosier*'s style short. Zuke jumped at the whirl of a golf cart as it passed through the quadrangle, not slowing down to investigate if anyone hid in the shadows.

"It felt like that for me too," Abby said, her face awash in the faint light coming from the inside of the residence hall. "Why didn't we?"

"Not yet," Zuke said. "I want to kiss you, but I don't want to kiss you when you have a boyfriend. It seems like a bad place to start, as if everything would have to be bad after that." There was another part of Zuke that didn't think it was a good idea to let Abby have her cake and eat it too. This, he translated, meant that perhaps a line in the sand at kissing might cause Abby to take action.

"I've decided to tell him this weekend," Abby said, as the two rose up from their respective crouches. Abby straightened Zuke's jacket.

Inside Zuke's chest, there was a romantic explosion of light, launching like a Fourth of July fireworks finale, zipping up his throat, spraying out into his head and pelting his eardrums from the inside. "Tell him what?" Zuke couldn't believe it. He'd really thought that it would take Abby a few days to digest the locket's message.

"I'm going to break up with Brett on Sunday afternoon. I want to wait until after the game. You know, he has the record and all to think about." Cheese was only seven little points away from breaking Coach Miller's record and becoming the all time leading scorer at Pison College.

"Three sleeping nights," Zuke said.

Abby laughed. "What?"

"Three sleeping nights," Zuke repeated, smiling like he hadn't smiled since he'd discovered Colleen waiting for him in his Chevette outside the Pizza King. Zuke couldn't believe it. Over four hundred days of waiting and hoping was now down to three nights? Zuke held up his hand so that he could count the nights on his fingers. "Thursday night," he said, extending his index finger, and putting out another each time he rattled off a night. "Friday night, Saturday night, and then Sunday will be here." Zuke's fingers showed his foggy calculations to be true. Three sleeping nights and Abby was scheduled to break up with Cheese.

A group of students, chattering excitedly, came walking through the quad, the de-facto social center of campus, one of the few places along with the gym during basketball games where male and female students could come together and talk. If the weather was nice, then there were also the athletic fields, the Lincoln house, the cinder loop that circled the perimeter of Pison, and if one had a car—both Zuke and Abby did—the quiet roads by the river along the Kankakee Cemetery.

Cheese had cut the corner on the far side of the quad and was now close to Barrett Hall, where as per the couple's Thursday night custom, Abby was scheduled to meet Cheese for a date. By his own decree, Cheese only saw his girlfriend three days a week: these were usually Thursday nights for ice cream (and Zuke suspected make out sessions after), Saturday nights unless there was an evening road game, and Sunday afternoons when the couples' families ate a late lunch after church and watched sports for the rest of the day.

"Sunday," Abby repeated, taking hold of Zuke's wrist but staring off to Cheese, as if she were trying to convince herself of what she had already said she would do. Zuke watched Abby watch her current boyfriend. Previously, Zuke had hoped for a romantic relationship with Abby the way fervent Christians hoped for the world: he prayed for it daily but believed it would ultimately fall. There had always seemed to be too much history and circumstance working against his desires: not only were Abby and Cheese's parents best friends, but also Abby and Cheese had gone to the same church their whole lives, played in the nursery together, went to the same vacation Bible schools, and even gone on mission trips (two times) to Honduras. Leave it to Zuke to try and crack in versus such impossible odds. Cheese had been an Illinois All-Star in basketball and occasionally someone would stop him for an autograph—he was the only player in the state's history to play for three state champions—and he had scholarship offers from Bradley University and Illinois State, while Zuke's one and only offer had been a partial from Pison.

"I'll tell him Sunday."

That Abby had repeated this for a third time caused Zuke to worry. "With your families around?" Zuke was skeptical.

"I've got to go, Sweetheart," Abby said, another first, using that term of endearment. She leaned forward and kissed Zuke on the cheek. In the cold air the moisture of it seemed to burn his skin. Her hand was on Zuke's arm. "I'll definitely call you Sunday night." She gave his arm a squeeze before she hurried off to meet Cheese.

Emotional happy bombs exploded in Zuke's thoughts, leaving him speechless and nearly thoughtless, completely unable at first to critically examine anything he had been told. A countdown toward Sunday night fired up on the big screen of Zuke's mind, ticking away the four days until he and Abby were scheduled to debut as a couple in the main feature. Zuke watched Abby hurry off toward the residence hall, her red hair free and bouncing on her back as she moved. As the mental smoke cleared from Zuke's mind, questions rolled up into his thinking like numbers on a gas pump. Will we start dating right away? Was her desire to kiss me just a momentary weakness? Had she really planned on breaking up with Cheese or was it just my gift that swayed her for a second? Oh no, Zuke realized, she doesn't really mean it. She'll never go through with it. It had taken less than thirty seconds for Zuke's joy to transform itself into anxious worry.

"Idiot!" Zuke said to himself. "You should have kissed her." Zuke began to see his whole life stretching out before him, a life during which he would surely always regret not kissing Abby. There he was an old man sitting in front of a television, watching sports, and telling a married friend of his about the time he almost kissed Abby Grant.

For at least the fiftieth time since he'd seen *Say Anything,* Zuke questioned how it was that one pursued *greatness.* Had he done a great deed to hold his character and not kiss her? Or was it that he had faced the cliff overlooking greatness in the form of a forbidden kiss that would have stolen Abby away from his rival, but instead, he'd stood paralyzed with fear, done nothing, and therefore missed his chance?

Over in the lobby of Barrett, the images of Hussein were gone from the projection television and replaced by the artificial intelligence character Max Headroom, which flickered on the windows where Zuke could see Abby's silhouette pass through the glass doors. Cheese rose up from a couch and several young women tried to ease away inconspicuously at Abby's presence. Cheese was a man with basketball groupies. He looked at his watch, possibly to indicate to Abby that she was late, but then the two pecked each other's lips. Thinking that those lips had just been on his own cheek, Zuke turned and began the short walk back to Chapman Hall.

During some of the darker days of Zuke's pursuit of Abby—when she'd seemed destined to marry Cheese—Zuke had entertained thoughts of a transfer from Pison College for some of the following reasons: he was firmly rooted on the basketball team's bench, the rules against female visitation in the dormitories were a drag, Zuke did not particularly like the mandatory two chapel services a week, and although he wasn't a drinker, he wouldn't have minded a few parties or nights out at the bars (for the girls) when he was old enough. With this new promise from Abby, Zuke felt relieved that he hadn't pursued his transfer daydreams, and he tried to focus his mind on something more useful.

"I've got to get that paper done," he said to himself, making his way to the back door to Chapman Hall. He was taking Professor Moore again—in a school as small as Pison there were only so many professors—and he had plans for a piece called "Chip off the Bloc: An Analysis of the Soviet Empire." Moore gave "+5" for creative titles, and Zuke hoped his would be good enough for the extra points. He'd already gotten a C and two B minuses on the first three papers.

Just outside Chapman Hall, under the feeble light of the moon, Zuke carried with him a measure of anxiety—a sickness he always felt when he knew Abby was with Cheese. Actually, he felt it every moment that she or Cheese wasn't in his presence, because each of those moments contained the potential for them to be together. Even in the middle of the night, Zuke would wake and find himself wondering if Abby might have sneaked out of Barrett into Cheese's apartment, something she'd once confessed to having done when she had just considered Zuke a good friend.

But on this night, Zuke possessed at least a partial remedy for his ailment: a dose of the same exuberance he'd felt the night after the high school Winter Ball, the night he'd first run his hand down Colleen Flannery's bare thigh. The two had been snuggled under a blanket in Colleen's living room, and had Colleen's spirited Irish Catholic mother come in, they would have said they were watching the movie *Mannequin,* which was rolling in the VCR. Zuke relished how far he'd hiked toward the summit of a relationship with Abby. For four hundred and fifty-three days he'd been trudging along, hanging in there so that one day he might come up through the wet fog and see the precipice. And now here it was—nearly miraculously so—in three days it seemed, Zuke would finally have his chance to date Abby Grant.

CHAPTER THREE

Coming up the last turn of stairs to the fourth floor of Chapman Hall, Zuke was so lost in his thoughts of Abby, of whether or not that she would actually break up with Cheese, that he nearly plunked his foot down into a fresh pile of human feces, which stinkified the doorway as if it were a dirty diaper receptacle. Likely, the responsible party for the poop lived down the hall opposite from Zuke, men who had recently been studying harder than they'd previously believed possible, driven by the fanatic desire to get their grades up to where they could transfer from the school they referred to as "Hell's College." The hall was busy with the hustle of late-evening, when everyone was up, no classes were in session, and the library had closed. Zuke gave the smelly inconvenience little thought, lengthened his stride to reach beyond the goop, after which he walked to the first room on his right, a room which contained his friends, those young men who alternately referred to themselves as the Fabulous Five or the Brothers in Pursuit. The door was partly open and Zuke entered.

Cowboy—the one who'd come up with Abby's nickname "Glory"—sat in the middle of the room, seated with his legs crossed on the worn and slightly warped hardwood floor, a plastic Chicago Bears souvenir cup just in front of him. He was a somewhat stout young man, handsome in a mature way, as if he were thirty and not twenty, with thick dark eyebrows and several days' growth of a beard. He sat across from Bryan Willingham, a guy whom everyone called Moon, a nickname he'd picked up from his grandfather when as an infant he seemed never to sleep at night. Moon sat across from Cowboy and was dressed in an L.A. Lakers "Showtime" t-shirt and a pair of mesh athletic shorts. Both Moon and Cowboy had played ball the previous year and given it up. Moon was a tall and thin young man, intent on becoming a Nazarene minister like his father, who was well known in church circles for going pew to pew at the start of revival week and securing from each parishioner a verbal commitment that he or she would attend all the services. With the concentration of a surgeon, Moon readied to toss a penny as if he were attempting to win some dishware at a local fair.

Moon and Cowboy were playing an invented game, one they'd named "Lincoln Shootout" for the pennies they tried to pitch into souvenir cups, and they had spectators: a pair of roommates named Phillip Leardini and Antoine Caldwell. They were both from Indianapolis. Everyone referred to Phillip as "The Dini," as if like Prince or Madonna, he only needed one name. When in one of his moods, The Dini could remind someone of a thinner and more stylish Richard Simmons for his sense of humor and hyper energy. The Dini roomed with Antoine, one of the two black members of the basketball team, a six foot eight inch sculpted mass of muscle whose little rounded pooch of a belly caused him to be given the rather ironic nickname of Flabby.

Nearing the end of a game of Lincoln Shootout, Moon leaned out as far as he could, an action which reduced the distance of his toss to less than five feet. He flicked the penny toward the cup in front of Cowboy, it caught the back rim, tipped the cup just a little (if it had fallen over, the point would have been nullified) and then the penny fell in to where it rattled the bottom of the cup.

"That's game, Loser," Moon said, his open-mouthed smile as happy as if someone had invited him into their home to talk about Jesus. He rose from his place on the floor and walked to his desk, where in black crayon, everyone's name had been written onto a massive poster board. It showed the Lincoln Shootout standings; there were columns for wins and losses.

"Dag gum it!" Cowboy said in a frustrated, almost angry voice. He was clad in a white t-shirt and a Cubs baseball cap was turned backwards on his head. "I get so sick of your cheating." Moon made a great show of slashing himself a line in the win column and one for Cowboy as a loss; then he turned around, obviously sensing his audience, knowing that this game of Lincoln Shootout had been played to a full house.

"All right you big baby, how was I cheating?" Moon asked. Behind him there was a poster of Earl Campbell clad in a light blue #34 jersey bowling over a defensive back for a touchdown.

Cowboy uncurled his legs from their playing position—it was a rule that each butt cheek had to touch the floor when a toss was tried—and when he stood, he immediately began to pace circles in the room. "Dude," he said, causing the rest of the Fab to look at one another. The previous week the Brothers had voted unanimously to impose a twenty-five cent fine on anyone who used the word. All of them were trying to stop saying *dude,* having determined themselves as eloquent as parrots with the habitual ways they used language. "It's like you're a freaking giraffe," Cowboy continued, "with that left arm of yours. I'm 6'0 and you're 6'3..."

"Six foot four and a quarter," Moon corrected, proud to be the second tallest Fab member behind Flabby.

"See!" Cowboy said, triumphant, his mouth opening wide in astonishment. He couldn't believe his luck, that Moon would emphasize his height at just the moment he needed it emphasized. Cowboy opened up his arms and talked as if he might be addressing Congress and not four people in a dorm room. "I move the point is voided and the game be resumed. All in favor?"

No one raised their hand in support of Cowboy's motion, and Flabby chuckled, enjoying Cowboy's moment of loss. It was Cowboy's stated goal to one day be President of the United States, and Flabby, who could be a little mean spirited, got a kick out of no one following his lead. "This game is on the books," he said, "but I do think you have a point about the reaching. We need a line that marks the point before which a penny must be tossed."

Before the debate could continue, the building began to quiver, something it had done before, much in the way that buildings in Chicago shook when the El went by. With a prophetic look on his face, The Dini held up his hands as if he were ready to conduct an orchestra.

Zuke laughed. Of all the members of the Fab, The Dini and Moon were the ones who most believed that supernatural powers regularly operated in the modern-day world. Within the past week,

The Dini had claimed to have been inhabited by the Holy Spirit, who'd *gifted* him a song, one which he'd copied frantically into the Mead composition notebook he carried on his person religiously. To hear The Dini tell it, he'd been channeling the Holy Spirit, but then Flabby had pointed out that The Dini's divine song contained two phrases prominent in the recent Michael Bolton song, "How Am I Supposed to Live Without You?" It wasn't just the movies that had a tricky way of slipping into the psyche undetected.

Everyone in the room had already heard The Dini's theory on the Holy Spirit's role in connection to the building shaking, and so they all stared at him good naturedly, expecting him to speak to what had just happened. "Okay, fine!" The Dini said. "Then what was it?" The Dini's large-round spectacles slipped a little on his face, the result of his excitement.

"You got me," Zuke said, feeling as if he were an actor playing his usual self. He spoke but didn't feel connected to his words for the way his guts churned at the propeller of anxiousness he felt about Abby. "I'm not laughing at you," Zuke explained to The Dini. "I just know you love it when Chapman gets the shakes."

Just a few weeks before, when there had been a similar sort of occurrence, the Brothers had completed a floor-to-floor inquiry, confirming that the whole building had shimmied from its pointed white roof to its marble-columned front porch. The shaking, which had happened enough that it was becoming somewhat accepted as a regular occurrence, stopped almost as soon as it started.

"Who's for a Power Dump?" Moon asked, looking around the room for someone to join him in the can. It was Moon who had coined all the phrases the Brothers used when they went down the hall to move their bowels: *a tandem* signaled two Brothers, *power dump* was for three, and *full house* reserved for the rare times all four of the stalls were occupied with a brother using the can. "At least a tandem?" Moon pleaded. "I want to talk about a *her.*" This word *her* took on important connotative meaning when it came to the Brothers. A *her* was a woman one of the Brothers was interested in dating, and it was often said among the friends that a man without a her is a man without hope.

"I think Bird has moved beyond *her* status," Zuke said. *Bird* was the nickname given to the daughter of the dean, easily enough conceived since her last name was *Parrot*.

Moon had been referring to Wendy "Bird" Parrot as his *her* for the past six months, ever since he'd seen her while in attendance at a resident assistants' meeting in her parents' home, a two-bedroom apartment on the ground floor of Chapman Hall. Although Bird had chosen to live with a roommate in the women's dormitory rather than live with her parents, she could often be found trekking through the lobby on her way for a visit with her mom and dad. It was on one of these visits that Bird had said "Excuse me," as she passed through her parents' living room on the way to the kitchen for a snack, and this was the one time she sort of spoke to Moon.

"All right," Zuke said, assenting to the tandem dump, "let's go."

The boys headed down the hall, which contained sixteen rooms housing thirty-five freshmen and sophomore men, all of whom shared a restroom with four stalls, four urinals, and a small shower (no stalls or curtains) that was filled to capacity as Zuke and Moon made their way into the restroom. They sat down on industrial strength toilets with silver flush rods while a fog of steam thickened around them. Voices of young men mixed with the rush of hot water.

"This morning, I was three people behind her at breakfast," Moon said, his sock-less feet clad in a pair of penny loafers plainly visible under the turquoise wall of the stall. Zuke recognized the voices in the shower as belonging to his classmates, one of whom was the likely culprit of the poop in the hallway.

"Didn't say anything?" Zuke asked, a smidgen of playful ridicule in his voice. It was how the Brothers got along, making fun of one another whenever they could.

Moon countered with a little grunt in his voice. "Look Zuke, it's not like everyone can just change their major to be around a girl." It was a low blow made possible by a confession of Zuke's at one of the Brothers' regular Sunday night meetings. It was for that reason—that Zuke had been relentlessly teased for at least a month—that now Zuke waited at least a day before he shared any major news about his life. It was for this reason that he thought he wouldn't just launch into the possibility that Abby would break up with Cheese.

"I'm calling her tonight," Moon declared. The guys in the shower were getting louder about something. The toilet paper dispenser jiggled in Moon's stall just as Zuke reached for his own roll.

"And what will you say?" As far as Zuke was concerned, Moon was on firm ground with his impulse to put in a cold call to Bird and ask her for a date. It had been just what Lloyd Dobler had done in *Say Anything* when he called Diane Court and had to explain who he was before he asked her out.

"I'm going to tell her she is the most beautiful woman I have ever seen, and that I'd like to talk with her."

It was only through good fortune that Zuke hadn't tried a similar plan. Circumstance had put Abby in his composition class, and this had negated any need for a random phone call. Instead, Zuke's boldness manifested itself in more of a silent and personal way: his choice of major allowed him to spend time with Abby and assume the role of question asker and listener, a plan of brilliance that he couldn't be given much credit for. Since Zuke had failed to notice any apparent flaws in Moon's phone-call strategy, the responsibility fell to Flabby, who had caught the tail end of the stall-to-stall conversation when he'd come in to shave at the sink.

"What could she possibly say to that?" Flabby asked, his tone accusing.

Moon had to respond to Flabby loudly since the din in the shower had grown tenfold.

"Thank you?" Moon suggested, "Let's go out? Let's make out?"

There was a jostling around in the shower now. What was probably going on was that the boys were now trying to pee on each other. What they liked to do was wait until a guy was immersed in washing his hair, eyes closed and scrubbing on his head. When that happened, they'd start to urinate on the unsuspecting victim who would eventually open his eyes and see what was going on. "Don't be such a faggot," one of the guys in the shower called out to another, laughing. *Faggot* was just the sort of thing the young men were always saying to one another, the worst they could think to call someone. Moon yelled from his seat on the toilet: "I thought I talked to you guys about that."

"Sorry Bossman," someone yelled back. "We forgot." Half-stifled laughter followed the apology. It was obviously not even close to sincere.

Moon, lowering his voice, asked Zuke, "Flush?"

Zuke assented and then in unison the two of them yelled, "Fluush!" In the shower, a complex rotation to the right got underway, movements which allowed its inhabitants to avoid the 2-3 seconds of scalding water that followed any flushed toilet. Because of this, naked and burned bodies no longer collided against one another.

Zuke and Moon exited the stalls and looked to where Flabby stood naked and shaving. When going to and from the bathroom, the man never covered himself. Moon said it was because he had a giant schlong, but Flabby said he just liked to air dry and that his life in sports had taught him to not think about whether or not he had clothes on. Flabby's towel was draped on a hook by the entrance, and he had to lean down to see his face as if using a child's sink, his neck crinked against his shoulder. "Okay," Moon said, "I'll work on what I'm going to say, but I've got to call her. This has gotten ridiculous."

Zuke and Moon left the bathroom and entered the hallway, which was wide enough that the men of Chapman Hall sometimes staged three-on-three knee football games. As they approached Cowboy and Moon's room, they could hear James Taylor on the stereo. The door was still open and Cowboy lay on the bed dressed in a white t-shirt and a pair of black dress pants reading a biography of Jimmy Carter. Both roommates had designs on futures that involved leadership positions. Cowboy fancied himself a politician, possibly even the President of the United States, while Moon knew he'd grow up to be a Nazarene preacher like his father. Cowboy—along with 90% of the rest of the student body—was a Republican who considered Ronald Reagan a personal hero.

Cowboy's reading of the Carter book was driven by his curiosity about what had gone so wrong in that man's presidency. Cowboy was a student who took his own eventual presidential bid seriously enough that he was often NOT doing things (for example dressing as a woman for a class homecoming skit) out of fear photographs might later surface out of context and cause damage to his reputation. Although Cowboy had never been on television or quoted in a newspaper, he sometimes preceded statements with the phrase, "This is off the record...."

As soon as Moon and Zuke returned to the room, a fellow fourth-floor resident named Nate Herman—he was Zuke's roommate and everyone called him Pee Wee (again the last name)—came rushing through the dark-wooded door frame. As he sliced between Zuke and Moon, Pee Wee, never a hitch in his step, impressively slammed the door behind him. "Lock it, lock it, lock it," he said, as if a killer pursued him down the hall.

There was something about Pee Wee that was slick, as if he could stereotypically become a used car salesman but perhaps someone more like Donald Trump. Pee Wee had wavy-blond hair that he tended to comb straight back, and when he wasn't fleeing from danger, he carried himself as if he were already a commercial real estate mogul. Pee Wee favored—but wasn't able to afford—gold watches, fine suits, and boats. He admired the golfer Greg "The Shark" Norman, Jimmy Buffett, and Michael Jordan for their moneyed empires. That Buffett had amassed such a fortune drinking, womanizing, and fishing—at least this was how Pee Wee explained it—showed that he was one of the ultimate geniuses in the history of mankind.

Pee Wee opened the shades to the window, which looked out toward the clock tower, Darby Hall of Science, and Burke Administration. The buildings were lit softly against the night sky as if they were pieces in a museum. "Oh, please lock it, Roomie," Pee Wee said. And when everyone looked to him for an explanation, he added, "Jesus. He'll be in here any second." A deep voice boomed from down the hall, loud, but the words were not yet discernable.

Pee Wee was jittery, as if he'd drunk an entire pot of coffee, and he frantically raised the window. For a moment, probably because he'd just recently re-watched Cusack's *Better Off Dead*, Zuke thought Pee Wee was going to jump, but then he turned away from the window and rushed to one of the cedar-colored massive wardrobes provided to each resident of Chapman Hall. He opened it and discovered a large cardboard box Moon used as a laundry bin. It was full of an overripe pile of smelly garments, including skid-marked tighty whiteys, and unfortunately for Pee Wee, the best available location to hide. A cold December breeze came in through the window and swayed the curtains as if a ghost had entered the room.

"Pee Wee," a voice thundered, closer now and amplified as if in a cave. "It's going to be worse if I have to chase you." Pee Wee stepped up onto Moon's pile of clothes, jammed his right leg down into the crease along the side of the box, then did the same with his other leg. Zuke grimaced a little when he saw Pee Wee grab an armload of dirty clothes—especially the grizzled underwear—and begin to burrow under them as if he were a rodent. "Close the door; close the door," Pee Wee begged, meaning the door to the wardrobe. His voice was muffled under the pile as he wriggled deeper toward the bottom of the cardboard laundry box. Somebody continued to bang their fist on the door, which was at least four inches thick and sturdy enough to withstand a police battering ram.

"You little son-of-a-bitch," an angry man yelled, a voice recognizable in the room to everyone as a football player with the last name Mulligan. "Are you in there? Open the door you snake."

Zuke eased the door to the wardrobe shut; Cowboy remained on his bed; and Moon, a little red in the face—probably from the cursing—unlocked the deadbolt to the door. The door burst open immediately, and Mulligan came into the room with the same intensity he used to bull-rush offensive linemen on his way to opposing quarterbacks. He was a pale-white version of Antoine, at least when it came to physique, and he seemed inhumanly fast and strong compared to Moon, who seemed to sometimes possess the motor skills of a toddler, wobbling his way around the campus as if he were on stilts.

Mulligan had thrown his forearm into the door with the full expectation that he'd find Pee Wee on the other side of it. The thick wood door just missed catching Moon in the face and instead glanced off his torso with enough force that it had knocked him to the floor. Mulligan had fallen too, the result of the way he'd planted his foot firmly onto a throw rug Cowboy kept next to the bed. The rug had slid on the hardwoods and although this had sent Mulligan flopping to the floor, he showed some of the same dogged perseverance that struck fear into the hearts of quarterbacks. He sprang to his feet like a cat and looked around the room. Pee Wee was nowhere to be seen and Mulligan, uniformed in the t-shirt of his favorite wrestler, Rowdy Roddy Piper, suddenly appeared confused.

"Oh," Mulligan said. He was sort of King Troublemaker, at least in Chapman Hall and Moon had already written him up many times for various violations, the worst of which was a hunting knife found in his desk drawer. This had gotten him a one week suspension not only from the football team, but also school. "Pee Wee's not in here?" The room was cold and before anyone answered Mulligan's question, he approached the open window.

"What's this about?" Moon asked, sort of gathering his splayed limbs as he worked his way back to a standing position.

"Uh," Mulligan hesitated on his way to answering Moon's question, "me and Pee Wee just needed to rap about some stuff. He owes me a little money." Mulligan, who had shoulder length curly hair, stuck his head way out the window and eyed the ledge in both directions. "Why is this window open?" He turned to the three young men with a suspicious stare. If not for Moon's status as resident assistant, Mulligan would have been *kicking ass and taking names,* a favorite phrase of his.

"I'm a little gassy today," Cowboy said.

Moon stared at Cowboy. It was probably Cowboy's use of the phrase *a little gassy* that gave him reason for pause. "Are you gay?" he asked, squinting at Cowboy as if one could stare intensely at a person and determine their sexual orientation. Cowboy shook his head. He probably had no idea what Mulligan was talking about. "Can I look in there?" Mulligan asked, pointing to Cowboy's wardrobe.

"You want to see my clothes?"

"No dipshit," Mulligan said, obviously realizing that he'd cursed in front of his R.A. again. "Sorry Bryan," he said to Moon. "I just want to see if you guys might not be hiding him." Then he turned to Zuke. "You're his roommate."

"You probably see him more than I do." That much was true. Pee Wee was from the same little town of Horseshoe that Zuke was from, but the two had only discovered during the last month of high school that they were both going to Pison, Zuke to play basketball and Pee Wee because his father would only pay for him to attend a Nazarene school. Mulligan opened the door to the wardrobe and began to slide Cowboy's clothes around to see if anyone was hiding behind them.

"Ever read *The Lion, The Witch, and The Wardrobe?*" Cowboy asked, a tint of sarcasm on his voice.

"Huh?" Mulligan asked, closing the door to Cowboy's wardrobe and going for Moon's. When he opened that door, he stared at the clothes as if they might tell him where Pee Wee had gone. The smell of week-old workout clothes began to cloud into his nose, a sort of olfactory torture that also worked as Pee Wee's saving grace, buying time over which Mulligan's anger might fade. Mulligan continued his interrogation: "He didn't go out on that ledge and into another room?" Mulligan stared at Moon, as if the question were only for him.

Once Moon had conceded that sometimes it was okay to lie, as in the usual example of Nazis knocking at the door for Jews during WWII, but it was a line of thinking he was apt to have trouble believing in as he applied it to present-day situations. Moon told Mulligan that Pee Wee certainly hadn't used the ledge and that there'd be a hefty fine for anyone who did.

"I hear that," Mulligan said, surveying the room. He'd received many a fine, both from Moon and other representatives of the college. "Can I look under the bed?"

"This is not a game of hide and seek," Moon said, reasserting his residential powers. "Your inspection is over. If we see Pee

Wee, we'll tell him you're looking for him." It was certain that Mulligan didn't like the tone of Moon's voice, but even he was likely to understand that this wasn't the spot for him to challenge his R.A.

"Cool," Mulligan said, starting for the doorway. "Catch you guys on the flip side." Mulligan left the room, and Zuke moved over to the door, pushed it shut, and turned the deadbolt. Then he reached over and opened the wardrobe just in time to see Pee Wee pop up as if he were a jack-in-the-box.

"That never happens to Jordan," Pee Wee said, dirty underwear, a sweater, and a pair of stiff workout shorts clinging to him as if he'd just come from the dryer. The Jordan reference was something Pee Wee had begun to say after one day at the park he jammed a basketball into the side of a rim and fell to the blacktop on his back. With flattened lungs, desperate for air, Pee Wee had wheezed, "That never happens to Jordan." The phrase had caught on among the members of The Fab, who were now always on the lookout for times to say it.

Clothes spilled out onto the floor as Pee Wee stepped from the wardrobe, and he smiled the way he did when his father sent him a surprise check in the mail. "It ain't easy being cheesy," he said, ala the Cheetos commercial. Pee Wee gave the double-thumbs-up sign that everything was A-okay.

"What's Mulligan so ticked at?" Moon asked.

"That big lummox?" Pee Wee had already seemed to forget how frightened he'd been when he'd first come running into the room. "He thinks I stole something from him." Cowboy asked him if he did; Pee Wee said he didn't, and then he headed for the door. "I've got to see a man about a dog," he said, turning the deadbolt, easing the door open, and sticking his head out into the hallway so that he could look both ways and make sure Mulligan was not in sight. As he left, Pee Wee closed the door softly behind him.

With Pee Wee gone, Zuke thought about telling Moon and Cowboy about Abby, but before he could launch into it, Moon went over to his desk, where he picked up his phone, obviously intent on making the call to Wendy "Bird" Parrot. "You're really going to do it?" Zuke asked. It was an amazing thing to see, to have Moon wait so long and then suddenly take action. "Right now?"

"What's he going to do?" Cowboy wondered.

"I'm tired of all this," said Moon, who looked as if he was talking to the phone, holding it responsible for the fact that he had never spoken with Bird.

"What brought this on?" Cowboy asked, getting interested. He smiled and leaned forward on his bed.

"No more talking," Moon said. "Time for action." He started to press the buttons on the phone.

"He knows the number," Zuke said.

"Of course he knows the number," Cowboy responded. "How many times do you think he's done this when we weren't here?" The ring on the other end was just perceptible to Cowboy and Zuke. Moon stood from his chair, the darkness of night behind him, and he began to pace the length of the room, the extra-long phone cord trailing behind. First Moon walked toward Cowboy, who still sat on the bed, and then back to Zuke, who stood near the door. Someone answered the call, and for Zuke and Cowboy, there was the barely audible sound of a woman's voice.

"Is Wendy there?" Moon asked. He sounded calm enough; good thing she couldn't see him, his arms tense against his body while he held the phone as if it were a lifeline stretched down from the edge of a cliff. A few seconds passed where nothing was said, and then Moon must have given his answer to the question of who was calling. "Bryan Willingham."

"What's she doing?" Cowboy hissed. Moon shook his head vigorously no, that he didn't want anyone talking to him. Five or six more seconds passed, and Moon rested his forehead on the door to the room, as if his anxiety were about the overtake him. "No thank you," he said into the phone and popped it into the cradle. "Oh my gosh," he said, turning around. "I almost had an aneurysm." He carefully set the phone onto the floor. Moon was cautious with everything he owned, including his new car, a 1989 Buick LeSabre in which not only was there no eating allowed, but he didn't even let anyone roll down the windows.

Moon howled as if he'd missed a game winning shot, and he ran toward the bed, stepped on the end-board and vaulted himself up onto the top bunk where the springs gave several inches toward Cowboy's head.

"That was her roommate," Moon said, lying back and looking up to the ceiling where he'd strategically placed an inspirational Christian poster. It had three photographs on it: a majestic looking eagle soaring over a mountaintop, a lion roaring on an African Plain, and a bear swiping a meaty paw into the whitewater of a stream. The fore-grounded caption read, *His Power Has No Limits.*

"She was out," Moon said, simply enough, seemingly pleased with his own attempt at action and probably relieved that Bird hadn't been there.

"Didn't you think it took the roommate awhile to tell you that Bird wasn't in?" Zuke was thinking this through. He imagined them all over there wearing boxers and t-shirts, or else since it was winter (who knew what the temperature was in the girls' residence hall?) maybe sweatpants and hoodies.

"You think she was lying?" Moon responded. "I wouldn't expect the daughter of the dean to room with a liar."

"Doesn't she room with Magic?" Cowboy asked. Just as in the NBA, Pison Nazarene College had a Magic opposite its Bird, a young lady whose real name was Marie Barrett, as in Barrett Hall, where the school's most beautiful women all seemed to choose to live. The dorm was named for Marie's Great Grandmother Orla, who was Pison's first-ever teacher back when the school had just been a high school and classes had been held in the church sanctuary.

"Magic moved back home," Moon said. "She's a commuter now. Wendy dorms with some girl named Heidi."

"Good looking?" Cowboy asked, always in search of a new girl to add to his list of *hers.*

Moon shook his head. He couldn't be bothered with the roommate's looks. What was in question at the moment was who might have lied about what. "What if Wendy was in and just didn't want to talk to me," Moon wondered. "What if she's the liar?" His eyes widened as if the Lord had just whispered to him the day and time of the rapture.

"Does Bird even know who you are?" Zuke asked, leaning against the thickly shellacked concrete blocks that formed the room. Zuke didn't think that Bird knew Moon and so she'd really not have a reason to lie. "I mean like, would she hear your name and be able to picture you? Would she know you well enough to know that she didn't want to talk to you?"

"Right," Cowboy said. "Good job, Zuke. I think no matter how hot a girl is, she'd still be interested in who is calling her."

"Moon could be Tom Cruise for all Bird knows," Zuke said.

"Oh," Moon said with a certain aspect of regret.

"What?" Cowboy asked.

"I gave my name," Moon said. "She's probably got the yearbook out right now looking to see who I am."

"Isn't that kind of the point?" Zuke asked.

"It's a terrible picture," Moon said. "Last year's yearbook picture." The thrill of the phone call seemed to already be draining out of him. It was a low Zuke knew well, having put in over a year of riding the ebb and flow of Abby's last comment, riding the waves of how happy she'd appeared with Cheese each time Zuke saw the couple together.

Moon took a deep breath, a sigh loaded with the burden of a garbage bag's worth of thoughts. "Blow job," he said. The Brothers had a tendency to mumble such phrases under stressful or depressing situations, as if they could just order up a sexual pleasure anytime they felt in need of relief. French kiss, back rub, and boob were some of the other more common ones.

"Moon!" Cowboy chastised. At the last Sunday-night meeting, all the Brothers had agreed that the pursuit of God and compassion for others clearly overrode any selfish desire they had for giving or receiving sensual pleasures.

"Marital blow job," Moon said, correcting himself and amending the phrase so that it could be included under a desire for God's sexual gifts to a married couple.

Zuke and Cowboy laughed, and Zuke could feel at least a thousand word analysis coming on for every word that Moon had just said and heard from Bird's roommate. He had work to do, especially a paper due the following Tuesday in Professor Moore's expository writing class.

"I've got to get started on a paper," Zuke said, getting up before the conversation got going again. He picked up his backpack from just inside the door. Zuke left his friends lying on their beds, certain they would pass at least an hour discussing Moon's call to Bird.

CHAPTER FOUR

Zuke came into his room dreading the thought of writing another paper. As an English major who never really liked English, Zuke was beginning to not hate some of the stories he'd been reading—for example, John Updike's "A & P"—but the writing never went well. It was painfully slow. Each sentence had to be drawn out of his thinking as if it were a tiny splinter stuck under his skin.

Over by the windows in Zuke and Pee Wee's room, there was a television and VCR sitting atop a waist-high bookshelf which contained about forty of Zuke's favorite movies. Back in Horseshoe, Zuke had at least another hundred in his parents' basement. By now, Zuke thought, plopping himself down into his desk chair, Abby was out with Cheese, maybe already parked out along the Kankakee River deep in a heavy make out session. Zuke looked at the wall in front of him where he'd taped his cherished *Say Anything* poster for inspiration. It was the one (are there any others?) where Dobler holds the boom box over his head. It was from this action of Dobler's that Zuke had come to believe he was only the right combination of actions away from gaining a woman's love interest. This meant that he was always mixing some combination of flowers, love notes, poems, some apt phrase at just the right time, gifts of jewelry, or other romantic gestures. Right now, as if Abby's heart were secured with a Master Lock, Zuke had spun the dial one way with a locket, another with his exposed feelings in the engraving, and now he wondered if Abby would be the one to turn the dial for the last time and finally pop their love open like a locker door.

There was a sloshing behind Zuke and he turned to look. "Hey, Chet," Zuke said, to Pee Wee's pet piranha, so named—at Zuke's suggestion—after the big brother in *Weird Science*. A poster of Kelly LeBrock was appropriately taped over the aquarium on the wall, pictured as she had been seen in *Weird Science,* clad in a cut-off sweatshirt and a pair of skimpy blue panties. The picture was of that moment in the movie just after she'd blasted through the bathroom door, having been created from a Barbie doll by two teenage boys who wore bras on their heads. Her lips were voluptuous, her long legs crossed sexily, and she wore high heeled shoes. Her hair blew in an indoor wind, a fantastic red light glowed from behind her, and the fog that hung in the air placed her firmly in the world of make believe.

Of course Zuke didn't think he could create a woman, but the degree to which he'd hung a fantasy on his wall escaped him, even though it was fitting for the way he thought about romantic relationships. The Brothers, in their own way, over the many conversations in their respective dorm rooms, had done a fair amount of female creation themselves. Because the poster depicted LeBrock's bare stomach and her lower half was only covered by panties, it would have been illegal according to Pison guidelines to hang it on the wall. As a way around this, Zuke had made from construction paper a full length sweater and a skirt that extended to the top of Kelly's knee.

Zuke unzipped the middle compartment of his backpack and pulled out his run-off copies of *Time* magazine, *Newsweek,* and articles from the *Chicago Tribune*—he hadn't even read these yet, but one of them contained another headline from the Middle East: "Democrats Fear Gulf Consequences, Costs." The fourth floor of Chapman Hall had taken on an aspect of tranquility: the quiet before the storm of curfew, when everyone would return to the dorm.

"No Abby," Zuke told himself. "Concentrate. Time to write this paper." Zuke had barely told himself this when his phone rang, and he picked up the receiver thinking it would be Moon or Cowboy wanting his opinion about some nugget they'd sifted from the flow of Moon's phone call to Bird. "Yeah?"

"Hey you," Abby said. Her voice had already crossed boundary lines this day, and now she adopted a more intimate tone of familiarity. She never called him at night, and Zuke hoped that the unusualness of it meant that she had decided not to wait to break up with Cheese; she'd just gone ahead and done it, and now she was ready to begin her life with Zuke as her man.

"You didn't go out?" Zuke asked. He sat with both elbows on his desk, his left hand holding the phone to his ear, his right one clenched into a fist against his cheek. His momentary hopefulness ebbed away and he worried about bad news.

"We're just about ready to go," Abby said. She might as well have told Zuke she just wanted to say hi before she went to make out with Cheese. "You know how it is with him. Big man on campus has to talk to everyone. I just came back to my room for a second. No one is here. I wanted to tell you I was thinking about you." There was a knock at Zuke's door.

"Thanks," Zuke said, distracted by the knock, his mind spiraling for something to say. Usually his time with Abby was easily anticipated—in class or during the hours in the library after dinner—and he prepared for those moments by creating actual lists of topics and questions which he could bring up in the event that conversation stalled. After waking up mornings he spent a lot of pre-Abby time imagining the conversations they'd have, and sometimes he went so far as to scrawl notes atop a tablet where he could peek at them the way a comedian might place a skeleton outline of an act taped to the stage floor. The knock at Zuke's door grew more demanding; maybe Mulligan had come back for another shot at Pee Wee.

"Is someone there?" Abby asked. Zuke rose from his seat, went to the door, and when he opened it, there was The Dini, dressed for a performance in a heavily starched pin-striped shirt and a paisley tie. He was a member of the Pisonians, a four-person traveling singing group that visited area churches and often performed a song or two for on campus events. Zuke told Abby it was The Dini at the door.

"It's not what he thinks," Abby said. "I don't know how to do this. If I act differently, Brett is going to know something is up. He'd make a scene."

"Okay," Zuke said, his voice wobbling with uncertainty. Apparently they were getting to the real reason for the call. "What happened? What did Phillip see?" Zuke backed away from the door waving Phillip in, who listened closely now that he'd heard his name.

"He just saw us together," Abby said. "Just like always." She paused. "Look, I've got to go. Nothing is different for me. I'll call you Sunday night, okay?" Zuke told her okay and hung up the phone. The Dini walked into the middle of the room. The overhead light reflected onto his large round spectacles.

"That was Abby?" Phillip asked, lacking his usual pop of enthusiasm. Zuke told him it was, and that she'd said he saw something.

"What? That little hussy all over her boyfriend?" The Dini laughed rapid fire, in the style of a woodpecker. "Those two need to get a room." His head wagged with attitude. "Oh, I see. I suppose she thought I was going to run over here and be a tattletale?" The Dini waved his hand. "Shoot, she can do what she wants." The Dini knew how much Zuke liked Abby. "And the rest of it is between ya'll and that young man they call Cheese." Even though The Dini had been born in Indianapolis, he had an accent much like the ladies who were on the television show *Designing Women;* in fact, that was the very place Moon had theorized that The Dini had picked up his way of talking.

"So what's the latest dirt on you two?" The Dini asked. "It's all so David and Goliath, so scandalous and romantic; little ole you against the big stinky Cheese Man." Phillip sat on Pee Wee's bed. It had a white comforter with neon lines, a variety of colors that zigged and zagged across it. His hands were on his knees and his posture erect, as if he might be sitting for a portrait.

This was Zuke's first opportunity to share his news of what Abby said she'd do. He was sitting across from The Dini, and feeling as he did sometimes, that in The Dini he was talking to an older Southern woman of the sort he'd never met, someone who sometimes engaged in some harmless flirting. Zuke told the story of his night to The Dini who grew as serious as Ronald Reagan on Star Wars Defense.

"Well that's hard, Eric Zaucha." The Dini wasn't much for the nicknames and was one of the few people who used Zuke's actual last name. "I hope that happens for you. You're a good man, and I'll be praying for you."

Both men twisted their separate thoughts, like Rubik's Cubes, and the only noise was the hum of the water filter in Chet's tank. "So if it wasn't to tell on Abby," Zuke said, forcing a smile while a memory of Abby surfaced. It was something he'd seen her do quite a bit: go running at Cheese and then leap into the air so that he could catch her. Abby would then wrap her legs around Cheese's waist and they'd kiss. Zuke, who was pretty skinny, thought Abby would probably knock him to the ground if she tried that with him. "What brings you by?" Zuke asked, somewhat absentmindedly, pulled to some dark mental place by his ugly fantasy.

Phillip pursed his lips a little and looked at the floor. He was no doubt a member of the Fab Five, one of the Brothers, but also mostly apart from them, a business major with a minor in art history who didn't know if the Reds played baseball in Cincinnati or basketball in Chicago.

"I think everyone," Phillip began, his sentence giving out like a worn copy of a Beta tape. The Dini's demeanor suddenly had Zuke's full attention. Something was wrong.

"I guess people probably know this," The Dini continued, "but I haven't really ever said it explicitly." Phillip looked directly at Zuke; a single tear rolled down The Dini's left cheek. "I suppose it's that I don't want to go to hell." He said this quietly, with his voice going shaky all of a sudden.

"To hell?" Zuke asked, having not sensed the heat of that bit of information coming forth. A couple of seconds dripped away like water torture.

"You know," Phillip said, his voice softening, "because I might be gay." The Dini put his hand up to his temples and rubbed them, as if he had a migraine. The Fab had long suspected that The Dini was indeed a homosexual. There was his love of musicals, his long days of shopping out with the best looking girls at Pison, his effeminate mannerisms, and that he worked as a housecleaner preferring to do that job in his tighty whiteys.

With The Dini hurting, Zuke felt some sort of touch would be appropriate; perhaps a buck-up-little-camper punch on the arm, a clasped shoulder, or possibly even a hug. Had The Dini been another friend or even if this conversation would have been about something besides The Dini's homosexuality, Zuke probably would have taken action, but as it was, he stayed put. "I'm not super up on my Bible verses," Zuke said. "You know, they don't really debate homosexuality here."

The Dini had a Bible verse all loaded up: "Do you not know that the wicked will not inherit the kingdom of God?"

Zuke didn't know the exact verse, but he knew the Bible well enough to realize he was hearing it. Christian or no Christian—and Zuke would say he was some sort of one, not necessarily according to the Pison way—a student couldn't jump through the school's curricular hoops without gaining some sense of the Bible's message. "Does the Bible clearly say being gay is wicked?" Zuke had in fact once thought he might be gay—this was in late elementary school—not the result of his sexual preference, but because he thought he was developing pointy breasts. Back then, Zuke thought gay was something that just happened to a person, sort of like going bald, something you had to deal with that wasn't so pleasant. As for his current stance on homosexuality, Zuke believed his own life so full of sin (lustful thoughts, high school sex, personal vanity, lies, hopes for the demise of others, mainly Cheese) that he wouldn't think to look for it in someone else's life.

"The Bible calls homosexual acts indecent," The Dini said, "and says that those who commit such acts as deserving of death."

"Don't we all have lives that contain indecent acts?" Zuke could see that The Dini was certainly up on his theology, at least as it pertained to sexual orientation.

"Not ones worthy of spiritual death; not if we turn from sin, accept Christ, and ask for His forgiveness."

Zuke looked at the floor and then up to The Dini. His brown eyes had steeled themselves as if awaiting news from an oncologist. "Not something at this point you can do in good conscience?"

"And the worst is that I know. It's not as if I want to be with a man and don't know any better. I've read the truth."

Zuke wondered if The Dini had nailed down more of the specifics of his reference to *a man,* wondered if maybe he had a crush on one of the Fab. This didn't seem the spot to ask about The Dini's interior romantic life. If was more of a belief system kind of talk and because Zuke was uncomfortable, he did what he sometimes did in moments of pressure. He sort of made a joke: "Doesn't the Bible say not to eat shrimp?" This Zuke remembered from Old Testament class, a course during which he was supposed to have outlined the whole thing, an assignment he'd eventually given up on. The professor had made everyone sign a piece of paper as an affidavit the work had been completed, something Zuke chose to do rather than fail the course. "I don't think I'm going to Hell because I eat shrimp from Red Lobster." Zuke paused and then smiled. "Especially not the grilled ones that taste so good skewered with some beef and veggies."

"I don't want to talk about shellfish," The Dini said, his face flushed maybe anger at what he considered avoidance on Zuke's part. "I want your opinion, as a friend. From what you understand, do you think I'll go to Hell if I decide to act on my homosexuality?"

There it was. The Dini couldn't be any clearer than that. Zuke took a deep breath, not because he didn't want to tell The Dini what he thought, but because he didn't have the slightest idea of what to say. The Dini had actually been pretty convincing in his argument against homosexuality. Zuke, in fact, usually let Christianity's judgment on sexual orientation float up out of his thinking as if it was a helium balloon he didn't have any use for. "I want to say no," Zuke said to The Dini about his going to Hell. There were a lot of voices yelling in Zuke's head telling him being gay was a sin, but Zuke had come to think of what many people at Pison would call a conscience, the product of his environmental conditioning, whatever it was that had been told to him his whole life. "The question has never mattered much to me before today. It's something I've never taken the time to think about."

The Dini nodded his head in dejection. Off in the distance, College Church's bells gonged eleven o'clock. "I already know what I believe," he said. "I just keep hoping someone will say something that will give me reason to think otherwise. I've never acted on the way I feel. Maybe God understands and will give me some credit for trying so hard."

"Sure," Zuke said. "If homosexuality is a sin, and you haven't acted on what you've felt, then you're no worse off than me. I sin every day, at least in my mind." The Dini got up from Pee Wee's bed, ending the talk in the manner of a psychologist whose patient has stayed long enough. The Dini had a way, a manner which allowed him to share, make himself vulnerable, and still seem in control.

"It feels good to have told you," he said, rising from the bed. He pulled a cloth handkerchief from his pocket and blew his nose powerfully into it.

"I feel like I didn't answer your question," Zuke said, rising to stand with The Dini. "You're a great friend. You're a good person, a better man than me. Maybe we'll both have more to say after we think about it for awhile."

"I've had plenty of time to think about this," The Dini said. Zuke extended his hand and the two young men shook, an awkward exchange which Zuke forced because he wanted to do something to give an affirmation, to undertake an action that said, *I'm with you, Brother.*

"Good luck with Abby," The Dini said. "She's a nice person but confused. You're a good guy; I'll pray for you. The best thing might not be what you think it is." The Dini opened up the door and stepped out into the hall. Zuke was trying to think about what The Dini had said. He couldn't think of a great reason for Abby to pick a guy like himself, but he didn't think Cheese was so great either.

Cowboy's voice boomed from down the hall toward where The Dini was standing: "Tell Zuke I need someone to go eat some gut busters with."

This made The Dini laugh. "Lord help me."

CHAPTER FIVE

It was Crowe's Café that served the locally famous gut-buster, a half pound of beef hamburger, two slices of jalapeno cheese, an especially hot veggie chili sauce, along with a host of more standard fixin's including tomatoes and lettuce. The sandwich wouldn't actually fit inside a human mouth, and upon special request it could be ordered *Porno Hot*—one got a t-shirt for eating it that way—and Cowboy had been personally excluded from the offer after securing his fifth. The restaurant had formerly been a gas station and the protective awning for the pumps was still out in front of the building. There were two large windows on each side of the front door, by which the register was located. In the building's previous life, one could have bought convenience-store goods up where the counter was now. Most of the seating was where the garage had been and nearly thirty years of messages had been carved into the wooden tables. The menu said, "since 1964." It was twenty minutes past eleven when Cowboy and Zuke entered the premises. Cowboy had been chattering away about Jimmy Carter while Zuke tried not to think too hard about where Abby was at the moment.

It was a down time at the café. Those who had come for dinner were long gone and those who would crowd in after the bars closed were still a few hours away. "Well take a look over there," Cowboy said as he slid into the booth. Zuke looked toward the counter and saw the daughter of the dean—the woman known to the Fab as Bird—clad in a work apron and leaning languidly against the wall. She wasn't quite a bony girl, but she was tall and slender with high cheekbones and a straight thin nose, her pale complexion clear, and lips full, and she was smiling to herself as if relishing a joke she'd just secretly played on a co-worker. Her hair was long and dark, almost to her waist, with traces of blonde highlights, and she had a hint of a dimple when she smiled. Bird looked more like an aspiring actress than a preacher's wife, which was the role Moon had in mind for her, but one could see how in her church clothes—the place where Moon usually saw her—she might garner knight in shining armor sort of thoughts.

"Guess she wasn't in after all," Zuke observed. "I do admit, Moon has good taste." Zuke hadn't seen Bird much since the year before and certainly never working at the café. She turned her head right to where they were sitting, her startling brown eyes met Zuke's for a moment, and he had to remind himself that there was no way she'd heard him, no way she could know the name Moon, or that he'd been talking about her. Wendy hurried toward them, pulling a pen from behind her ear, her eyes showing more than a glint of recognition.

"Hey guys," she said. "Sorry about that. I totally spaced." Wendy stood at the edge of the booth, her bangs scrunched up and off her forehead. Zuke wondered what she had been thinking about, wondered what it was that would make such a woman smile the way she'd been smiling. "You're the guy with the fan club," she said, nodding to Zuke. By fan club Bird meant that some of his friends—including Moon and Cowboy—always dressed at Pison home basketball games in white t-shirts that spelled Z-U-K-E. Zuke was a bit surprised that Bird had put it all together, that he was the guy whose name was spelled by the shirts. It was kind of embarrassing, really.

"Eric," Zuke said, introducing himself and already feeling out of the ordinary, as if Kelly LeBrock had climbed out of her poster from next to his desk and asked him about how he liked Pison College. It had taken Zuke nearly a year to not at least visibly freak out in Abby's presence over how attractive he thought she was. "You're Wendy," Zuke said. "We know you from your dad." He regretted the line as soon as he said it knowing it had been predictable. Generally, Zuke tried to imagine people's usual comments and say something else.

"Doesn't everyone?" Wendy asked.

"I'm the *k,*" Cowboy said, raising up his sweatshirt to reveal that at that very moment he was wearing his lettered shirt.

"I've noticed," Wendy said, aggressive like a fairy-tale princess never would be. "I hope that shirt's going to get washed before Saturday." Zuke noticed that Cowboy's cheeks glowed. Bird was smiling easily and happily. It was instantly obvious that the two of them had great chemistry. Cowboy told Wendy his name, included his nickname, and then a bit abruptly—Bird seemed content to just chat away with them—Cowboy told her he knew what he wanted and ordered two Porno-Hot Gut Busters and a large Coke. The air felt electric, Cowboy saying the word *porno* in the presence of a girl like that.

Zuke ordered just one Gut Buster, minus the Porno, and Wendy left their booth undaunted by what she could have read as a brush off from Cowboy, who hadn't acknowledged that she'd said she noticed him at the games. Maybe Cowboy's red cheeks had told her all she needed to know. Zuke certainly felt the energy spring up between them, as if they were a nuclear reactor come to life, and their feelings, if acted upon, had the potential to enact their own Chernobyl upon Cowboy and Moon's friendship.

After Wendy moved out of earshot, Zuke shifted the porcelain container of sugar packets from the edge of the table and began to stack them on top of one another. Coming in to Crowe's, he'd thought he'd go over Abby's break up plan with Cowboy, but now there was something more pressing on the table of conversation. Zuke wanted to let Cowboy bring it up first, but then he couldn't wait. "Uh, oh," Zuke said smiling. He'd wanted to keep a straight face but failed.

"Uh, oh," Cowboy repeated, his smile matching that of Zuke's, and his legs jiggling so hard under the table that Zuke could feel the entire booth begin to vibrate. "Let's not get ahead of ourselves. Maybe she's just nice. Maybe it's good to see someone she knows at work. It's got to be pretty boring."

"Pretty boring," Zuke echoed, unconvinced and sarcastically playing along. He reached for the bottle of ketchup on the tabletop, turned it upside down and tried to make it balance. "But let's pretend for a second that she is interested." Zuke wondered why he felt so exhilarated that the *her* of one of his best friends seemed interested in Cowboy. Maybe he felt the excitement of meeting a movie star sort of woman—that's the aura the brothers constructed with their dorm-room conversations—or else possibly humanity can't help but feel just a tiny bit of zip at the sort of conflict that arises between men over women.

"Well if she's interested," Cowboy said, "it doesn't matter. Moon's my Brother. He's made it plain how he feels about her."

"He's never even talked to her," Zuke said. "In the last two minutes you said more to her than he has."

"Well if she's interested," Cowboy said again, his voice sounding just a little more hopeful, "maybe I'll talk to Moon and see what he thinks."

It was nearly midnight when Cowboy polished off his second Gut Buster, just a little sweat on his brow, the only consequence of spices hot enough for some patrons to lose their stomachs. Eventually, they'd gotten to the latest on Zuke and Abby, but not reached any conclusions about what they thought she'd do. It was good that she'd said she was breaking up, and both men agreed that she might or might not follow through with her plan. Sunday certainly would be an interesting day.

Zuke had taken the paper off both his straws and rolled them into tiny balls, where he created little piles off to the side of his plate. Cowboy had resigned himself to the fact that he could not pursue Wendy at the moment, probably not ever, not unless by some freak accident Moon began to date someone else. Wendy walked toward them with the check; she had that same bedeviled expression on her face she'd had when Zuke first saw her.

"I hear that's a sign of sexual frustration," she said nodding to Zuke, who looked down at his shirt to see if he'd drooled on it. "Whatever it is that you did with the wrappers on the straw." Wendy winked at Zuke before she turned to Cowboy. "Can I ask you guys a favor?" Cowboy told her that she could. "There's this new guy in the back. He hasn't really done anything; I'm probably just being stupid, but I don't like the way he stares. Anyway, I'm off in a second; do you mind walking around the back while I get into my car?" Cowboy and Zuke agreed, still a little razzled at suddenly talking with Wendy "Bird" Barrett. "Besides," she said, looking at Cowboy, "I've got something I want to ask you." Zuke and Cowboy both thought of T.W.I.R.P. weekend. It was a weekend where the girls were supposed to ask out the boys and the letters were rumored (at least on the fourth floor of Chapman Hall) to stand for "The Woman Is Responsible to Pay."

Wendy went over to the register, and it was obvious that everyone at the cafe liked her: the other waitresses, the high school boys who bussed the tables, and especially the older woman who counted out Wendy's tips from behind the counter. Cowboy laid a fiver on the table.

"She's going to TWIRP you," Zuke said.

Cowboy grimaced. "I'm in big trouble." He couldn't help but smile.

Outside in the parking lot, it was still windy and very cold. Zuke sat in Cowboy's car, a massive Lincoln Continental, thinking that by this time, Abby ought to be on her way back to her dorm room, and he was thinking about how a year's worth of planning, silent prayer, and countless thoughtful gestures, had hopefully now put him in position to be a good boyfriend. Zuke was banking on kindness and common interests to win out over good looks, basketball skills, and campus fame.

Cowboy and Wendy stood in front of her Buick Monte Carlo, shiny white, with black t-tops, two thin red-racing stripes running along the bottom with a red *SS* on the door. She stood opposite Cowboy and hugged herself inside her grey wool trench coat. She wore a knitted cap pulled down low over her long dark hair. Cowboy stood just a few feet from her and shifted his weight nervously from side to side, laughing occasionally. His ears were exposed and red. He wore a Chicago Cubs baseball cap turned around backwards on his head. Once the two of them looked right at Zuke, Cowboy seemingly impressed, as if Wendy had told him of some great achievement, even though Zuke had never spoken to her before this night. Zuke thought maybe when he returned to the dorm he'd have a call from Abby. Maybe tonight she'd just gone ahead and gotten it all over with.

The door to the Continental opened, and a blast of December air puffed inside, jerking Zuke from his thoughts. Cowboy plopped into the deep cloth seat; his car had a bench that went all the way across—perfect for snuggling, he'd always said—if only he had a girlfriend. Obviously cold but very excited, Cowboy hurried the key into the ignition. "You were right," he said, staring straight ahead at the white cement blocks of the backside of Crowe's Cafe. "I've been TWIRPed." Cowboy put his hands on the wheel at the ten and two position. Wendy's Monte Carlo crunched the gravel from behind them, and she gave her horn two quick toots. There was a brand new silver Mustang parked next to where Wendy's car had been. Cowboy waved. "And so have you." Cowboy turned and looked right at Zuke. "That is if you're up to it."

"Who?" Zuke asked, even as his mind leapt to images of Abby, her toned long legs erupting off the floor to spike a volleyball into the hardwood.

"Magic," Cowboy said. "Marie Barrett! Can you believe it? Bird and Magic want to go out with us."

CHAPTER SIX

T he next day, Friday, Saddam Hussein was front page news again, gas was $1.53 a gallon, the metal bands Warrant and Poison were set to play a show up the road at the Rosemont Horizon, and Zuke was down to two sleeping nights before Abby's alleged break up was to occur with Cheese. The previous night had not brought any news from Abby. Friday was not a study-in-the-library day for the two of them, and now the Pison men's basketball team was near the end of practice. As usual, Zuke was doing what he could to defend the team's star attraction.

Cheese was 6'4 with exceptionally tan skin, broad shoulders, thick wrists, and lips that, at least on the court, seemed fixed in an eternal sneer. Cheese set up under the basket as the point guard brought the ball across the center circle, and Zuke set up to block Cheese's intended path. There was a new dimension to practice on this day, that now Zuke could consider the repercussions should Abby actually follow through with her breakup plan. At the moment, Zuke couldn't imagine Cheese competing any more fiercely than he already did. As Cowboy was prone to saying the year before, Cheese was an absolute bearcat to guard.

As Zuke and Cheese's bodies came together under the basket, Cheese gripped Zuke's practice jersey with both hands and pulled him close. He was redolent with the musky cologne he applied *before* practice. Cheese grunted as if readying to pull a Buick from a ditch, an act he seemed nearly capable of accomplishing.

From out toward the sideline, Flabby came over with the intention of chipping Zuke off of Cheese with one of his big hip bones. Although the two were best friends, Flabby relished his regular screening of Zuke and often liked to tell the Fab about his biggest hits in the evenings. Cheese twisted to the baseline and stuck his elbow in Zuke's chest, using his other hand to grab his own fist and thrust his arm like a piston, driving the point of his elbow into the center of Zuke's body. This sent Zuke backwards, which created the space Cheese needed to begin his sprint out to the wing where he was supposed to receive the basketball.

With the determination of a mosquito going for an eardrum, Zuke slid past Flabby without being hit. At one hundred and fifty-five pounds, Zuke was no easy player to screen because he was so skinny. The point guard's pass was wide and although Cheese had to turn his back to the court, he was still able to reach out and snag the ball. Zuke pressed his knees—like two small spades—into Cheese's hamstrings, and he lay his chest on his back, sticking his face close to Cheese's neck.

"Rip it through," Coach Miller instructed. He was a big man with unkempt caterpillar eyebrows and thick black hair he shellacked straight back just like Pat Riley. Coach's teams were known for their competitive ruthlessness, and he was of the philosophy that practices should be harder than the game, more akin to street brawls than anything else. No player embodied this spirit more than his star player.

Cheese did indeed rip it through, leading with his elbow as he squared to the basket. The elbow caught Zuke just above his mouth— likely an offensive foul had this been a game—and the blow forced Zuke's teeth into his upper lip, and snapped his head back as if he'd received a Mike Tyson punch, vengeance for his embarrassing loss to Buster Douglass. While all this went on, the rest of the players on the court moved and pushed for position, reading for Cheese to either pass or else shoot. A dribble left Zuke behind, and Cheese's muscled thighs, hamstrings, and calves pushed him forcefully up into the air. Cheese's right elbow at first cocked and then unfolded where his arm, wrist, hand, and finally his fingers released the ball. The leather didn't graze the rim as it passed into the net, briefly defying gravity as it spun and then dropped to the floor.

"Atta boy," Coach Miller said, a smile spreading onto his face when he saw that Zuke's teeth were pasted crimson with blood.

"Let's run it all the way through this time," Coach Miller said, fingering the gold Super Bowl ring on his right hand, an adornment he'd picked up during his two-year pro football career during which he was a second string tight end for the Pittsburgh Steelers. "We know you can score on the third team; I just want to see us execute." Miller took a few steps closer to where Zuke stood. "Too easy, Zaucha," he said. "I'm never going to be able to play you if you keep that up."

While the team manager retrieved the basketball and got it back out to center court for the next play, Zuke followed Cheese as he jogged back down under the basket. The two players battled every day, Zuke the third string guard who sought to prove to Coach Miller that he deserved a little bit of playing time. Of course Abby provided extra motivation for the two competitors, but it wasn't exactly clear how much Cheese understood, and so all that tension lurked under the dark waters of practice, like a hungry shark that had caught a whiff of blood but couldn't quite find it.

The next play unfolded like the first, that is until Cheese came at Zuke's nose with his elbow again, this time using it more like a spear, an action for which Zuke was prepared. He tilted his head back to where only the breeze of Cheese's devilish intent struck his chin. The swing and miss—as powerful as a Jose Canseco homerun swipe—put Cheese just off balance and caused the ball to move out and away from his body to where Zuke was able to pop it with the palm of his hand, sending the basketball up into the air and bouncing along the end line. Because it was hustle that delivered Zuke a measure of solace for the guilt and shame he felt at not playing, he repeated the same mantra over and over again during every practice: *look for a chance to dive; look for a chance to dive.*

Zuke dove for the ball before Cheese really even became fully aware that he didn't have it. He went skidding across the floor, face down as if he were on a slip and slide, and got hold of the basketball just before Flabby, who pounced on Zuke like a lion might envelop a gazelle. The two rolled over once as Flabby snatched the ball from Zuke's grasp, and Coach Miller used his lips, tongue, and slightly gapped teeth to blow his natural whistle. Miller was angry when he strode over to where Flabby and Zuke hustled to their feet. It was always a quandary for anyone on the second team. Play well against the first team and piss the coach off, or play badly and prove you're where you belong.

"How many times am I going to have to watch you miss a screen?" Miller was after Flabby, and he came in close, a white spray of his spit visibly hitting the subject of his derision in the face. Everyone else in the gym watched; they'd seen it before, and as Flabby held the ball, Coach took his fist high above his head and drove it down onto the top of the basketball, meaning to bust it loose from Flabby's grasp. Even though Miller's move was probably a surprise to Flabby, his fist landed on something secured more like a tree stump than a basketball.

A look of surprise flashed on Flabby's face—it was as if he'd accidentally popped coach with one of his iron fists—and Miller was surprised too, a condition that caused him to get even angrier than he was. "Give me that ball," the coach yelled.

Flabby did as he was told, and the coach drop kicked the ball up to the balcony, where it hit the windows, bounced twice on the track, and then rolled along one of the banked curves before slipping under the guard rail back to the hardwood. "Go get it," Coach told Flabby, who, showing no emotion, took off on a casual jog to retrieve it.

"Johnson go for Caldwell," Coach said to Flabby's back up. "Williams, go for Cheese." Coach's second substitution was a superficial one, meant to make it seem as if everyone was accountable, but Cheese certainly was not. He was a player seven points away from becoming the all time leading scorer, and he took his time leaving the floor, where after a few shuffling steps toward Coach Miller, Cheese paused to spit a big green hacker on the court, rubbing it in with his purple and white L.A. Gear basketball shoes. A few feet over, on the sidelines now, Zuke worked the cut in his mouth with his tongue and wondered what the next two days would bring.

Following practice, Zuke showered and hurried over to Ludwig Hall where in a few minutes the serving lines would close. The area just inside the doors was reminiscent of the lost luggage area of an airport, and the floor was littered with at least a hundred backpacks. The room was shaped like a full-bodied tree, one that a child would draw, thin at its base where the students entered, but round like an umbrella at the top where everyone sat.

The hall had two distinct sides, each with its own serving line and a giant, three-story-high window of glass looking out to campus. Through the windows of one side, diners could see the library, the landscaped quad, and the Tree of Knowledge; while those who sat on the other side had a view of College Church and the main parking lot. Each group of students made wise-cracks about those who sat on the opposite side of the room. The church side was thought to be the more academically minded side, the less fashionably conscious side (or as they would have said, the less vain side), and the more seriously religious. On the Tree of Knowledge side, there was a more developed taste for all aspects of college life social, and it was the hub of where young men and women might make plans with one another, the place where a night of nothing to do might produce some excitement: a trip north up Interstate 57 to Ed Debevic's in Chicago, maybe indoor miniature golf at the Navy Pier, or possibly bowling or roller skating in town. These were the activities permitted to the students by the rules of the college.

Four of the Brothers—Moon, Zuke, Flabby, and Cowboy— concerned about the segregation of the students, especially concerned that their desire to sit on the Tree of Knowledge side might rise out of unChristian vanity, decided at an early-year Brothers in Pursuit meeting that they would eat breakfast and lunch on the church side and sit on the social side for dinner. This plan, they reasoned, allowed for the desperate circumstances of their romantic lives, since none of them had shown any signs of having a date.

Flabby had been the first to benefit from the alternate side sitting guideline when he met his girlfriend Tara one day when she just walked up with her tray and asked if she could sit with them. Now Flabby took all his meals with Tara—sometimes with the Brothers, sometimes not—while The Dini—the one Brother who would never sit on the Church side—ate at the self-proclaimed most popular table, which convened at 5:30 and required that three large rectangular tables be pushed together. The popular were great in number at Pison.

As Zuke made his way across the maroon carpet embroidered with bouquets of flowers, Cowboy got up from a table near the window. He'd been sitting with Moon and Flabby's girlfriend Tara, and he hurried toward Zuke who was trying to beat the close of the serving line doors.

"Zuke," Cowboy hissed, as if he were whispering in a quiet classroom instead of a crowded cafeteria. The students had to dress for dinner, and so Cowboy wore freshly pressed khaki slacks and a red polo shirt. Zuke tried to block out his friend's insistent demand for his attention and instead focus on what was most important: that he enter the serving line before it closed. To make it, he broke into a light jog which Cowboy picked up too.

"Don't bring up Bird," Cowboy instructed as he reached Zuke. "I haven't had a chance to talk to Moon yet." Zuke grabbed a tray and stepped up to the counter, the hot lamps shining down on what was left of dinner. "Okay?" Cowboy pressed, always wanting some sort of response when he said something. Zuke told him no problem and smiled at a woman he recognized as Olga, a retired schoolteacher, who regularly worked the serving line Friday nights and weekends.

Zuke chose breakfast for dinner—scrambled eggs, French toast and sausage links—and as he exited the line and headed for the fountain drinks, he saw Wendy "Bird" Parrot on the church side of the room having dinner with her father. She was dressed in black stretch pants and a purple sweater, sitting way in the back with only empty tables all around them. Her father the dean was a silver-haired and usually stern man who rarely smiled. To Zuke, he always looked ready to deliver a fine or suspension, but sitting next to his daughter, all his dean-ness fell away.

Because Zuke stood in the center of the dining hall where the salad bar was, the people on each side of the cafeteria were visible to him, but invisible to one another. This meant Zuke could see Wendy and her father, see Moon and Tara, but they could not see each other.

Wendy saw Zuke and waved—the action caused a surge in Zuke's heart, not of the romantic sort, but a feeling of buoyancy to know her, and also a guilty excitement at the knowledge of the conflict which could arise between Cowboy and Moon. Without a free hand to wave back, Zuke could only smile and nod to Wendy. Dean Parrot looked up—most fathers are suspicious of the young men who wave to their daughters—and his look changed, as if he'd just been told that the university would begin allowing coed residence halls. He adjusted the glasses on his nose and showed little response, only a slight shrug of the shoulders and maybe even a look of concern. It was entirely possible that the dean knew Zuke hadn't been to College Church for seven Sundays, and that his religious life had backslid into the two weekly required chapel services. Zuke went to church when he knew attendance would be taken.

"So, why is Miss Bird over there waving to *you*?" Flabby had come up from behind Zuke unseen and caught him off guard with the question.

"Uh," Zuke couldn't think of anything to say, and he felt as guilty as if he had been the one Bird TWIRPed. "It's a long story. Don't say anything at the table. I'll tell you later."

"Oh, I see," Flabby teased, "now we have secrets from one another."

The tables in Ludwig Center came in either rectangles or circles and the chairs were pleather with high backs. Flabby sat down next to Tara, who was an elementary education major with light brown hair that reached her shoulders. Tara was barely five foot tall, bronzed from weekly visits to the tanning bed, and on this evening, she wore a red cardigan sweater, a white turtleneck underneath, and large silver-hooped earrings dangled along the sides of her face. The prayer chapel on campus bore her last name, the result of her grandfather's monetary contributions to the school. Tara's parents, upon their most recent visit to campus, had met their daughter's black boyfriend over dinner. Later in the evening, after Flabby had departed, they quietly suggested that Tara date a young man who was a deacon (and white) in their home church. According to Tara, they wouldn't be hearing from her anytime soon.

At the table, Cowboy at least gave the appearance of contentment as he licked his swirled chocolate and vanilla ice cream cone. Perhaps he felt as if he'd covered all the bases, at least for tonight, and that Zuke had been properly notified to keep the previous night's events out of conversation. Moon polished off a second bowl of Batman Cereal, his preferred dessert. Two tables away, Mulligan and his friends let out a big laugh. Pee Wee was with them, having evidently reached a peaceful reconciliation with Mulligan.

"I get so tired of those guys," Tara said, pushing a blonde highlight back behind her ear. She'd heard from a girlfriend that Mulligan had said something in the lobby of Barrett about *black meat,* and when she'd talked to Zuke about it, they had both agreed that it might not be a good idea to tell Flabby. Both thought Mulligan was on the edge of being dangerous, and that if Flabby found out about it, he was likely to confront Mulligan, something that might get him into pretty serious trouble.

Flabby shrugged about Mulligan and his buddies. "What a bunch of clowns."

"I think one of them pooped on the floor again," Cowboy told Tara, who pretended as if Cowboy hadn't spoken. Conversation flowed along its usual course: practice, youth ministry, sports, and the pep band of which Tara was a member.

Zuke could see that the subject of TWIRP weekend was likely to surface. Tara had talked about it for at least a week, needling the brothers about what girls they hoped would ask them out. She'd already informed Zuke that Julia Roberts was not a proper response. Zuke wondered if Abby had TWIRPed Cheese. She really wouldn't have had to. Saturday was already sort of their regular date night.

Because of where Zuke and Cowboy were sitting at the table, they were the only two who could see that Wendy and Dean Parrot, having finished their dinners, were approaching the conveyer belt that moved the dirty dishes back to the kitchen. Cowboy glanced at her and then kept his head down. It would be terrible for him if Wendy came over.

Zuke probably looked Wendy's way a little too long because his stare caused Moon to turn around just in time for him to see Wendy deposit her leftover food and dirty napkins from her plate into the trash.

"I'm going to talk to her," Moon pronounced, his voice full of resolve. "She wasn't in."

Tara looked accusingly at Flabby. Everyone knew Bird was Moon's *her* but this latest business—whatever it was he said about "she wasn't in"—didn't make any sense. "Why don't you ever tell me what's going on?" Tara asked Flabby.

"I don't know either," Flabby responded. Wendy had unloaded her tray now, and from halfway across the cafeteria, she waved toward the table. Of course only Zuke and Cowboy would know why.

"Oh jeez, Dude," Moon said, turning his back to her while his face reddened with color. Moon was the sort of guy who might read Wendy's wave as meant for him; maybe even the sort of guy who would see her approach as some sort of divine intervention in answer to his prayers. At the sound of the word *dude,* Flabby rubbed his fingers together signaling another twenty-five cent fine. "Do you think she already figured out that I'm me?"

Zuke wondered if Wendy had received the message from Moon upon arriving back to her dorm room after work. She'd known him, known at least Cowboy's appearance, and so she could conceivably put together that Cowboy and Moon were friends.

Bird kissed her father on the cheek and began to walk toward the table. Cowboy appeared white, as if he had the flu and might throw up.

"Guess I'm going to find out now," Flabby said to Zuke, a satisfied look on his face.

Tara appeared angry. "Tell me what's going on," she demanded.

Moon had turned away from Wendy and was now gripping his tray with two hands, possibly trembling with fear. "Is she coming over here?" Moon asked. His head started to bob, as if he were trying to psych himself up.

Wendy arrived at the table, standing right next Moon, who still had his back to her. "Hi," Wendy said, looking right at Cowboy, who smiled and began to say something before Moon turned, clearing his throat for what he had to say. Moon was a big throat clearer.

"Hello," Moon said, scooting his chair back, bumping it a little into Wendy's leg as he moved. His right thumb went to the v of his collar as if he were situating it. Wendy took a step back. "I called you last night," Moon informed her. From the way everyone within the range of a couple of tables turned to stare, it was as if a spotlight shone down upon the two of them.

"Moon don't," Zuke said, trying to save him from what would surely be a humiliating situation.

"You called me?" Wendy asked, awkwardness spreading over the table like the glow of a red light at an intersection: *Stop, Stop, Stop,* it warned to no avail. Zuke could already see that Wendy had not received the message that one Bryan Willingham had called for her.

Moon could be ferociously persistent, a quality that served him well when he witnessed for Jesus, but was likely going to cause him trouble here. He remained in his seat, looking up at Wendy as if he were Romeo in the balcony scene, the sort of man who might propose at a major league baseball game via the jumbotron.

"I called last night to tell you that I think you're the most beautiful girl on campus," Moon said, happily baring his emotions within earshot of at least twenty people.

"I didn't get the message," Wendy said, a young lady who seemed no stranger to surprise declarations of love. Her expression softened as if she'd seen an injured deer limping alongside the road.

"I know you don't know me." Moon seemed oblivious to the paradox of loving a woman who didn't know who he was. "But it would be an honor to take you out, go get a cup of hot chocolate, or attend the Sunday services together. You know, just something where we might get to know one another."

Flabby mouthed a *wow* to Tara, who'd unconsciously put her hand on Moon's shoulder. Zuke looked to Cowboy, who'd momentarily dropped his head into his left hand, with which he massaged his temples. He wasn't watching (maybe he couldn't) but then he took a deep breath which gave the impression that he'd inflated himself:

his posture straightened, he made fists of his hands and rested them on the table.

"Moon," Cowboy said. "I wanted to talk to you about something, and I realize this isn't the place, but last night Wendy and I made plans to go out with each other."

"I TWIRPed him," Wendy explained.

Moon's lips tightened and he forced a smile. "I'm sorry for embarrassing you," he said to Wendy, and when she tried to respond, Moon held up his hand like a traffic guard at a school crossing. He glared at Cowboy, probably not because he believed Cowboy had stolen his girl—there was likely no one more aware of how silly and childish Moon's claim on Wendy Parrot was than Moon himself—but Moon surely could see that for the past twelve hours or so, his emotions had been handled as if they were a carton of eggs. Moon had to feel as if he had been pitied and it was probably that knowledge that filled him with a scalding vat of anger. "I won't have this conversation," Moon declared. "Not now. Not ever." He rose from the table. "I'll be fine," he said, taking a glance around the cafeteria. A wide circle of rubber-neckers were looking his way. "You two have a good time." Moon brought his palm down softly on the table, as if his touching it would start the world to spinning again, as if he'd given the quiet order to "carry on."

Most of the students on the Tree of Knowledge side of the cafeteria watched Moon weave his way through the tables, his head up and eyes on the prize, the place where he could empty his tray of trash and send it back into the kitchen, a passage through which he'd probably have preferred to exit the building.

As Moon made his way along the long walk of shame, out to the row of double doors that would take him out to the hallway and then another row of glass doors that would lead him to the quad, the crowd of diners inside Ludwig Hall began to return to their own conversations. The Dini came hustling over to the Fab's table, pulling up a chair. Moon appeared out the windows walking through the quad toward Chapman Hall, his head down in hangdog fashion.

"Bless his heart," The Dini said, motioning Wendy toward the chair Moon had vacated. For once, the table of the Fab was the place to be. "Exactly how did this all happen?" The Dini put "happen" in air quotes, taking for himself an idiosyncrasy of a character from *Say Anything.* Because of Zuke, all members of the Fab had seen the flick quite a few times.

Cowboy explained to those at the table that he and Zuke had run into Wendy at Crowe's Cafe. "We can't go out," he said, dejectedly, as if he were a politician who had to face dropping out of the race after what had been a promising start.

"At least not right now," Wendy agreed. She was the sort of person who could plop down at a table anywhere with just about anyone and fit in quickly. "What's the hurry, right?"

"I don't think that's fair," Tara said. "And I don't think Moon would want it that way. Isn't that part of the reason he's so hurt?" Tara looked to Flabby to see what he thought.

"No reason to embarrass the man," Flabby said.

"Which means what?" Tara asked.

Flabby shrugged his shoulders. "It's a woman thing to want to hash it all out. Moon'll get over it. And if he doesn't, that's his problem, not Cowboy's." Flabby picked up one of the hamburgers on his tray—it served as a sort of period at the end of his sentence—and he consumed nearly two thirds of it in one bite.

"Zuke?" Tara asked, leading the discussion, her teacher self taking over.

"I'm not sure," Zuke said. He felt largely off the script thinking about Cowboy and Wendy in light of Moon's well-known interest. In the movies Zuke watched, the lead actress usually had a jerk boyfriend, there was a nice guy who liked her, and the film was largely a matter of the actress suffering enough emotionally that she eventually saw the error of her ways and fell for the nice guy. "When I was in high school, me and my friends said all is fair in love and dating. We used to go with each other's girlfriends all the time."

"That's taking it a little far," The Dini said, "don't you think?"

"The idea was," Zuke explained, "if your girlfriend messed around on you, then you probably shouldn't be dating her anyway."

"Amen," Wendy said.

Flabby gulped the rest of his hamburger so he could say something. "Let's be clear: sure, Moon has liked Wendy here for a long time, but if there's even the smallest beginning of anything starting to happen, it would be between the two of you." Flabby was looking right at Cowboy and Wendy. "Right?"

"But what about the Brotherhood?" Cowboy asked. "Isn't the whole point that we're to support one another? That we're for one another?"

"Brotherhood?" Wendy asked. "All of this is because of a TWIRP date?"

Tara laughed and shook her head. "Girl," she said, "you don't even know what you're getting yourself into with these guys. They have a little club where they strip down to their matching and embroidered boxer shorts and play games."

Cowboy took a tone of seriousness: "We pursue truth, compassion, God, and women. I don't know why Tara chooses to emphasize those other points."

"Sounds cute," Wendy said, "can I watch?" Then her face went serious, perhaps sarcastically but definitely the result of Cowboy's tone. "And important. I mean, who takes the time to consider what they are in pursuit of these days? Seems like a little reflection and fellowship would be good for the soul."

"I like this girl," Flabby said, nudging Tara.

"It's not even like you asked out Cowboy over Moon," Tara said. "You didn't even know Moon liked you. All of this is just a matter of how people match up." She looked to Cowboy, who listened in earnest as he brushed his black hair off to the side and out of his eyes. "You're good for girls who want a nice guy. You're fun loving and cute enough in your own way."

"In my own way," Cowboy said. "Not sure that's a ringing endorsement."

Wendy patted his shoulder in playful sympathy. "I think you're adorable."

"Right," Tara seconded. "You're cute like a guy who's going to be a good daddy."

"Whoa," Wendy said, laughing. "I think I'll hold off on that one."

"So what about Moon?" Flabby asked. "Is he cute too?"

Tara scrunched up her shoulders. "I imagine him pounding a pulpit for change. Urging people to follow God. He feels so serious to me; some girls here are totally into that. They actually talk about sitting in the pew listening to their husband preach."

As if it had dropped from the heavens, a valentine-red grape landed square in the middle of the table. Everyone looked around. Nearby and along the windows, two international students wiped down vacated tables. Over by the serving lines, several staff members pulled silver tins of what was left from the salad bar. Snickers of laughter bubbled up from Mulligan's table, and a crumpled piece of yellow paper came up from the middle, tossed by an unseen hand, where it landed on Wendy's shoulder and clung to her hair like a fallen leaf. With the patience of a chess player, she plucked the paper bomb from her back and began to un-crinkle it.

"Say the word," Flabby said to Tara, "and I'm on them."

"You'll sit right there Antoine Caldwell," Tara said, moving her hand over onto Flabby's massive thigh, as if she could hold him down if he really wanted to get up.

Overhead on the ceiling, the heating vents had kicked in and the temperature inside the cafeteria rose. Wendy un-crumpled the green sheet of paper, an announcement for the university singers upcoming concert. There was a pencil-scrawled message on the back which she began to read: "Dear Fag Five." Already she couldn't resist an aside: "Real mature," she said, then continued reading. "Let this notice serve as your invitation to Pisonmania I. We challenge you to a no-holds-barred wrestling match, five on five, tonight in the confines of the fourth-floor hallway of Chapman."

"Pisonmania?" Wendy asked.

"Like Wrestlemania," Flabby said, a smile breaking out onto his face. "You know, Hulk Hogan? The Macho Man?"

"The Iron Sheik," The Dini added with a touch of sarcasm. "Watch out for the Camel Clutch."

Flabby waved over toward Mulligan and his friends. "Those

boys over there are obsessed with it, always acting out matches in the hall."

"They even have a title belt they pass around," Zuke added.

Mulligan rose from his table and outstretched his hands as if he were in the ring and part of one of the pay-for-view extravaganzas. "What's it going to be?" he asked.

Wendy, at the sight of Mulligan, appeared as if something from a nightmare had come walking into her reality. Flabby called back to Mulligan, "Don't know about these fellas, but I'd be happy to wrestle you all at the same time."

Mulligan pumped his fist in front of his face and turned to his buddies, who didn't seem as excited as their leader at the prospect of a Friday night wrestling match with Flabby. "Let's go guys," Mulligan said. "We have some pre-fight preparations to go through." He turned back to Flabby. "See you at eight," he said. Mulligan and his buddies stood from their chairs and headed for the exit, leaving their leftover food, trays, drinking glasses, and dirty napkins for someone else to clean up. Two of the guys flipped over their chairs. If Moon had been there he would have written them up.

Zuke noticed that Wendy was looking at Mulligan intensely, holding her stare as he left the cafeteria.

"Did that really just happen?" Tara asked. "Did you just agree to *wrestle?*"

Wendy leaned into Cowboy. "That's him. The big obnoxious guy at work; the one who gives me the creeps."

"No wonder," Cowboy said, "He is creepy."

"What's this?" The Dini asked.

"That guy," Wendy said, nodding to where Mulligan and his buddies appeared out in the quad through the windows. "Works at Crowe's Café with me. He's a cook. You guys are all friends with him?"

"No," Flabby said, "definitely not friends. He's more like the Joker to my Batman."

"I don't care what ya'll say," The Dini said, flipping his wrist with a gesture meant to include everyone at the table, "but I am not going to wrestle anyone, especially those boys." He looked right at

Wendy. "They pee on each other in the shower."

"Ewww." Wendy scooted back from the table as if a herd of roaches were coming for her. With Pisonmania on the horizon, the mood at the table had lightened. "Are we going out or what?" Wendy asked. "That is if you survive your little engagement."

Cowboy looked around the table. "Let's go out," he said, sounding almost convinced that it was a good idea. "It might be just because it lets me do what I want, but I'm kind of buying that Moon might feel even worse if he knows we aren't going out because of him."

"He'll think it through," Zuke said. "Sure, it's embarrassing but not any more embarrassing than lots of things that have happened to us." Zuke was thinking of one time when he'd come in late to a basketball game and the point guard (who seemed as fast as Carl Lewis) had whipped by him three times in a row and laid the ball into the basket.

"A double date?" Wendy asked, looking to Zuke. Tara popped Flabby on the arm again.

"No way," Flabby said, defending himself. "Stop hitting me. I don't know about this either." Flabby looked to Zuke and mimicked his girlfriend's voice. "Why don't you ever tell me anything anymore?"

Zuke was thinking of Abby. The Dini and Cowboy were the only ones at the table who knew that Abby had said she'd break up with Cheese.

"My friend thinks Zuke is fantabulous," Wendy said.

"Who's your friend?" The Dini asked.

"Marie Barrett," Wendy answered. A hush fell over the table. Had the dating stars aligned for the Brothers? Had God decided this was to be the year of the Brothers in Pursuit?

"Mmmm," The Dini said, "that girl's got a rockin' body."

"Phillip!" Tara chided.

"Well she does," The Dini said, "and I'm not even sure she knows it."

"So what do you say?" Wendy asked Zuke.

"I don't know…" Zuke answered. He felt that one little date

didn't have to be a big deal. It could just be a friendly night out, but on the other hand, he was supposed to know if Abby was single by Sunday night.

"She was all over him last night," The Dini said. Everyone at the table except for Wendy could surmise that *she* would have to be Abby Grant. "She ratted her own self out," The Dini began to explain. He looked down at his hands as if he was inspecting his cuticles. "As I've previously stated, those two need to get a room."

"From what I have observed," Flabby said, "Abby Grant has a boyfriend. The same boyfriend she's had for the year and a half I've been here. I don't know; you may have heard of this guy, some big dude everyone calls Cheese who's scheduled to become the all time leading scorer of this here college tomorrow afternoon?"

"Actually," Tara said, "if you really want to get Abby interested, it might be a good idea to have a date." Wendy was obviously in need of an explanation and Tara provided it to her: "Zuke's got a crush on Abby Grant. If you ask me, she's led him on a little."

Zuke smiled weakly. He could fire off the perfect retort, that Abby had told him she was going to break up with Cheese in two short days, but he didn't think this was quite the spot.

"C'mon Zuke," Wendy said, a big smile breaking out onto her face. "Don't take that crap from her. It's not like I'm saying you have to put out. Just meet the poor girl."

"I wouldn't exactly describe Marie Barrett as a poor girl," Zuke said. He'd never talked to her but definitely knew who she was. The Brothers were often cataloging Pison's women, and Marie was always mentioned early in any conversation.

"There you go then," Wendy said. She laughed. "All you have to do..." Wendy didn't finish her sentence. "What are we doing tomorrow night?" She looked to Cowboy who'd just taken a big lick from his ice cream cone.

"Don't know," Cowboy said, his mouth half full. "I was TWIRPed, but I'm sure the gal who asked me out will think of something good."

No matter what Abby had said, Zuke didn't think she seemed

that confident in her plans to break up with Brett. Plus, he knew
that in high school it was Angel the homecoming queen's interest
in him that had finally bowled Colleen over his way. Abby had a
boyfriend; why couldn't he at least go out on a harmless TWIRP
date? The alternative would be to sit on the bench and watch Cheese
break the record, probably go out to eat with his father who was of
course coming up for the game, and then what? An evening in his
dorm room worrying about the following day. "I'll go," Zuke said,
kind of surprising himself. The table erupted into excited applause,
once again garnering the attention of those sitting around them.
Zuke was going to have a date, not with Abby.

CHAPTER SEVEN

For the first time in Chapman's long history, there was a four on four wrestling match. The Dini had escaped to Ruby Tuesday for cheese cake with girlfriends, and Pee Wee had agreed to don Mulligan's referee jersey and officiate the match. With the band Europe's "Final Countdown" blaring from Mulligan's stereo, the members of the Fab, dressed in the matching plaid and embroidered boxer shorts they wore to their Sunday night meetings, began to spread out a little: Cowboy and Zuke took a few cautious steps along the sides of the hall toward their opponents, who wore various items of wrestling fan gear, mostly tank tops and cut off shirts.

Mulligan's replica title belt hung on a radiator that had just clanked to life. He'd already told practically the whole floor that he'd bought it when he was one of ninety thousand fans who witnessed a wrestling event in Michigan. The black leather belt shone with an oversized gold medallion, bejeweled with red, white, and blue flags on each side. Flabby stood motionless by Moon, who'd been relieved to have his friends return from dinner, not with talk of Wendy Parrot and questions regarding his feelings, but instead with news of a challenge. With that, he had been able to fall back into life as if nothing had happened, the way that many men prefer to do, as if his friend hadn't become the recipient of his own impossible fantasies.

Except for Zuke, the boys who'd signed on for Pisonmania (both sides) seemed unsure of how to begin the match. There was a certain tentative awkwardness that permeated the hall, as if it were the first day of classes and the teacher had assigned an awkward icebreaker. Surely, the seriousness of a fist fight wouldn't be warranted, but then again, everyone knew the intensity level would likely rise above that of a touch football game.

"Let's get it on," said Mulligan, mostly to Flabby, the only

Fab member he'd assumed would be willing to tangle with him. Mulligan's friends Sheldon Anderson and Mark Phillips, two boys who'd tried to capitalize on all things related to the New Kids on the Block, exchanged a look, silently deciding on their attack points: they each inched toward Moon and Cowboy.

Unlike the other men in the hall, Zuke had discovered a switch in his gut, one that after it was thrown seemed to automatically bend his knees into the athletic stance that Coach Miller was always harping about. The muscles in his arms and legs shivered with adrenaline and the air around him seemed to grow thin—he felt as if maybe he could fly. Zuke thought of Abby, of his hopes for Glory, and that he might very well have a more violent encounter ahead, punches allowed, with Brett "Cheese" Chezem. There was a thrust of power in his right hamstring, and Zuke yelled as if he were hauling down the first hill of The Beast at Paramount's King's Island. He tore at Mulligan, jumped into the air as he neared him, and as Zuke came down from flight, he grabbed Mulligan in a side headlock, a move that jerked the defensive end toward the floor.

Zuke's high school friend "Road Dog" had always said he had a good fireman's carry for a basketball player, and it was shocking the way Zuke was able to use the momentum he'd created with his run and jump to fling Mulligan over his hip and onto the carpet, under which the hard cement helped Zuke push the air from Mulligan's lungs. Too bad Zuke didn't know what to do with an opponent once he got him on the floor. "Where's the count?" Zuke hollered at Pee Wee, who was drawn by Zuke's crisp and authoritative voice from the wall to where Mulligan was pinned to the carpet. Pee Wee slid in next to them as if he'd just stolen second base.

"One," Pee Wee said and slapped the carpet as he'd seen done nearly every day in Mulligan's room watching videotapes of WWF action. Pee Wee raised his hand for the two count while Randy, Sheldon, and Mark all rushed Zuke and pushed him onto his side as if they were about to roll a log down the hall. Zuke was knocked free of Mulligan over onto his back and all three men began to pile upon him. Now Zuke was in danger of being pinned and Pee Wee turned his count to him.

Flabby grabbed Zuke's arms, which had been flapping weakly over his head, and pulled Zuke partly to his feet. Mulligan rose up, not just a bully as one might have suspected, but also a fierce fighter, temper blown, rules of engagement forgotten. Mulligan wrapped his hands around Zuke's neck and squeezed.

"FOUL," Pee Wee yelled as he rose to his feet. "FOUL, FOUL, FOUL. Do you hear me, you big lummox? FOUL."

Flabby barrel-hugged Mulligan, anxious to get at him, anxious to quiet the chuckles he could still hear in his mind, chuckles that he'd probably always connected to the fact that he was a black man at Pison with a white girlfriend. Flabby grabbed Mulligan as if he were a rolled carpet and tossed him aside like he was an unwanted remnant. Mulligan's death grip on Zuke's neck was broken, and the big defensive end thrashed out for another piece of Zuke, getting instead a fistful of his t-shirt, which tore away as Flabby took Mulligan all the way to the floor.

Nearby, Mulligan's friend Mark had used his high school wresting moves to put Moon into the awkward position where his nose was pushed directly between Mark's butt cheeks. Moon was faced with the not so great choice of leaving his face where it was or biting into Mark's nut sack. As the referee, Pee Wee had more to do than he could manage.

Mulligan dug his fingernails, intentionally kept long, into the skin of Zuke's chest, who instinctively threw his left forearm into Mulligan's beaked nose. Zuke had never been in a fight but his initial instincts proved to be good. There was the crunch of cartilage in Mulligan's nose. Moon pursued his lips and worked the best he could to rack Mark with his chin.

Mulligan's buddy Sheldon pulled his right arm back, as if to throw a roundhouse punch at Cowboy, who somehow had the presence of mind to lurch forward, saving himself the brunt of the blow and instead only receiving a glancing shot to his ear. The whole mess of young men was a violent traffic snarl of appendages, a medievalist tortured game of twister, during which anger that had lain within a year's worth of what were supposed to have been good-natured wisecracks, finally came to the surface like a scaly rash.

"What the hell are you all doing?" Pee Wee yelled, the veins in his neck pulsing. Perhaps for the first time of his life, Pee Wee found himself the voice of reason. "Jesus!" he said, as if maybe calling on the Lord Himself to stop the brawl.

A subtle whine sounded in everyone's mind, and Chapman Hall trembled. Zuke's eyes watered at the sound, he felt suddenly nauseous, and he had to remind himself that he lived in Illinois, a place where tornadoes wreaked destruction and earthquakes were novel squiggles. The sound made everyone squint, and the intensity of the wrestling match dropped as if they were all demonstrators hit with the water of a high pressure hose. Their fury was gone, and as they lay tangled on the floor, strewn about like children's toys in a playroom, the very foundation of Chapman quivered.

Away from the pile of young men and toward the door to the restroom, a crack opened up near the base of the wall, where water as clear as the glass pulpit on the stage of College Church oozed out into in the hall. Mark separated from Moon and put his hands over his ears. Moon was the first to see the miniature river gurgling down the hall toward the melee.

"Look at that," Moon said, nodding toward the middle of the hall as if an angel hovered in the air. "Get up!" he said. "The toilets probably overflowed." Moon and Sheldon scrambled to their feet.

From in the bathroom, something broke loose and a four-inch flash flood of water sprung free, gurgling down the hall and saturating a ten yard patch of carpet. Sheldon was the only one who'd heard Moon.

Zuke, who was still lying on the thin carpet of the hallway, felt a cold sensation atop his head, then on his shoulders and back. Moon hurried toward the restroom to find the source, and down at the far end of the hall, a good fifteen yards from the action, a door creaked open. A student named Barry Sanchez rolled his wheelchair out into the hallway. He was a guy who'd once asked the members of the Fab to please address him as Captain Midnight, the moniker of one of Barry's heroes, someone who in 1986 successfully jammed HBO's satellite signal. Barry was a sort of Buddha figure, overweight with a shaved head, and he sometimes wore a dark cloak and the amplified Darth Vader mask he'd made from a mail-order kit. Now, at the other end of the hall, as if he were some sort of Dark Lord, Barry scientifically surveyed the scene, and his stoic gaze remained unchanged. Without a word, he rolled back into his room.

"Did we do this?" Mulligan asked, denial already in his voice. Flabby's left side was wet, and his boxers clung to his skin like a cotton wetsuit, but Randy and Mark only had damp knees.

"Somebody must have stopped up the urinals," Pee Wee offered.

"That's completely disgusting," Sheldon said. He raised his arm and sniffed it for any tell-tale urinal stench. Cowboy put his hands on his knees as if he might throw up.

"It's coming from the wall," Moon yelled to them. "The water's not from the toilets or the urinals." Moon hurried across the hall, feet splashing as he went, to where he picked up his phone to call Dean Parrot, who in his dual role of dean and resident director of Chapman Hall, could surely bring aid quickly. Mulligan and his friends, no strangers to the actions necessary to appear innocent, quickly headed back to their rooms to change into dry clothes. The Fab, quick learners who'd just begun to consider how they'd look soaking wet and clad in matching boxers, also retreated to their rooms.

The fourth-floor hall of Chapman, only moments before full of violence, emptied. The lights which ran along the center of the hallway's ceiling—those that still worked—shone down into the water below, which created little gleaming halos, so bright that it was as if they were electrified. Zuke's torn shirt lay soaked in the middle of the hall, and water trickled into the rooms, but fortunately for the residents of the fourth floor, the ridges of wood across their doorways kept most of the water headed for the stairwell, where it ran down the steps eventually creating a light running waterfall. Mulligan's title belt, still dry, hung forgotten over the box that held the fire extinguisher. A champion of the fourth floor had not been crowned.

CHAPTER EIGHT

Following the Fab's customary Saturday morning breakfast in the Ludwig Hall dining room, Moon and Zuke sat on the freshly cleaned carpet in the fourth floor hallway of Chapman. The cleaning crew had arrived even before the sun was up, first sucking up all the water and then giving the carpet a good shampooing. The crew was still down the hall working on repairing whatever had given way in the walls near the restrooms.

Because the Pison basketball team had an afternoon game versus Eureka College, Zuke was dressed in his team-issue purple sweat pants, a grey hooded sweatshirt, and a cheap baseball cap with Pison Basketball embroidered across the front. Like most Saturdays during basketball season, this would be a busy day for Zuke, starting with what he liked least and working up to more interesting events: there was Coach Miller's pregame walk through which Zuke generally found mind-numbingly boring, some time for studying, the pregame meal, the long wait for the game to get started, Cheese's likely breaking of Coach Miller's scoring record, dinner at Denny's with his father, and then the grand finale of his TWIRP date with Marie.

Zuke had boiled down Tara's comment from the night before—the one about attracting Abby—into his own little axiom for human attraction: people tend to want those they aren't sure they can have. If there were any wrinkles of doubt in Abby's break up plans, a date with Marie might be just the thing to iron them out. Zuke believed it was unlikely that Marie would actually be interested in him—what in the world had initially attracted her?—because he had always thought of himself as average looking and without a chance with anyone who didn't get to know him.

Moon sighed next to Zuke. The previous night hadn't exactly been a great one for him. He was faced with moving on from his two-year infatuation of Wendy and probably trying to come to grips that his own dreams—his own dreamgirl—had ended up happening for his roommate. Although Moon wasn't on the team any longer, he also had a game day uniform of sorts: Levi ButtonFly jeans and the white t-shirt onto which he'd colored an enormous black "Z" with a permanent marker. Also, he wore his old-school purple and gold Converse Weapons, the basketball shoes that Larry Bird and Magic Johnson had endorsed.

"So what do you think about last night?" Zuke asked. News of the fourth floor water leak had spread over the campus like smoke from a fire. Various theories abounded: the spirit of God was on the way (it had come memorably in the spring of '66 and many students ached for a similar revival), a minor earthquake had occurred, or possibly it had just been the pressure from the ruptured pipes that caused the entire dormitory to shake.

"Do you mean that the woman of my dreams seems to like one of my best friends, or do you mean Pisonmania, or are you talking about the water?"

"The water," Zuke said. "What do you think?"

"Weird," Zuke answered, flinching at his own word. Ever since he'd for the most part successfully extricated the word *dude* from his vocabulary, Zuke had begun to think of the other ways he used language. Professor Moore had written on one of his essays that clichés replaced thinking, and so Zuke had been on the lookout for them. Now he wondered if the word *weird* wasn't something else—not a cliché but maybe an abstraction. Whatever weird was, he felt a little trapped inside it.

"This all reminds me of something that happened to me in high school," Moon began, sliding his voice into the polished coat he dressed it in for his pastor-at-the-pulpit persona. Even though he was only twenty, Moon had preached several sermons at his home church in Danville, and he'd also begun to promote himself as a public speaker. So far, he'd developed the following talks that he could give on the spot: The Art of Witnessing, The Hope of Jesus, The Ten Commandments Today, and the one which he was about to deliver to Zuke, God's Faithfulness.

"It was the summer before my senior year," Moon said. "I was doing my morning devotional when I was struck with a feeling not unlike what I had last night during the wrestling match. It must have been around nine o'clock in the morning, Mom and Dad were gone to work, and I didn't have to be anywhere until noon. As I sat there at my desk, I was struck with the feeling that the rapture had occurred."

"Why did you think that?" Zuke asked. Once at a meeting of the Brothers in Pursuit, Moon had referred to something God had told him, as if maybe they'd met for breakfast over at Crowe's Café.

"I don't know how I knew it," Moon said, seemingly a little chafed at being interrupted. "How do you know you love Glory?" Moon often worked this little rhetorically savvy move, turning people's challenges into questions for themselves. "I was really freaked out, and so I decided to call my mom at work. I figured if she answered, then the rapture hadn't happened. But no one answered."

Zuke stopped listening to Moon, and started thinking about Glory, about Moon's question regarding how he knew he loved her. Professor Moore was always demanding supporting details. What details would Zuke cite as evidence of his love?

"You see Zuke," Moon said, drawing Zuke back into his story. Moon was good at those little tricks, tricks like saying a listener's name, if they weren't paying attention. "If the rapture had really come, it would make sense that no one was answering the phone at church."

"Because everyone at church has accepted Jesus," Zuke said.

Moon ignored the little challenge and continued. "So then I tried my dad. He's an accountant for the Bischoff Corporation. His secretary answered—no surprise; she was on our prayer list; not a Christian—and she told me Dad was in his office, but when she tried to put me through, it turned out he wasn't there. 'Maybe he stepped out to the plant,' she said, but I figured he'd been taken. So I called everybody I figured was a for-sure Christian: both sets of grandparents, my youth minister, my vacation Bible school teacher, and none of them were home. I decided to go to church and wait for a sign of what to do.

"As I was driving, I started to cry and tremble so hard that I pulled over into a strip mall parking lot off Keating Road. It wasn't that busy, the lot was huge, and I stopped the car near the sign way out by the road." Moon tapped his finger onto the carpet to denote his parking spot. "All the cars were way over here," Moon said, pointing to a spot further out into the hall.

"I tried to read my Bible, and I was so shaken that I accidentally tore one of the pages in half. I sat the good book down on the passenger seat, grabbed the wheel with both hands, put my head on the steering wheel and asked God to help me. I was near my absolute breaking point. All of the sudden, there was a tapping at my window. Scared the crap out of me. It was a young guy, maybe as old as we are now, with shaggy black hair he kept out of his eyes with a white headband. He had green eyes, but get this, his eyes were a color that human eyes can't be, almost like a neon sign."

Zuke raised his eyebrows.

"They were very bright."

"Like maybe he had in those special contacts? Like in the 'Thriller' video?"

Moon stood and went into his room where from his desk he picked up his Bible. He kept it between two golden-lion bookends along with C.S. Lewis's *Chronicles of Narnia* and a Major League Baseball encyclopedia. When Moon returned, he opened his Bible to a page which had been torn in half, now repaired with a yellowed piece of tape. The hair on Zuke's arms prickled at the sight of the repaired page, evidently the same page Moon had torn on the day he'd believed the rapture had come.

"The guy signaled for me to roll down my window," Moon said, pulling what almost looked like a parchment from the crevice of his Bible. "He gave me this." Moon handed over the brittle-thin paper to Zuke, who felt a jolt of adrenaline delivered to his throat, chest, and arms, as if he'd been sitting around a campfire listening to ghost stories and one had finally gotten to him. He unfolded the paper and looked at it. Shapes leapt from the page which appeared as if they might have been drawn by a quill dipped in ink. In the upper left corner was an unmanned trumpet blasting over a three-pronged crown. The pictures were crude, undeveloped, more like rough outlines of what might be, or the stamp of a child's toy, except for the occasional artful flourish of where the ink swooped. Toward the middle of the page was the drawing of a cylinder of paper, unwound, which asked, "Who is worthy to break the seals and open the scroll?"

Zuke thought the question sounded Biblical, maybe from *Revelation* or *Daniel*. A horse galloped on a string of clouds, there was what looked like an *A* attached to an upside down horseshoe—that would have been the Alpha and Omega—there was also a butterfly, a woman battling a dragon in the corner, several kinds of crosses, one of which was on fire, and various other phrases that must have been Bible verses too. The one across the bottom of the page stated, "Whoever acknowledges me before men, I will also acknowledge him before my father in heaven." As Zuke looked at the verses, he thought it odd that none of them were cited chapter and verse. It was as if whoever—dare he say whatever—had transcribed them onto the paper had known them by heart or else experienced them in a way a war veteran would experience a battle: first hand with little need to check a book to see what had happened.

"The man at my window asked me if I'd accepted Christ as my savior. I told him I had, and then do you know what he said to me?"

"What?" Zuke asked, nearly pulled all the way into Moon's story.

" 'Then you have nothing to worry about.' "

Zuke pursed his lips and wrinkled his face. "Are you telling me you got a note from an angel?"

"How did he know what I was worried about?" Moon asked. Zuke returned Moon's parchment to him just as two men—one dressed in overalls and the other in jeans and a flannel shirt—emerged from the restroom.

Moon shrugged his shoulders. "It got handed to me right when I needed it." He re-inserted the sheet back into his Bible and snapped it shut as if it were a gavel and he'd just banged a case shut.

A door creaked open down the hall and here came Barry rolling out again from his room, just as he had the night before. He was dressed all in black, cloak adorned, and had on his Darth Vader helmet. "Zuuuuuke," he called, his voice a raspy hiss through the faux breathing machine he'd constructed. "I am your faaaather."

Zuke laughed. "I don't think so Lord Vader."

From the end of the hall opposite Barry, Flabby emerged from his room, carrying a bucket of shower supplies and wearing only a royal blue robe, which he allowed to trail behind him as he walked. He could have been a naked king or maybe a superhero. "What's happening Vader?" he yelled down to Barry, who shook his fist like a champion and then whipped his wheelchair around once before rolling back into his room.

"You shower before practice?" Moon challenged.

"It's supposed to be a walk through," Flabby said, "What am I supposed to do, just stink all day because we have an afternoon game?"

"Fair enough," Moon said. Flabby made his way on down the hall to where the maintenance crew had stopped their clean up to watch the approach of this giant and naked man.

"Perfect timing," Flabby said as way of greeting.

"Awful proud of yourself, ain't you?" one of them asked.

"Yes sir," Flabby said, breezing past them and rounding the corner into the bathroom. Both of the men laughed and started to walk down the hall toward the exit. With the carpets clean and bright rays of December sun shining in from the windows at each end of the hall, Chapman seemed baptized by the water that had poured forth from her pipes the previous night.

"Hell of a story," Zuke said, rising up from his place on the wall. He'd chosen *hell* specifically to irritate Moon. "But I sure don't know what it means."

"We aren't to know the hour," Moon said going over to replace his Bible on his desk. "Good luck today." He meant the game; Zuke hadn't given it much thought, and didn't think he needed luck to sit on the bench.

"I'm going to go get some studying in before walk through,"

Zuke said with a sigh. On game days, Coach Miller conducted what Zuke thought of as slow-motion practices, extra boring affairs that lasted anywhere from one to three hours. With Moon and Cowboy off the team, and Flabby nearly always in the game, Zuke didn't even have anyone he liked to sit next to on the bench. Eureka College, the players knew—contrary to all that Coach Miller had said leading up to the game—was supposed to stink. Maybe, Zuke thought, I'll finally get into another game.

"See you at dinner?" Moon asked, as Zuke walked toward his room to get his stuff.

"Nah," Zuke answered. "Dad's coming."

CHAPTER NINE

From Zuke's seat two spots from the end of the bench, he stared across the gym at Abby, who wore a brand new custom-made Pison jersey with Cheese's number twenty-four on it. Zuke shook his head—Abby in a brand new jersey?—she might as well have had a shirt on that read *Property of Cheese.* It was situations such as this one—where Zuke faced a long day on the bench watching the girl he loved cheer for her boyfriend—that Zuke thought he needed to get the heck out of Pison and go to some other college, perhaps over to St. Joseph's for another try on a team or to Indiana University where surely his social life would go on the rise. Zuke tried not to jump to conclusions about Abby. The jersey could have been a gift, perhaps from Cheese's parents, who were sitting right there with Abby along with her own mother and father.

The gym at Pison was small, with only eight rows of bleachers on each side, but it was also packed, so full that people stood and filled the corners, and even stood up in the balcony, along with the pep band, where a small track circled the gym. Looking across the way at Abby as she chatted with Cheese's parents, Zuke remembered from the film *When Harry Met Sally,* that the character played by Princess Leia—Carrie Fisher would always be known by the name she carried in the first movie Zuke had ever seen—kept saying that she didn't think her married boyfriend was ever going to leave his wife. This was something in the film that everyone else seemed to know. Zuke didn't want to be that kind of stupid, the sort of stupid where he was the last one to realize something about his life.

A whistle blew on the court, and Zuke looked at the scoreboard. Pison College was nuking Eureka, a squad which could have used some inspiration from their most famous alumnus, former president Ronald Reagan. Back when Reagan had played guard for the Red Devil football team, he had been known as Dutch, a nickname which had eventually given way to The Great Communicator, or depending on your political leanings, The Teflon President.

An illegal screen had been called, and it appeared that Cheese would be given two free throws. This was Cheese's big moment: one point would tie Miller's record and if he could make them both, then the record was Cheese and Cheese's alone. The gym grew quieter as the players walked to the other end of the court. The score was 20-4 in favor of Pison. Zuke looked to the corner opposite Abby where his dad sat making a note on his program. He kept track of points, rebounds, assists, and a running score of the game.

"Hey Miller!" The Dini yelled, "put Zuke in." There were a few nervous *yeah*'s that seconded the request, and most of Zuke's teammates looked down his way and smiled. The Dini's yell was particularly funny given the contrast between the two men: The Dini, a stylish singer who appreciated art, film, and fine food while Coach Miller intimidated most of his players and his favorite restaurant was the Golden Corral Buffet. Miller appeared always on the verge of emotionally snapping, and Zuke figured that if anything, the Fab dressing in t-shirts that spelled his name probably hurt his chances for playing.

The cheerleaders in the corner across from Zuke raised their arms above their heads and shimmied their pom poms as Cheese went through his elaborate pre-shot routine. When the ball finally rolled off Cheese's fingertips, it splashed the net, and the cheerleaders along the base line dropped their hands from above their heads and yelled, "Swoosh!" One more point and Cheese would tie the record.

Zuke looked back to Abby, who sat between two sets of parents, her own and Cheese's. "I'm an idiot," Zuke said, too loudly in the small gym which had grown quiet out of deference for Cheese's approach of Coach Miller's record. From Zuke's spot on the bench, he was less than ten yards from where Cheese stood, and Zuke could see that what he'd said caused a little hitch in the great scorer's release. The ball hit the back of the rim hard and flew nearly straight up. Cheese actually looked from the court toward where Zuke was sitting. No doubt, he'd heard somebody talking, but Zuke thought it was unlikely that Cheese would actually realize the voice had come from the bench. Zuke knew his own penchant for paranoia well enough that he worked to not give himself away and to talk himself down from paranoia's precipice.

Flabby jumped up into the air but his leap was ill-timed and his hand whiffed at the leather Wilson basketball. As can happen when large crowds come together to watch a live event, a disappointed chorus of "oh" sounded throughout the gym. Faster than if he were on a pogo stick—it was one of the gifts that made Flabby such a dominant post player—he jumped again, and this time he was able to tip the ball up and back toward the middle of the lane. Cheese, who at least on the court could have been dubbed The Great Anticipator, had sensed what Flabby would try to do. He snatched the ball from the air, his shoulders crashing into two Eureka players, sending them both to the hardwood. He dribbled the ball once, took a big hop to just under the rim, gave a fake that sent a Eureka player up into the air, and as the defender crashed down on him, he powered the ball up to the basket drawing another foul. The ball went straight through the rim. Cheese had the record, and the gym erupted into a frenzied celebration. The bleachers bent under the crowd's jubilance and the track above shook as Chapman Hall had the night before. Cheese, with sweat pouring down the sides of his face, on his chest, and down his back, pointed to Flabby, an acknowledgement for his part of the play. Cheese ran over to Flabby and then slapped him on his giant rump.

Inside McClain Gymnasium, with 11:02 remaining in the first half, it began to rain cheese, specifically Kraft singles. Through some sort of massive organization, it seemed as if every member of the crowd had gotten hold of a package of individually wrapped slices. At first it only trickled cheese: a square landed at the center circle, another near where Cheese had scored, but then as the crowd grew more confident that there would be no serious judgment issued upon the act, the slices began to become more frequent in the air, a floppy hailstorm of yellow dairy product. It must have been that while the game had been going on, people had secretly freed the slices from their packaging, tucked them into their pockets or otherwise had them ready for the record-breaking basket. Zuke looked up to where Abby had stood and now flung cheese slices toward the center of the court, waving her hands as if she'd won the lottery. There was no way, Zuke thought, she was going to break up with Cheese. Look at how excited she was for him.

From behind, a slice hit Zuke in the shoulder—not one that Abby had thrown; that would have been a particularly cruel turn of fate—another sailed over his shoulder, still another slapped onto his neck, and then two more hit him square in the head. He had become someone's target.

When Zuke turned to look into the stands directly behind the team bench, yet another slice hit him directly on the forehead and clung to his skin like a Wacky Wall Walker, crawling over and plunking down onto his nose. After peeling the cheese away, Zuke could see Wendy Parrot sitting a few rows behind the bench, gleefully armed with a package of Kraft singles and laughing at him. Zuke laughed too, and he saw that Wendy was sitting with Marie "Magic" Barrett, the girl he was supposed to go out with that night. Of course Zuke knew who she was; the year before the Fab had done a superficiality top ten, a list which only took under consideration sheer physical appearance. Marie had ranked anywhere from two (on Moon's list) to eighth (on The Dini's). So while Zuke had acknowledged that Magic was extremely good looking, he'd always been enamored of Abby, and so he hadn't given her any more thought than he'd given, say, Samantha Fox, the British pop singer he also admired from afar.

"Zaucha," Coach Miller said, deadpan as if he were a grumpy license branch employee calling out the next number. The coach had caught Zuke red-handed staring away from the game having his little moment with Wendy. "Get some guys to clean up this mess." The pep band had started into the school song, while back on the court, the players from both teams looked around bewildered, except for Cheese who had begun to grin as if witnessing his first snowfall.

Zuke looked up and down the row of players on the bench; none had heard Coach Miller. The crowd began to chant, "Cheese,

Cheese, Cheese," and as they did, they bounced up and down to the thump of the drum from the pep band up on the balcony. The athletic director walked in front of Zuke, stepping on Zuke's foot as he made his way to the scorer's desk holding a plaque and the game ball. Zuke bent over and picked up two slices, moved a few feet out to pick up some more—he'd now removed two of what were at least five hundred slices—but then he heard a creak that reminded him of the days he and his father had spent in the woods when they lived in the country outside a small town named Grass Creek. Back then, this was before Zuke's family moved to Horseshoe, they'd had a three-acre woods and Zuke had been charged with hauling firewood out of it in a red wagon. The sound that Zuke remembered was the sound of the final creaks of a tree before it fell, and the one he heard now came from the upper corner of the gym where the band was. It was a sound that Zuke heard even over the chants of Cheese, the clang of cymbals, and the wallop of the drums.

The portion of the balcony that was directly over Abby's head, the corner that held the pep band, rippled like a piece of kindling that has just caught fire, and then it dropped down nearly as if it had been a trap door, not giving way completely so that a short and wide slide angled down toward the bleachers below. Zuke could see the drum set in the far back corner, half on the ramp that had been created and half off, begin to crawl forward just a little. Several members of the band slid right down into the guard rail, which had bent at the partial collapse of the floor but was holding for now. Those band members not on the actual width of the damaged floor were at first confused, but every second that passed more of them stopped playing and started to figure out the danger they were in. Down on the floor level, the crowd in the one corner, the corner closest to where Cheese had scored his record-setting basket, realized that something not good was happening, but the rest of the fans continued to celebrate with exuberance.

Abby turned from watching her boyfriend to the scene up and behind her, where band members pushed against one another trying for the exit. It was as if Glory had been hypnotized, as if she waited for an alien space craft to land.

"Watch out," Zuke yelled. He was sprinting into the hurricane of sound across the floor before he even realized he was no longer on the bench. A tire-sized piece of concrete fell from under the balcony, just missing Cheese's dad's head, before it splintered a section of the bleachers and fell to the McClain gymnasium floor. The father of Pison's all-time leading scorer sank down to his waist as if he'd fallen into a woody quicksand. The corner of the balcony bowed and cracked a foot or two more and one member of the band flipped over the guard rail onto the bleachers. A few more students clung to the rail, their feet smacking some of the crowd below in the head.

While the rest of the families scrambled to safety, Abby grabbed the arm of her boyfriend's father. Zuke rushed into the growing puddle of space under the balcony as people cleared away from the location of its impending collapse. Up the rows of the bleachers he went: one, two, three, and he noticed a tuba slide forward on the balcony with a set of drums scooting along behind. Zuke felt a splash of sweat on the side of his face, and the knock of a broad shoulder against his arm. Cheese had come up the bleachers too, step for step with Zuke.

Simultaneously, the two of them reached the spot where Abby was, and she struggled to maintain her grip on Cheese's father's shoulder, just as Zuke saw the tuba turn over the top of the rail, coming straight for Abby's head, moving so slowly—at least in the way Zuke experienced it—that he felt as if he were back in his bedroom working the frame advancement button so he could study each little movement of Chris Mullin's sweet jump shot. Zuke thrust his forearm up in the direction of the brass instrument's crushing path. It smacked the open palm of Zuke's hand—he could hear his wrist snap with the impact—and then the tuba rolled over the length of his forearm, and fell to the bleachers where it rattled down a few rows until it came to rest where the broken concrete had gone through.

At the same time Zuke had executed the successful tuba deflection, he had also placed his right arm around Abby's waist, and his hand locked into place on her hipbone as if it had been created for this very purpose. Cheese had grabbed his own father—it was the sensible thing to do given his location respective to Zuke's position on the bleachers—and Moon arrived with Cowboy, two steadfast brothers holding true to the pursuit of compassion. Flabby was down on the gym floor waving Tara over toward the door where she'd been able to avoid the jagged cliff that formed in the corner of the gym.

Zuke and Abby fell to the bleacher she had been sitting on. Cowboy and Moon were assisting Cheese with his father, who'd been at risk to fall through the woody-toothed gap in the bleachers. The drum had clattered to the rail but not gone over.

The distances, emotional and physical, between Zuke and Abby were erased. Her cheek was against his, and he felt the powerful exhalation of her breath on his neck. After Zuke had landed on his back on the bleachers, most of Abby had landed on him. Zuke tried to savor their closeness, to experience what it was to have her body next to his. Abby's mother arrived at their side and two medics, on standby in an ambulance parked just outside the front doors to the gym, were there too. With his father now safely seated on the bleachers, Cheese turned to see how his girlfriend was. With surprise, Zuke recognized true concern in Cheese's eyes as he lifted Abby up from the bleachers and into his arms as if she were a little girl. Zuke wasn't sure he was even strong enough to do such a thing. The first tweaks of pain began to spider in Zuke's wrist, which felt as it had the previous time he'd broken it: not too bad, probably in need of a cast, maybe only a splint. Starting with stitches when he was two, Zuke was accustomed to torn skin and cracked bones. Already, there was the sound of a fleet of rescue vehicles, whistles blaring, the sound of the rapid approach of the men and women who in the village of Beau Flue rarely had reasons for action. Little Pison College had fallen, and the town's men and women were coming to its rescue.

With help from Flabby carrying their supplies, medics attended to the young man from the band that had fallen onto the bleachers. The student didn't appear to be hurt severely: a compress had been applied to his arm and a medic was wrapping his ankle. With her parents and Cheese leading her, Abby moved away from where

Zuke was, and she was looking at Zuke as if he'd dyed his hair blue, as if he'd undergone a befuddling, not necessarily negative, transformation. Zuke pressed his left forearm to his chest and winced as he tried to make a fist.

"What is it?" Zuke's father asked. He'd hustled over to where Zuke was at the first sign of trouble. He was four inches shorter than Zuke, sixty years old, and ran two miles a day. His smoky brown hair had flopped partially into his eyes. "Your wrist again?" he asked, swiping his hair back into place. Just over his shoulder, Zuke could see Moon directing Dean Parrot's attention up to the balcony as he explained what had happened to the man he'd only days before fantasized would one day be his father-in-law. Zuke looked around the gym for Wendy and Marie. Where had they gone?

"Eric!" Zuke's father said. "Can you hear me?" Zuke looked at his dad, whose voice had quavered a little, and he thought to himself that he'd never seen his father worried about him before. Zuke thought to answer and told his dad that he believed he'd broken his wrist.

"Let's get you to the emergency room," his dad said. "I guess that's the end of your basketball season."

Thank God, Zuke thought.

CHAPTER TEN

Following two hours in the emergency room, Zuke sat with his father in a window booth at Denny's wondering how he'd tell him that he was thinking about transferring. From what Zuke had just experienced—Abby wearing Cheese's jersey, her enthusiasm for his breaking of Coach Miller's record, and the authentic concern for Abby that Zuke believed he'd seen on Cheese's face—Zuke thought maybe the time had arrived for leaving Pison. Yes, he possibly had a date coming up if he somehow hooked up with Cowboy and Wendy, but the possibility of one woman, a woman he'd never met, was no reason to stay at a school. Zuke and his father had already covered their usual conversational paths. Via payphone at the hospital Zuke's mother had reported that his sister's basketball team had won, and she was glad that all had escaped serious injury during the balcony collapse.

"Do you realize," Zuke's dad asked, looking up from his program as if he'd just read that *E.T.* was a true story, "with 11:02 to go in the half, it was 20-4?"

A waitress came walking up to their booth. Her nametag signaled her as Lucy. "You guys know what you want?" Lucy wore a forest-green dress, a sort of conservative maid's uniform with a frilly apron tied around her waist. She had a mountain of blonde hair which she'd wound up into a bun. Zuke had seen her before, at the restaurant and on campus. He thought she worked at the radio station, 89.7 The Light.

"Lumberjack Slam," Zuke said, "scrambled eggs, hash browns, wheat toast, orange juice to drink." Boomba! This was the sort of efficiency Zuke wanted from the way people ordered in a restaurant: placed straight from the menu in less than ten seconds. It had been the movie *When Harry Met Sally* that had given Zuke the language he needed to think about this aspect of his personality, that he held high contempt for those of the brand of high maintenance explained in the film. When the Brothers had developed their lists for what they looked for in a woman—and Zuke had stopped his own when it flooded onto the third page—he had been sure to include low maintenance, a characteristic Zuke explained with the examples that any girl he dated should wear little make up, be able to go from waking up to the car in less than thirty minutes, and in the case of a restaurant, order quickly from a menu accepting the food as it was generally prepared.

But in the instance of Zuke's father, in the case of family relations rather than romantic ones, there was no such thing as making a list of desirable traits. Zuke's father was his father no matter how many lists Zuke might make, and in a restaurant, he was a whole different kind of ordering beast. And so it was with a certain amount of dread, nearly as if he were settling back into a dentist's chair that Zuke leaned back into the cushiness of his booth seat and stared out the window waiting for his father to begin to try and communicate to Lucy what he wanted to eat. Outside it was nearly dark, a steady rain was turning to ice, and a string of cars splashed through a giant puddle as they rounded the corner headed for Interstate Fifty Seven.

"Do you know what you want, Sir?" Lucy asked. Zuke's dad glanced up and then back to his game program, where he zigged a little blue line on it to mark his place. Still waiting for some sort of response, Lucy looked to Zuke. Was there something wrong with his father?

"Dad, what do you want? Do you want chicken?" Zuke talked to his father as if he were two years old, which was in fact nearly his mental age in a restaurant, this even though he was quite capable of quoting longish passages from writers such as Milton or Defoe, two of his favorite writers from the senior literature anthology he'd taught from for over thirty years.

"Sure," Zuke's dad said. "That sounds good. Give me some chicken and maybe some French-broasted potatoes." Zuke's father had just ordered the potatoes from his hometown Pizza King in Horseshoe. It was possible that he'd order a Whopper next or more likely a Frosty for dessert. Because Zuke's father was just three years beyond a heart attack, Zuke had been thinking grilled chicken breast for his dad, but now he didn't know.

"I don't think they have broasted potatoes," Zuke said. "You want fried chicken?"

"Mmm," his dad said thoughtfully, "I probably should go with grilled. Grilled chicken and broasted potatoes? Remember, my heart."

"You guys need a minute?" Lucy asked, looking down the row of booths that made up her section. The last two had just been filled and the hostess had begun to start a wait.

"Just bring me a grilled chicken breast and the broasted potatoes," Zuke's father said. He still hadn't bothered to open the menu. Whenever he went somewhere, he just ordered what he wanted. Probably he'd been fine if a plate of bread had been placed in front of him. "Do you have salad?"

The exchange—one couldn't really call it a conversation—between Zuke's father and Lucy—began to remind Zuke of a Sesame Street skit he'd thought hilarious as a child, one where the restaurant is out of something—let's say macaroni and cheese—and so the character, Bert or whoever, continues to order different combinations all of which contain the item which the restaurant doesn't have. Zuke laughed at the thought of it.

"No broasted potatoes," Lucy explained. Her face was nearly as white as the coffee cups on the table, and she wore bright red lipstick—possibly she'd emulated Annie Lennox of the Eurythmics or maybe someone from the Cure—but what immediately impressed Zuke was that Lucy seemed to actually be smiling at Zuke's father, entertained when she had good reason to be a bit angry. Somehow, Zuke thought, Lucy understood that his dad wasn't messing with her; this was actually the way he was. "French fries, baked, or mashed," Lucy said, on the brink of laughing. "That's how we do our potatoes here. If I knew what broasted meant, I'd try and get somebody to make you some."

Lucy leaned and opened Mr. Zaucha's menu, an action which caused him to scoot his game notes away from her and toward where the salt and pepper shakers were. He seemed to believe that given the chance, Lucy would have liked nothing better than to snatch the program, make a dash for the women's restroom, and lock herself in so she could pore over the statistics at her leisure. For the first time in his life, Zuke wondered what happened to his father's game programs. Surely, eventually, they made it to the trash, even if it was Zuke's mom who had to sneak them there.

"Mashed," Zuke's father said. "What about a salad?"

"Here's the choices." Lucy pointed to the lower, left-hand corner of the menu. There were at least five different kinds: Zuke could read Cobb, Caesar, and spicy chicken.

"Can't I just have lettuce and French dressing, maybe a couple of those miniature tomatoes?" Lucy told him that she'd scrounge up some lettuce with French dressing, but that their tomatoes were diced. Then she asked him what he wanted to drink.

"Lite beer, draft, could you put some ice in the glass?" There it was; the sort of order Zuke treasured, at least when it came to an efficient turn of phrase. But of course most Denny's don't serve beer—this one didn't—and it's a pretty unusual request to want ice in one's draft, but that's how Zuke's father drank it unless the glass was cold, and then no ice was okay.

"No beer," Lucy said. "Soft drinks, lemonade, juice, tea, coffee, or water." Mr. Zaucha settled on ice water, and Lucy took a deep breath of relief and went off to turn in the order.

"Dad, I want to transfer," Zuke said, having just decided to bonk his father over the head with the news. He hadn't totally decided this but he knew he had to sound confident.

"Where does this come from?" Zuke's dad leaned back and folded his arms; he didn't seem angry, not confused, mostly he seemed curious. It was just the sort of reaction he was a pro at delivering, one that made Zuke wary. He felt that no matter what he said, he'd be back at Pison the following semester. "Your injury? You came back from this before; you can do it again; you just have to be patient."

"Dad no, not my injury. I've been here a year and a half; it's a stupid college, a terrible fit for me. Even if I'm good enough to play, I'm not going to change Coach's mind. I'm not that much better than the guys in front of me. I want to find somewhere else that needs a shooter, or I just want to go to Indiana."

"It's a stupid school?" Zuke's dad asked, attacking the weakest point of his son's argument.

"Not a stupid school; just a stupid school for me."

"You don't want to play sports anymore?" Zuke's father likely knew what connection his son would make next, a zip of logic that would cause him to think, *and just be an ordinary student? Ordinary* was quite a few rungs below what Zuke was after, maybe not even on the same identity ladder as *greatness.*

Zuke looked down at the table where the menu pictured the variety of Grand Slam breakfasts offered at Denny's. The condition of ordinary student already existed for him; no, it was worse than that. He was an embarrassment, practically a mascot. After a few seconds of silence, Lucy came with their drinks and looked quizzically back and forth between Zuke and his father. She'd noticed the change in the atmosphere at the table.

"What did you do to your hand?" she asked. Lucy had a soft-looking oval face, and Zuke thought she was pretty in a Melanie Griffith sort of way. He told her he'd fallen on the bleachers.

"That sucks," she said, a little flippantly for Zuke's taste, but added, "Sorry," before turning her attention to the next booth down the aisle.

"You didn't fall on the bleachers," Zuke's father said. "You knocked a trombone out of the air and kept it from cracking some girl's skull." Zuke's father, or his mother for that matter, had never heard the name Abby Grant or her nickname, Glory.

"It was a tuba."

"Right, a tuba, even better." Zuke's father turned and looked over his shoulder to the next booth where Lucy had begun to take an order. "Excuse me," he said. Lucy looked warily at him, as if maybe he had decided on a bottle of champagne, a lobster roll, or some other nonexistent item on the restaurant's menu. "A part of the balcony collapsed during the Pison basketball game." Zuke's father had Lucy's attention now.

"Oh my God," Lucy said. "Was anyone hurt?" The older couple

who'd been giving their order looked to Zuke's dad. Given their apparel, they'd obviously come up from Eureka for the game, and they were probably the parents of a cheerleader or player, maybe the manager.

"Not too bad, but my son here, he ran up into the bleachers and saved some girl from a falling tuba. Don't you think his modesty is taking things a bit far?"

"Why yes it is," Lucy said, looking at Zuke's cast with fresh respect.

"Oh yeah," a woman at a different table across the aisle said. "This young man was quite the hero. I would have liked to have seen you play." She winked at Zuke. "These coaches, they take it all too seriously sometimes; don't you think?"

Zuke faked a smile, a twenty year old who planned to take it all very seriously when and if he ever got a coaching job. Here he was again, in the spotlight for not playing, his shame outed for all to discuss.

Through the gap between Lucy and the couple from Eureka, Zuke saw Wendy Parrot come through the door followed by Cowboy, who had been holding it. Marie wasn't there. Zuke thought she must have got a good look at him and changed her mind.

Wendy wore blue jeans and a Pison College sweatshirt, and she was holding something in her hand. When she saw Zuke, which was almost right away, her gold Nike running shoes seemed to come right up off the floor in excitement. It was an unexplainable action to Zuke, who'd never really felt as if any woman who wasn't his mother had enjoyed his company. From adolescence, back before his freshman year of high school when he first spotted Colleen Flannery on the pitcher's mound, Zuke had always been in pursuit of the approval of others, always felt that it was his job to win people over to liking him.

Wendy took Cowboy's hand; he was still dressed in his *K* t-shirt, and she led him back to the table where Zuke and his father sat. The two appeared as if they'd been dating for years. Zuke's father knew Cowboy—who wouldn't know one of the letters of his son's name?—and Cowboy introduced Wendy, who suggested that they join them. Without waiting for an answer, she plopped down beside Zuke's father and slapped a baseball card onto the tabletop. Zuke made room for Cowboy. After the new couple was filled in about Zuke's broken wrist, he asked about the baseball card Wendy had placed on the table. "What do you have there?"

Wendy looked at Cowboy and smiled. "Let me see." She held up the card next to her face, as if it were a bottle of Pantene shampoo and she were Kelly LeBrock in preparation for a television commercial. "What I'm holding here is a gift from Paul: a 1983 Ryne Sandberg Topps Rookie Card."

"In mint condition," Cowboy added.

"You gave her a baseball card?" Zuke asked.

"Can I see that?" Mr. Zaucha asked. He went right for the back of the card and started reading.

"She likes it." Cowboy said, quickly looking to Wendy now that it had occurred to him that she might have been fooling him or worse: just being nice. "Right?"

"It's my first one." Wendy looked around the table; she had what Zuke thought was the most authentic looking smile he'd ever seen, like a bed of dewy-morning flowers. "It's important to him," she said. "He's being sweet. I've always wanted to meet a sweet boy."

"He's probably got five of them," Zuke said.

"Still," Zuke's father said, "even if he does, great present." Zuke's dad handed Wendy back the card.

"Do you have another one of these, Paul McClain?" Wendy asked. Cowboy raised his eyebrows and looked ten years younger, as if he'd just denied eating the last piece of a forbidden pie and the empty tin had been found in his bedroom.

"How many, Paul?" Zuke asked.

"The truth?" Cowboy asked.

"The truth!" Wendy said.

Cowboy hesitated and shuffled his mental cards. He sighed and exhaled powerfully. "Twenty-four," he said, pausing to let the number move away from him, as if it were some sort of nuclear warhead. "That is now that I've given one of them away."

"Shame on you," Wendy said, mock horror on her face.

"If we're dating in a year," Cowboy offered, "and all is going well—well, hold on, maybe I meant more like two years and not one—you can have an autographed card." Wendy shook her head in pretend disappointment. "At least as long as we're together, I mean." Cowboy was getting nervous now and each word he spoke revealed himself further as an idiosyncratic, overly compulsive devotee of all things Chicago Cubs. "And if you want," he added, now lost in what he was saying, not really aware that he was talking to anyone, "I'll hold that one you've got right there for safe keeping." Zuke expected that Wendy and Cowboy's first fight was to come.

"Crazy," Wendy said, making the *loco* sign by pointing her index finger to her head and spinning it around. She didn't seem bothered in the least by Cowboy's quirkiness. Zuke was starting to think he didn't know anything about what it was that attracted women to the men they fell in love with. Lucy came over to take Wendy and Cowboy's order.

For all Zuke's father's awkwardness at the art of ordering, he was a master of the interview, which was what he did when he met people. He interviewed them. He had thirty years of experience running high school newspapers, teaching students to ask questions, to follow the lead of the answers they were given, and when he applied that experience to the young woman who sat next to him; well, that was like throwing a lighted match into a gas tank: there was an immediate detonation of conversation. As Wendy began to talk, Zuke knew that if his date was still on—he'd forgotten about it for stretches of his afternoon given Cheese's record, the collapse of the balcony, the trip to the E.R., his decision to transfer, and his overall wistfulness for Abby—his father was going to hear about it. This happened even sooner than he expected.

"My friend Marie can't wait to go out with your son," Wendy said. She was emotionally open with a sense of humor, talking with a man in Zuke's father who had never discussed romantic relationships and all that went with them—dates, proms, sex, conflict, and insecurity—with his son. "She's cute and smart." Wendy opened her eyes wide at Zuke's dad. "Ideal daughter-in-law material."

"Is that right?" Mr. Zaucha asked. Wendy was teasing him in a psychological place where he was most vulnerable, but Zuke was surprised to see how much his father seemed to enjoy the news. He wondered if it wasn't because it meant that he might stay on as a member of the basketball team, or if it was just that he'd never thought his son had a life outside of class and practice.

"If all goes well," Wendy said, "I'll have your son out of here by seven-thirty and on a pair of roller skates by eight." Zuke thought of his friends at Indiana University, who were probably drinking into their second keg of the weekend. It wasn't necessarily that sort of atmosphere that Zuke wanted, not crowds so thick in the bars that he was pushed up off the floor by the force of them, but he sought company he couldn't name, company which he imagined was more accessible at a state school. All he wanted shimmered in foggy remembrances of relationships he'd seen on the big screen. Zuke wanted to be in the kiss at the end of the movie.

After everyone finished dinner, Cowboy and Wendy went outside to her car while Zuke stood near the counter and waited for his father to return from the restroom. From the front of the restaurant, Lucy the waitress came toward Zuke, and as she passed him on her way to clearing the table, she smiled and placed her hand on Zuke's shoulder for a moment. True, the gap between the booths and the counter was narrow, but even to Zuke, who was commonly ignorant of flirtation, Lucy's touch hadn't been necessary. While Zuke had been sitting at the table, he hadn't realized how tall Lucy was, probably close to six feet, and he hadn't realized how attractive she was either. Zuke's dad emerged from the restroom, walked up to his son, and folded his arms in a pose that was well known to the residents of his hometown of Horseshoe, where he'd spent many years as an athletic director standing in a similar way off to the side of sporting events.

"We'll talk about this transfer later," he told Zuke, as if he was the general manager of the Zaucha team and had reached his decision for the time being. "There's no way to get anything done by the spring semester. So for what it's worth—and of course you can do whatever you want—if it were me, I'd just stick it out on the team and make up my mind before summer. With the wrist, you're going to have a little vacation from it anyway."

Zuke nodded his head and thought of the hours he'd already spent watching practice and listening to Coach Miller talk. Already boring, Zuke wondered how dreadful practice would be if he were not even able to go through the drills.

"Have fun on that date," Mr. Zaucha said, nudging his son. "Good daughter-in-law material," he said, "or so I hear." Zuke smiled and his dad stuck out his hand. The two shook as if they'd just completed a business agreement, and then Zuke's father strode out of the restaurant. The Zauchas tended to hurry their goodbyes.

"Hey," Lucy said from behind Zuke. She'd just finished cleaning off the table and was tucking into the pocket of her apron the ten dollar bill Zuke's dad had left for a tip. "I just thought of something. Don't I see you all the time in the library with Abby Grant?"

It was an innocuous enough question from Lucy, but Zuke always felt adulterous when someone asked him about Abby. "Do you know her?" he asked.

"No, but I know who she is, and I know that dick she dates."

Zuke was surprised at Lucy's word choice; not that it was a word he wouldn't use too, at least outside the world of Pison, but still, it was not an ordinary choice for a Nazarene girl, especially one who worked for the radio as part of what the station called "The Voice of the Oracles." Zuke shrugged his shoulders. "I guess I feel like you do, but maybe I'm not such an impartial judge." Lucy smoothed out her apron.

"Well," she said, "if you ever get over her, you ought to come by the radio station. I'm on Monday thru Wednesday, seven to ten in the morning. Maybe I'll sign your cast." She laughed and with her note pad, she smacked Zuke's unbroken side on her way to the register. Zuke thought for a moment, staring at the floor, and he remembered something The Dini had once told him, an axiom related to dating: when it rains, it pours. The Dini had meant that one can go through long droughts across various seasons of dating, but all of a sudden there can be unexpected downpours, more options than even practical. Zuke smelled ozone in the air and thought that maybe a storm—of the dating kind—was on the way.

CHAPTER ELEVEN

B uilt circa 1930, the inside of Lane's Roller Rink was noisy and hot as skaters spun through the colored rays of light that came off the disco ball and cut through the darkness. Originally a dance hall, the rink was rectangular, three sides open to the crowd, and the skating surface was accessible through a royal arch. Faux crystal chandeliers hung in three rows across the length of the ceiling, which refracted the lights of a giant disco ball. The DJ booth was on the fourth side of the rink—the only walled side of the skating surface, and from the giant speakers in the four corners of the room blasted the song "Funky Town," by a band named Lipps, Inc., a pun on the phrase "Lip Synch."

With the smell of popcorn in the air and the sound of Donkey Kong beating his chest nearby, Zuke sat at a picnic table across from Cowboy and Wendy, and next to Marie, his TWIRP date. He poked around in a strawberry sundae he'd ordered even though he wasn't hungry. At a place like Pison—and this may be the norm in all American church societies—if one was going to have a social life then it meant that one was going to do a lot of eating. Rather than choose ice cream, Marie munched from a small bag of jelly beans, and her outfit—matching acid-washed jean jacket and pants—had Zuke silently singing David Bowie's "Blue Jean" to himself.

Cowboy had just explained the girls' nicknames to them, an action that had fallen flat. As it turned out, they weren't too thrilled with them. Zuke, whose mental attention teeter tottered between Abby and Marie, had unconsciously grown a little quiet and lost in his thoughts. In an attempt to pick up the spirit of the evening, Cowboy, who was an inventor of games, who had in fact invented the Lincoln Shoot Out the Brothers played in their dorm rooms, tried to introduce a game of a different sort. It was a game meant to save the date, a way to rebound the shot he'd missed when he'd decided to tell them that they were *Bird* and *Magic*.

"All right," Cowboy said, a silly grin on his face as he sat with both hands flat on the table in front of him. "Here's what we do." Cowboy was always good for picking up the energy of an evening, or at least attempting to do so. With the four of them that made up the TWIRP date, the feeling was a little like the huddle of a pick up football game, Cowboy the quarterback. "Slap the table twice with your hands and then clap." Cowboy began to do this lightly to the table while the rest of them watched. "C'mon," he said. "You guys join me."

Wendy and Marie looked at Zuke, who with some sense of embarrassment took a quick glance around to see if anyone was watching. Nobody was. He shrugged his shoulders, smiled, and with his cast-less hand, began to smack the table to Cowboy's beat. Tentatively at first, Marie and Wendy joined in, but it wasn't long before they smiled, as if experiencing their first carousel ride. At some of the neighboring tables, children began to join in, and there hung a *what are we doing?* look on their faces.

"Now," Cowboy said loudly, over the hullabaloo that he had begun, "start making horsey noises." Zuke burst out laughing at the phrase *horsey noises*—so hard that he stopped clapping. Wendy looked at Cowboy as if he'd dared her to skate in her underwear, but he remained undaunted and called out even louder than he had before: "C'mon everyone; horsey noises!" He looked to the table next to him, full of elementary-aged students and asked, "What sounds do horseys make?" One kid whinnied. Another made a quack-quack sound.

Against his better judgment and level of comfort, Zuke began to make whinnying noises of his own, and then something surprised him: their dates joined in Cowboy's game. Zuke noted the development, which went against his general philosophy of relationships, which was that he was never silly. In the spirit of Lloyd Dobler, Zuke's goal was always to be *a great date,* which meant that he often showed up on first dates with flowers and tried for romance in the form of candlelit dinners or else sunset walks along the banks of the Tippecanoe. Before Zuke had actually met Marie and Wendy—certainly a key point Zuke had not yet considered—he'd imagined that women such as them would want to date artists, maybe a guy like Cheese, or more likely a business major headed for big money in Chicago. And if it wasn't that, if they happened to be people who were not superficial, then, at least at Pison, they were likely to want to be preachers' wives.

But here were Bird and Magic, sitting at a picnic table in a roller skating rink, gleefully making horsey noises. With Abby on his mind—and quite a few other items hovering like roaches waiting for the cover of night—Zuke hadn't had time to over-think his date with Magic. He'd just showed up with no expectations, showed up without caring very much how it turned out, and it seemed to be turning out fairly well. There was a lot for Zuke to notice about how dating and love worked right here, but nothing had sunk in quite yet.

Marie and Wendy continued their various attempts to make horse noises—Marie had switched to a sort of *klip klop* meant to sound like galloping. Far trickier than rubbing one's belly and tapping one's head, it took focus to clap and slap hands, make noises, and listen to Cowboy as he extended the instructions. As it turned out, it was the very point of the game to not realize what you were saying. What Cowboy wanted Marie and Wendy to do was choose a horse's body part, and to the beat of their two-table slaps, say it out loud and add the word *hearted.* They each took turns doing this as fast as they could one after the other. Cowboy had to explain the process several times before everyone began to catch on.

"I'll start," he said, already beginning to laugh again. A crowd of twenty or so had gathered around the table clapping and continuing with their horse noises. Cowboy, it seemed, was born to run a day care center, a children's camp, or else teach in an elementary school. There were noticeably less people on the skating surface as the song "Macho Man" came onto the sound system. Cowboy was out-drawing The Village People, a band generally thought of as a guaranteed-to-fill-the-floor entity. "Tail hearted," Cowboy said, nodding to Zuke who sat across from him.

"Nose hearted" Zuke said, trying to see where the game was going, if it indeed would go anywhere. With Cowboy running the show, it could be some sort of trick along the lines of a practical joke. The year before, Cowboy, when he'd been on the basketball team too, had joined forces with Zuke several times to baby sit Coach Miller's kids when he brought his family on a team road trip. Coach Miller, who didn't trust either of the young men with the basketball on the court, did trust the two benchwarmers with his kids in the motel room. One night, Coach's children had gone a little crazy doing dives from the chest of drawers on the bed and eventually a bucket of ice got knocked over onto all of coach's paperwork. To settle everyone down, Cowboy had suggested "The Amish Game." It had lasted for nearly an hour, a contest that had as its only rule that there was no talking or noisemaking (this included, say, rumpling a piece of paper). There was no keeping score, something that was certainly a minimal requirement of Zuke's for an activity to be considered a game. Admittedly, the game had worked perfectly and the kids had fallen asleep during the course of the game, but when the night was over, Zuke had wanted to know what was Amish about the game—there were quite a few Amish in the area surrounding Horseshoe where Zuke had gone to high school—and Cowboy had said he didn't know. Wasn't it quiet at an Amish person's house?

"Hoof hearted," Marie said, jumping in after Zuke and right before Wendy was to speak.

"I can't think of anything," Wendy said. "Body? Is that good enough? Body hearted."

"How about *eye*?" Cowboy said. He was red-faced, as if he'd been out in the cold or just finished fifty push ups, a laughing volcano near eruption.

"Eye hearted," Wendy said.

"Tail hearted" Cowboy said. "Faster. We've got to go faster. Round and round." Everyone clapped more rapidly. The words began to run together.

"Hoof hearted," Wendy said. And as the speed with which each of the four of them said their words increased, the more each member of the circle's words ran together. "Hoof hearted. Hoof hearted. Who hearted. Who Farted?"

"I hearted," Marie had said, immediately following the first time

Wendy had spoken her part. Eventually her words also morphed into something else: "I hearted. I hearted. I farted."

Although the young women were baffled at what they were saying, to Cowboy, the game became as funny as one of Gallagher's smashed watermelons. Tears rolled down his cheeks, and the girls laughed but didn't know for sure why they were laughing. Zuke had realized what they were saying, but only because Cowboy was a man who often had gas on his mind. Once the year before, Zuke had proposed a competition played by him and his high school cross country teammates. The game was to see who could audibly fart in the presence of another Brother in Pursuit. If it was silent but deadly (SBD) it didn't count. Cowboy had easily blasted his way to victory by registering 43 "toots" in a week's time, and for awhile it appeared as if he might become Methane Man.

"Did you like it?" Cowboy asked Wendy, who along with much of the crowd that had gathered around them, was shaking her head in mild amusement.

"Paul McClain," she said, "what am I going to do with you?" If it had been a movie, Cowboy would have answered *marry me*.

Later, when Cowboy and Wendy had moved off to skate, Marie and Zuke sat talking.

"I've actually known who you are since last year," she said. "I used to live on campus." Zuke told her that he knew she'd lived on campus, and that he'd heard she'd moved back home. "Every day at about the same time," Marie said, "I'd be at my desk reading pysch, and I'd see you go walking by to practice."

Zuke felt as if he was listening to himself talk about Abby, except for he'd never told her about the first day of class, the time when he changed his major just to be around her. Zuke wished he'd never even told his buddies. He asked Marie why she'd moved back home.

"All the rules," she said, a surprise answer for Zuke, who'd assumed he was out with a model Nazarene, mostly because one of the residence halls bared her family's last name. "Don't get me wrong; I believe in God and my family has invested a lot in the school, but I'm just not into all that regulation. I can't go see *The Little Mermaid* at the movie theater?" She wrinkled her nose. "You and me can't sit in a dorm room and study together? I mean, c'mon. Didn't God give me a mind and the ability to choose Him or not choose Him?" The two thought on what Marie had said for a moment. "How about you?" she asked. "You're a Nazarene?"

"No. I came for the basketball. I thought the rules would be no big deal, that I could put up with them, especially because the atmosphere is so great at the games." Zuke thought back to some of the other schools he'd considered, one of which was an all boys school he'd avoided because he thought he and Colleen would go to the same place. "But I'm not getting to play, and it's not a big deal to be barred from the movies, but when that's added to required chapel, a dress code, the rules against visitation, and not being allowed to go shirts and skins playing pick up ball, it starts to be a major drag." Zuke picked at a splinter on the picnic table. "But I guess most of it has to do with basketball. If I was getting to play, I wouldn't mind the rest."

Marie turned to Zuke and swung her leg over the bench of the picnic table so that she faced Zuke and was close enough that he could smell jellybeans on her breath, also the scent of vanilla on the skin of her neck. "Do you know what I liked about you?" she asked. "That is before I met you?" This was the other side of Zuke's fantasies. Here was a girl who'd imagined an identity for him in the same way he'd created one for Abby. Ten yards away from where Marie and Zuke sat, couples moved slowly around the rink, a swirl of colors blipping the air, with the Cutting Crew's "I Just Died in Your Arms" on the sound system. It all reminded Zuke of a high school dance, except for the sound of Ms. Pac Man in the background chomping pellets. "I thought you were brooding," Marie continued. "You know? Every day you looked so serious: brows furrowed, head down, and I don't think I ever saw you speak to anyone. I imagined you reading Thoreau and Keats, serious about your writing and grumpy."

"You thought I was one of the seven dwarfs?"

"What?"

"Grumpy. You said I was Grumpy. He was with Snow White, right?"

Wendy laughed. "See what I mean? You're not brooding and intense at all."

Zuke wondered if he'd come across as naively blithe. Marie reached out and squeezed Zuke's arm. "But that's okay. You're funny. Nice. Friendly. And you're still an English major, right? You read books. You've read Thoreau." Zuke thought Wendy sounded as if she were trying to convince herself of him, and when he didn't respond to her line of inquiry with regard to his reading habits, she said, "Hey! You've read Thoreau, right?"

"Sure," Zuke said. "Maybe ten pages. I've heard about living deliberately, but I think I got most of that from *Dead Poet's Society.*" Zuke felt as if he were meeting a female version of himself, at least in the unguarded ways that Marie communicated. Usually it was Zuke who offered too much about what was happening in his head, too early in the time he was getting to know someone. And as he listened to Marie describe the Eric Zaucha of her imagination, he felt as if maybe he wanted to become more like the person he was hearing about. It was sort of like seeing Farmer Ted or Lloyd Dobler and taking a little bit of that character for one's self. Zuke thought of the assignment he had due in Moore's expository writing class, the European Bloc piece which he'd lightly researched but not begun. *What else could he write? What could he write that Marie would want to read? What about Abby?* Zuke felt a bud of guilt wriggle in his chest, a sprout watered by his time with Marie. With force, he tried to remind himself that Abby was probably, almost definitely, with the new all-time leading scorer of Pison College.

With skates returned and everyone outside the rink, the two couples stood on the sidewalk and looked out to the parking lot where freezing rain fell from the sky and pounded the aluminum awning over their heads. An increasingly thick sheet of ice had begun to form on the blacktop of the parking lot. The members of the double dating TWIRP party walked away from the rink toward the bowling alley to where Wendy had parked her car.

"Did you know," Cowboy inquired, mostly to Wendy, "that Jimmy Carter once filed a report that he'd seen a UFO?" It wasn't the first instance of the evening that Cowboy had mentioned Carter; in fact, for the past month he'd begun to pepper any lull in conversation with an increasing amount of trivia related to the nation's thirty-ninth president. Aside from his own desire to one day hold the position, Cowboy had begun his study as a part of a project for an education course he was taking where he was supposed to organize a unit by theme. It was no surprise to anyone who knew him that he'd selected a presidential one.

Out in front of them and beyond the edge of the parking lot toward the bowling alley, the Illinois plain stretched off to where the Pison campus was visible: the steeple of College Church, the lights of the football field, the library, and even the orange letters PNC on the smokestack of the King Power Plant. Bolts of light spidered the sky over campus, as if the town of Beau Fleuve was encased in a lightning bowl, and a giant had twice placed his hands on it.

"Did you see that?" Wendy asked, pointing in the direction of the college, where the flashes crackled against the black sky.

"Lightning?" Zuke asked.

"In December?" Marie wondered. They had arrived at the edge of the sidewalk and the end of the overhang which kept them from being drenched by the freezing rain.

"Want to loan me your keys so I can pull up your car?" Cowboy asked. Wendy looked him up and down as if to study him.

"Let me explain a few things to you," Wendy said. "Take the hierarchical structure of the United States government and imagine it as a way of seeing the way that I think about men."

"Okay," Cowboy said, grinning.

"Way down here, on the local level, where decisions are made about new sidewalks or whether or not the town is going to do a tree-lighting festival, this is where you'll find someone I'm willing to go out with."

"I'm down there," Cowboy said, a little dejectedly.

"A few rungs higher," Wendy explained, "because don't forget, I asked you out. I just bought you a Mountain Dew slushy."

"And I said *thank you*."

"You're very welcome, but just so you know, driving my car is still quite a few levels up there on the dating ladder." Wendy pointed up to the underside of the metal overhang where the freezing rain dinged away.

One of the double-glass doors to the bowling alley opened and out stepped Cheese and Abby, smack dab into the middle of Zuke and Cowboy's double date. Zuke's first thought was that the two sure did look like a couple, Abby clinging to Cheese's arm, not the sort of body language that foretold a next-day break up. Zuke realized at least for the span of the last hour, he had forgotten himself, forgotten his life and the anxiousness that squeezed his guts like a too-tight pair of pants. He was in the middle of what Lloyd Dobler surely would have categorized as a great date.

Zuke thought that it had only been that very afternoon when Abby had lain scared in his arms on the fractured bleachers. He felt guilty and thrilled at the same time seeing Abby, and he searched her face looking for any sort of reaction she might have at seeing him and Marie. So far she hadn't even looked at him.

"Hey guys," Cowboy said. He of course knew Glory and Cheese well, the first as Zuke's primary womanly pursuit of the past year and the latter as a teammate who had devised his freshman basketball initiation: the upperclassman filled his hotel bathtub with Captain Crunch, slathered Cowboy in Vaseline, and then tossed him in for a cereal bath.

"How is your dad?" Zuke asked Cheese, noticing that his teammate had his own monogrammed bowling ball bag. It was black with hellish yellow flames licking up toward the phrase *Up Your Alley*. Zuke's thoughts were engaged in a brutal tug-of-war, anywhere from *Did Marie know about this?* to memories of the way Colleen had dropped Knucklehead the week after she saw that the homecoming queen had been waiting for him after his first varsity basketball game.

"Sprained knee," Cheese answered, glancing to Zuke's freshly casted arm. "Hyper extended his elbow but he's going to be fine—he and Abby are both going to be fine—thanks to you."

"Glad to do it," Zuke said. This was the first time Abby looked his way. She had a smile on her face that he'd never seen before. It was as if he were a stranger.

"I didn't say thank you. I really appreciate what you did, Eric." It was a stunning thing for her to do, use Zuke's first name. He didn't know what to make of it. On the one hand it was as if she were distancing herself from him, changing names in preparation to disappoint him with bad news, but on the other, Zuke knew how Abby didn't like Cheese's nickname and so maybe the switch to Zuke's own first name was the first step toward their official coupledom.

"You're welcome." Zuke looked at Cheese. "I didn't do any more than you did, and also, congratulations on the record."

"Oh yeah," Cheese said, "Right. I just checked in with Coach. The points are going to stand. They're going to do a special thing for me the next home game. Eureka agreed to call that the final score rather than make it up."

"Great," Cowboy said, "quite an accomplishment."

Wendy stepped up toward Abby and Cheese, into the space that separated them. "Cowboy here isn't used to being in the company of a lady, so I guess I'll introduce myself."

"Dag gum it," Cowboy said. "I'm sorry."

"No need," Cheese said. "I know you two." He looked at Marie, who was obviously with Zuke, and then Zuke thought he could see a look of approval in the great scorer's face.

"Everybody knows you," Abby said. She turned to Marie. "It's good to see you. I miss having you around."

"Thanks," Marie said. This felt weird for Zuke. Obviously the girls knew each other pretty well. He wondered what secrets, if any, Marie might have, and he wondered to what degree she was aware of the *Glory Situation.*

Out in the parking lot the hail had changed to a thick sleeting rain and it appeared as if the lightning-bowl giant was now emptying his slushy machine onto Beau Flueve. It was windier than it had been upon entering the skating rink and that made it cold.

"C'mon girl," Cheese said, "it looks like hail out there." Abby laughed at Cheese's line; it was a big laugh, one full of happiness. Red faced, she shook her head in playful embarrassment as Cheese grabbed her hand and pulled her out into the rain. Zuke watched them run, hand in hand, toward Cheese's new Firebird, a metallic gold color for Pison College. Zuke swallowed hard and felt jealous at how Cheese had been able to get Abby to laugh.

"Did Cheese just make a joke?" Cowboy asked.

"A pretty funny one," Wendy said. "Is that unusual?"

"He's very good looking," Marie added, a comment that caused a whoosh of anxiety to gust through Zuke.

"I can tell you," Cowboy said, stepping off the curb into the parking lot, "about my experience with that man's sense of humor."

During the ride home in Wendy's Monte Carlo, Zuke and Marie sat in the back while Cowboy rode shotgun, where he'd turned almost sideways in the seat so that he could face Wendy. He'd just finished telling the girls about Cheese's towel flipping and described his freshman initiation. Nobody said anything and so Cowboy went back to Carter. "Did you know," Cowboy asked, "that Carter created the Department of Education?" Surprisingly enough to Zuke, who had only vague notions that Carter was a Christian with ties to peanut farming, Wendy seemed interested in what Cowboy was saying, even knew extra facts about Carter that Cowboy didn't know.

"Did you know," Wendy countered, taking it easy as she made a turn onto Mahoney Boulevard, "that Amy Carter was arrested three years ago?" Wendy was a political science major, and Zuke could see that she had begun to develop a sort of contest with Cowboy to see who could out trivialize the other with random historical information. While the heat hummed to the growl of what must have been a powerful engine under the hood of the SS, the rain blopped against the windshield on the roof. Wendy drove carefully and confidently in the weather.

The inside of the car was covered with a velvety maroon fabric; the dash was large, black, and simple, except for a bright red Chevy logo, something that had been added to the car. The gearshift was between the seats and to Zuke, the Monte Carlo seemed a strange car for Wendy to drive. He would have imagined her more as a Volkswagen kind of girl.

"I actually brought you something," Marie said, reaching into the wide and deep pocket of her coat from which she pulled out a worn paperback book. Zuke felt a bristle of emotion on his arms. He had always been the one to drive any relationship, the one who had to come up with the ideas, initiate the dates with Colleen, and so it was amazing for him to have someone else do this for him.

"I read this last year," Marie said. "When I used to see you go by my window, I kept thinking that someday I'd run out there and ask you to read it. I figured if we ended up together, it would make for a good story." She kept her head down as she said that last part, an embarrassed smile on her face, but she looked up at Zuke when she handed over the book: on its cover was a star-filled sky and in the middle of it, as if it had floated down from Heaven, a bluish-white feather. The title, centered at the top, was done in fat, all-capital white letters: *Illusions* it read, and in smaller letters underneath, *The Adventures of a Reluctant Messiah.* It had a title that a certain sort of Nazarene would probably try to ban.

Marie's gift was the first book anyone had ever given Zuke. Up to this point in his life, except for what he'd been assigned in school, Zuke's reading had been confined to C. S. Lewis's Narnia books and Louis L'Amour westerns. So it was of no surprise to him that he'd not heard of the author Richard Bach, and as he flipped open the first few pages, he noticed the words looked as if they'd been copied from someone's hand-printed journal. Zuke read the first line: "There was a Master come unto the earth, born in the holy land of Indiana, raised in the mystical hills of East Fort Wayne."

"At least he's got the right state," Zuke said. Marie asked him what he meant, and he told her he was from Indiana.

"Oh yeah," she said. "I knew that." And when Zuke's look

questioned where she'd gotten her information, she reminded him of the basketball media guide and told him that she'd read his page. "And just so you know," Marie said, "my first concert was Jackson Browne." She winked at him and Zuke blushed. He'd written Jackson Browne in the "likes" category of the program. Zuke turned the book over in his hands and Moon's "Angel in the Parking Lot" story came to mind for its suggestion that supernatural powers still worked in the day-to-day-world.

Holding the gift of the book from Marie, Zuke felt something: maybe the hand of fate, possibly one of those God-incidences that had been the subject of a chapel service, or perhaps it was just the chemistry that one experiences when meeting another who is obviously meant to be a friend. Zuke had theories regarding circles of friends; people who were destined to know each other, who in fact couldn't avoid knowing one another no matter what they did. It was within these circles of humanity, Zuke hypothesized, that people located opportunities to pursue love.

"If you're willing," Marie said, "I'd like for you to read this and tell me what you think." Zuke looked up at her and nodded his head, then looked back to the pages, to where after the journal-like section, the book seemed more conventional. The words were typed and the text divided into chapters. Marie had carved up the book with a pink ballpoint, using check marks, circles, underlining, and on one page she'd written *what?* with an arrow that pointed to a particular sentence. Zuke felt his heart shimmy in his chest, thumping to the chill that comes with a special feeling of closeness. It was a feeling nearly identical to the one he'd experienced when one night Zuke's high school girlfriend Colleen Flannery had found his baby book and spent an hour browsing though his childhood. Zuke counted that night on the couch with Colleen as one of the most pleasant instances of his life, and now here was another such night.

Wendy eased the Monte Carlo in front of Marie's parents' house, a two-story cape cod, ornately landscaped, with lights glowing from basement half windows. Just as Cheese had predicted, the rain had transformed into tiny pellets of ice. Zuke wondered again to what

degree Marie had been told about the *Glory Situation* and he wanted
to explain it to her if she was willing to listen, but he wouldn't do
it in front of the others. I'll walk her to the door, Zuke thought,
but before he could ask, Magic dive-bombed in with her lips and
kissed Zuke. It was his first kiss in four hundred and ninety three
days—the Brothers kept such statistics—and the last one had been
two summers ago after his senior year in high school, a kiss that had
preceded Colleen's break up with Zuke. This one from Marie was
over before Zuke even thought to experience it. His lips quivered
in an invisible stretch for more as she pulled away.

"I'll have my people get in touch with your people," Marie said,
her hand on the door, pulling the handle down while the smell of
her, the feeling of closeness, her body—the whole experience of her
was gone before Zuke could give any sort of response. Hail rattled
on the ice-covered blacktop of the street, and Zuke didn't really
come to his senses until a wet and magical puff of cold Midwestern
air came into the backseat, burned his nostrils, and ignited a return
from the Narnia the kiss had been for him.

"Bye," was all that Zuke had time to say. The door slammed. "I
had fun," Zuke mumbled, too late for Marie to hear, but audible to
Cowboy and Wendy in the front seat.

"She did too," Wendy said. "You'll see her again if you want."
Zuke had thought his experiences with Colleen had prepared him
for all future relationships; that once he'd dated her, kissed her,
and gotten used to having a girlfriend, that he'd never again feel so
bumbling, immature, and helpless. He'd never return to that fright
that had caused him in the eighth grade to break up with Shawna
Russell because he sensed she wanted to kiss him. He wondered
again if it hadn't been honor that caused him to not kiss Abby, but if
it had been fear instead. Zuke knew that standing outside the library
Thursday night with Abby, he had felt all those panicky feelings he
felt in the eighth grade, as if he were back in middle school afraid
of girls, back behind the backstop in Horseshoe making two year
plans to say hello.

Marie's house was one of four lined up on the curve of a cul-
de-sac, and as she entered the front door, a light came on in the

big picture window, where the shadow of a man who must have been her father peeked around a thin curtain. Obviously Wendy's car was familiar to him, and even though he surely couldn't make out any faces inside the Monte Carlo, he gave a little wave. As a response, Wendy bonked the horn twice before shifting into first gear and driving the car around the curve of the cul-de-sac, under the yellow glow of a streetlight, where the tires spun a little on the slick road. Zuke heard a dog bark in the distance, and the world outside darkened as the car rolled away from the homes of the subdivision and onto a thin and deserted stretch of road that led back to the main thoroughfare of Beau Fleuve.

Parked off in the grass was a new-looking gray Mustang, strangely free of ice for the weather, and it was a car that Zuke didn't remember seeing on the way in. It looked as if a man, fairly large, sat slumped down in the driver's seat. Zuke thought maybe he was having a smoke, a puff of hashish, or maybe a beer.

Zuke's thoughts went to what he felt for Marie. It was much like the feeling he'd had when he first saw Colleen on the pitcher's mound and like the one he'd felt at the sight of Abby in the back of Professor Moore's class, but how could he feel love for Marie when he was already supposed to be in love with Abby?

Zuke wished Marie back into the car with him and tried to remember the sensation of her lips on his. He took a deep breath of the still light smell of vanilla that lingered in the back seat. It was a didactic moment of confusion for Zuke, who realized how easily the emotion he'd possibly mislabeled love could fire in his heart. It wasn't that Zuke was trying to discount the feelings he had for Marie, but instead he had begun to consider just how much stock he'd placed on what he'd felt at first seeing Abby in composition class. It had been that particular moment and feeling that had catalyzed his decision to become an English major and his year-long pursuit. He'd certainly believed that he had fallen in love with Abby but now found himself experiencing a similar emotion on his date with Marie.

Through the rear window of Wendy's Monte Carlo, Zuke saw the lights of the Mustang come to life. Glancing to the front seat,

Zuke saw Wendy frown into her rearview mirror.

"What's the matter?" Cowboy asked, his face hardening as if he'd just been threatened. He turned in his seat and stared out through the rear window of Wendy's car, so covered with ice that the world took on a muted wavy appearance. In the mirror, Zuke watched Wendy's eyes follow the car's path.

"I don't know," Wendy said. Zuke turned his gaze back to the car and wondered if Marie had a boyfriend she hadn't told him about. Not that there would have been anything wrong with that—Zuke had certainly left out all the back-story of himself and Abby—but if there was a boyfriend, maybe he had followed them on their date. It was the sort of thing Zuke had considered doing for himself, trailing Abby and Cheese on one of their ice-cream dates so he could see what really happened. The Mustang moved under the glow of the streetlamp and then whipped around the cult-de-sac doing a complete 360 before following the same route Wendy had driven. The Mustang's bright-white driving lights were book-ended by yellow parking ones, a feature that made the front of the car look like a feverish predator. In the front seat, Wendy noted, "You know, Mulligan's got a car like that: a silver Mustang."

Cowboy and Zuke both expressed surprise at this. "He sure hasn't bragged about a new ride." Cowboy said.

"It seems like he would have," Zuke added, looking back at the car, interest renewed.

"It looks like his," Wendy said. The silence in the Monte Carlo seemed to vacuum all the dust up from what had been such a happy night. Wendy stopped the car at an intersection, looked both ways, and waited for a salt truck to rumble past. She glanced again into her rear view mirror and checked the progress of the phantom car.

"Should we wait on it?" Cowboy asked, a young man who seemed to have grown a new and aggressive personality, one that sought to protect what it had never known.

Wendy offered an uncertain alternative: "Let's just pull out and see what he does?"

"Should we call the police?" Zuke asked, feeling more than a little cowardly offering such a proposition.

"If he follows us back," Cowboy said, sounding confident, "we'll just park someplace safe and report him to campus security." Wendy pulled out onto the road more quickly than she'd intended, and the back of the Monte Carlo fanned out to the side, the tires buzzing on the icy pavement.

With no small amount of anxiousness, Zuke and Cowboy looked back to the gray Mustang, which had just darted out of the subdivision, as if driven by an undercover officer who'd received an emergency call. At the main road, the driver turned the car away from the direction they were all traveling, away from the location of Pison College. All the air whooshed out of the tension balloon that had filled the car.

"I guess I'm just being paranoid," Wendy said.

"Maybe," Cowboy said, "maybe not."

Upon reaching the parking lot of College Church, Zuke took leave of Cowboy and Wendy, where he thought it likely they would partake of their first kiss. As he walked toward the street, pellets of ice fell mixed in with glops of rain. Zuke stared up at the church steeple, its white point shaped like a Phillips screwdriver, bright against the black sky. Concerned for his cast, Zuke tucked it under his coat as he crossed the street and headed for Ludwig Center, a sort of short cut to his dormitory on the other side. Women's curfew was at one, and so it was a fairly busy time on campus, a time when students were returning from wherever they'd been and were in the process of stopping off at the student center for some acoustic Christian music, a slice of pizza, a basket of breadsticks, or a root beer float nightcap. When Zuke came to the stairs, he bounded up them to the glass doors and felt filled with the desire to run, so much so that he had to make himself walk once he was inside the lobby. On each end of the hallway were stairs that led down to the basement. Zuke heard the sound of someone playing the guitar, a Steven Curtis Chapman song, and the pop of a ping pong ball being batted back and forth. It sounded as if the student center in the basement was fairly busy.

Zuke emerged from Ludwig and walked out into the quadrangle, where the Tree of Knowledge was lit up under a spotlight as if it were a monument in Washington D.C. It shone under a thick glaze of ice and there was Moon, his back to Zuke, standing there staring at it as if he'd been hypnotized. He wore a red sock cap with a white fuzzy ball on top, a shiny sateen L.A. Lakers jacket, and he was drenched as if he'd been standing there for hours. Zuke knew that when Moon was depressed he went for what he called prayer walks. Zuke wondered if maybe thoughts of Cowboy's date with Wendy had prompted one such walk.

"You all right?" Zuke asked, frowning a little when he got close enough to Moon to see that he was soaked and shivering. His glasses were covered in a foggy film of water. He seemed disoriented, as if he'd just been deposited back from somewhere else. "It's not *The Tree of Knowledge*," Zuke said, going for a joke.

Moon took off his glasses, reached under his jacket, and used his shirt to clean them. "My friend," he said, in an oddly formal voice, "this has been one of the strangest, most personally embarrassing nights of my life."

At hearing this, Zuke wondered if maybe his friend had become confused about what day it was, that it had been the day before when he'd professed his love for Wendy in front of about thirty people while sitting next to her TWIRP date—Cowboy—for the following night. The windows of Ludwig glowed warmly, and as Zuke stood in the cold rain—which, if anything, had grown more intense—he considered suggesting to Moon that they go get a cup of hot chocolate, that maybe the singer in the basement might be just the thing to lift his spirits.

But Moon resumed talking before Zuke had the chance say anything. "Tonight at dinner, after a couple bowls of Batman Cereal, I sat alone and looked into the yellow swirl on the surface of my leftover milk. I got to thinking that it looked liked representations I've seen in science books of the universe. Of course that got me thinking about the Creator, and I felt like all of the sudden He was listening very closely to me, as if He knew this was a moment where I really needed Him." Moon, wet like a dog who'd gone for a swim in the river, asked Zuke, "Do you know what I asked Him?" Zuke raised his eyebrows. It always gave him the creeps when Moon talked like this. "I asked Him for a sign of what was to come in my future. I asked God if I was meant to live alone."

"Any word back?"

"Edie Greathouse came to sit with me."

"Edie Greathouse?" Zuke asked in disbelief. Was there some supernatural dating power that had determined the Brothers' time had come, that they would be delivered to the Romantic Promise Land? Edie was president of the freshman class, tall, thin, and blonde, and The Dini had already determined her to be the most talented member of their traveling singing group. She swam in the thick of every spiritual event on campus and in a paraphrase of a line from *Say Anything,* Zuke had once remarked that she was a missionary trapped in the body of a supermodel, just the sort of woman Zuke would have thought his friend to have idealized as a future wife instead of Wendy.

Moon looked down at the ledge that circled the Tree of Knowledge and put his foot on the knee-high brick wall. "She TWIRPed me," he said. "That beautiful creature with such a tender smile TWIRPed me. 'Let's go for a walk tonight,' she said, right away, without even saying hi. I figured she just felt sorry for me, that maybe someone had dared her to ask me out."

"Edie doesn't seem like the sort of person," Zuke began.

"No she doesn't," Moon finished. "She said she had some work to do, but that she'd meet me in the lobby of Chapman at nine, and we'd take a nice long walk out by the track and have a good chat."

"Chat about what?" Zuke asked, rummaging his thoughts for what it would be that would make Edie want to take a walk with Moon. Not that there was anything wrong with Moon, but Edie Greathouse? It didn't make any more sense than Bird or Magic did.

"I think she saw the thing the other night," Moon said, "but we didn't get to talk about it. Wait till you hear this." Moon lowered his head—almost shamefully. "I was just so excited," Moon continued, "glad for the time with her—just to walk with such a woman, to see what she was like, to enjoy thirty or so minutes that I might remember forever."

The words and tone Moon used sounded ridiculous to Zuke, but it was Moon's way, to try and live his life up in the King's English, in the lines used in the Biblical story of the Song of Solomon: "Thy lips, O my spouse, drop as the honeycomb: honey and milk are under thy tongue; and the smell of thy garments is like the smell of Lebanon." Moon loved the book and often cited it as an example of what sex was supposed to be, the gift the Lord had bestowed on married couples. Zuke listened and at the same time began to theorize about what would make a girl like Edie Greathouse TWIRP Moon.

"I came down at nine, and there was Edie waiting for me. She wore two pink barrettes to keep her hair out of her eyes and the cutest fluffy white earmuffs. She looked like a little bunny, and I couldn't believe she'd actually changed clothes for me."

"That's what you wore?" Zuke asked, almost as a challenge to Moon's good sense, his tone flat as he took another look at Moon: his Laker jacket, too-tight soaked jeans, and red sock hat. If he'd been going for Chevy Chase in *Fletch;* well, maybe he'd pulled that off. Zuke wondered if the boldness of what Moon had done the night before had impressed Edie. Without question, Moon had at least thrown a Hail Mary in the direction of greatness. Maybe his wild pass had just been caught by an unintended receiver, sort of like the Pittsburgh Steeler's Immaculate Reception but this one snagged on the field of romance.

"It was starting to rain," Moon continued, "and I told her possibly we shouldn't go. I wanted to let her off the hook in case she'd changed her mind, but she said it would be fun. So we went out to the track—not the track track, but the gravel walking one. I was nervous, you know; it's not safe to be out in freezing rain."

"And you were nervous," Zuke said, smiling, "getting TWIRPed by a girl who made our superficiality list of top five good looking girls at Pison."

"The rain got worse," Moon said. "It was really coming down, and I thought if the hail got larger that we could actually be hurt."

Zuke remembered the sparks they'd all seen from in front of Lane's Roller Rink, thought to interrupt Moon and ask him if he'd seen them, and then also remembered that he wanted to tell Moon about their running into Cheese and Abby. "Remind me," Zuke began, but Moon stopped him.

"Please friend," he said, "just let me get this last part out. We were walking, and I felt the hair on my arms, my back, my chest and neck—all of it prickled, stood right up on its end. I've always heard that's what happens right before you get hit by lightning. But it's December, and so I was confused but also frightened and trying to figure out what was going on. There was a loud pop; I swear it could have been a gunshot or maybe even a cannon. It scared me to death and without thinking, I just hit the deck, dove to the cinder track surface and covered my head." Moon sighed as if he pushed out the last bit of air in his lungs. "I showed absolutely no regard for Edie. What I did was indefensible." He looked into Zuke's eyes and then stared at the icy ground.

"It's not the best thing in the world to have happened," Zuke said, "but I wouldn't call it indefensible. It's not like you're used to having someone around you're supposed to look out for."

"That's not even the worst of it. While I was down there hiding on the ground like a big weenie, the transformer blew. It was just like the final scene in *The Natural*." Moon laughed with disgust at himself. "When those sparks began to rain down all around us, I looked up at Edie and took off on a sprint. I'd like to convince myself I told her to 'come on,' but I know I didn't say anything. I just ran. At first I ran because I was scared, then I ran because I didn't know what else to do. I knew I couldn't go back and have any explanation for what I'd done."

The way Moon looked reminded Zuke of the time he'd slipped on the riverbank of the Tippecanoe and slid down through the ice into water that, lucky-for-him was just several feet deep. Zuke's ears, nose, and cheeks were freezing; Moon must have been borderline hypothermic.

"I can't explain it," Moon said. "What must she think of me? What am I to think of myself?" The only sound in the quadrangle was of giant raindrops landing on ice; it was almost the sound of a crackling fire. Moon continued to shiver, and Zuke could see his lips were turning blue. A single bell tolled from College Church that marked 11:30.

"You think she's okay?" Zuke asked, a rush of panic filling him as he realized Edie Greathouse might be lying hurt or worse on the track.

"I heard sirens," Moon said. "The police. The sparks were done before I even got a hundred yards. I'm sure she just walked back to the dorm. I'm such an idiot."

"No matter what," Zuke said, "you should call her. As soon as we get up to the room. It doesn't matter if it's too late. You should just tell her you're sorry, even if she doesn't want to see you again." Moon took a deep breath, held it for a few seconds, and then exhaled.

"You're right."

The exposed hand on Zuke's good arm was numb, but underneath his jacket, he could feel sweat trickle inside his cast and a powerful itch start to develop. He tried to convince himself the sensation had been created by his mind. He'd forgotten how his senior year he'd taken to inching knives down his cast for a scratch. "At least you know you can predict electrical accidents," Zuke offered, trying to lighten the mood. As long as Edie was okay, then this would all pass; big deal, Moon had been surprised by a loud noise and not responded so well in crisis. "What I don't understand," Zuke said, "is how you run toward a balcony collapse and away from a blown transformer."

Moon shook his head. "It's so humiliating. No, it's cowardly. How can a coward be a preacher?" Moon kicked the pavement with the ball of his foot.

"You don't have to be that guy," Zuke said. "Not the guy you were tonight. That was one decision in what will be a thousand. Someday you'll be thirty years worth of decisions. This could end up the one time you did the wrong thing. Tonight can be the exception to the person you will become."

Moon nodded his head. "Let's go." As they started to walk

toward Chapman Hall, he took his sock hat, removed it, and wrung it out like a dish towel. "What a crappy weekend."

Zuke shrugged his shoulders. His hadn't been so crappy. There was a broken wrist and the tension he felt about Abby and Marie, but there was so much more happening than usual. Sometimes life felt empty of energy, as if he was stuck in the same routine of study, wish for Abby, and the dull beatings he received from Cheese on a daily basis at practice. "At least you know a girl like Edie could be interested in you." Zuke gave Moon a little push as they walked up the incline to their dorm. "That is until you took cover like a little girl." Moon and Zuke walked into the darkness that separated the Tree of Knowledge from the security lights of their residence hall.

"I thought Edie was the answer to my prayer," Moon said. "I just don't get how God works. Not one bit."

CHAPTER TWELVE

Moon arrived to Zuke's room having changed into a dry T-shirt and Houston Oiler baggy-blue leopard-print muscle pants. He came bearing the news of a brief conversation with Edie Greathouse's roommate, who relayed that Edie was fine but didn't feel like talking at the moment. Then Moon plopped down into Pee Wee's desk chair and patiently listened to Zuke's account of the TWIRP date, including how they'd all run into Abby and Cheese. "So what do you want to happen?" Moon asked, after Zuke had especially highlighted the attraction he felt for Abby in relation to the new spark fired by his first date with Marie.

"I think I need to decide," Zuke said. He was lying flat on his bed, the bottom bunk, with his fingers intertwined in the springs of the underside of Pee Wee's mattress. His wrist felt better elevated. "There was this guy I knew in high school, Derrick Kruzick. He tried to date two girls at once, and he ended up losing them both." Zuke stared at the mattress overhead, old and a faded brown. He wondered how many Pison men had slept on it, wondered how many nights those who'd come before him had lain there thinking about the same sort of problem.

"I hate it when you do that," Moon said.

"What?"

"Bring something up and then just let it go. You wait until someone asks you for more, or you don't say anything. It's totally annoying."

"I wasn't waiting; I was thinking."

"Derrick Kruzick?"

"My freshman year there was this Halloween Party. Not a beer party, but a watch-scary-movies-and-eat-cookies party. Derrick's mom picked us up. I was staying the night at his house, and there were some girls in the car too. Derrick's mom gave them a ride

home. There were four of us in the backseat: me by the window,
the girl Colleen I was in love with sitting next to me, Derrick next to
her, and then this other girl named Laura. Plus there was one more
girl in the front seat who doesn't figure into the story.

"Now, this guy Derrick knew you liked Colleen?"

"Maybe. Not really. At least not how much I liked her. Everyone
kind of liked her; I mean if she was interested in you and you were
single, then you would like her back."

"Colleen knew you loved her?"

"No, I don't think she thought of me, and back then I was afraid
to talk to girls."

"Back then," Moon said. "Thank goodness those days are behind
us."

"From my seat, I could see that Derrick and Colleen were holding
hands. Of course it crushed me. There I was, thinking that I was
seeing one of my friends end up with the girl I liked."

"Yeah," Moon said sarcastically, "that would be terrible."

"But when we finally got to Derrick's house, he tells me that he
had been holding Colleen and Laura's hands."

"He said that in front of his mom?"

"No, not in front of his mom. Why are you messing with me?"

"Seriously. From the way you said it, I thought he told you right
in front of his mom."

"Who would say that in front of their mom?"

"I would," Moon said. "Maybe. Why not?"

"So that whole night we went over all the pros and cons of who
he should go out with. Of course, I wanted him to date Laura,
but I couldn't say that. The bastard—sorry—would have probably
picked her for just that reason. But he couldn't make up his mind,
so get this: he decides to date them both. He talks to Colleen before
school, and Laura after third period. He calls one and then he calls
the other. He took Colleen to the movies on Friday night and went
to the fair the next day with Laura."

"He sounds like an idiot."

"He definitely wasn't the kind of guy who could get away with
something like that."

"Who can?"

"I don't know. Magic Johnson. The star of the football team. Someone who doesn't go to school with both girls every day of the week; someone who lives in a town big enough that not everyone at the grocery store knows who you are."

"Are you telling me that Glory and Magic both want to date *you*? Is that the point of this story?" When Moon put it that way, the proposition did seem unlikely.

"I don't know. What the heck is Abby going to do? She had Cheese's dag gum jersey on at the game." Zuke could not logically imagine the following string of events for Abby: wear Cheese's jersey, go bowling, attend church with him in the morning, and then when their families got together in the afternoon, break up and return to campus to begin dating someone new. "She laughed at something he said. Who would go bowling with someone, laugh at a joke, and then break up with them the next day?"

"People have definitely gone bowling and broken up. What's so special about bowling? It's not like she planned a romantic dinner at the top of the Sears Tower."

"And I can't be sure about Marie. She just met me. I'm no treasure."

"You're the apple of God's eye," Moon said. When Zuke laughed, Moon added, "Seriously, you are."

"I've written Abby three hundred notes, met her in the library four days a week for over a year. You have to understand, I've invested a lot of time to get to the point where there is even a possibility for us to be together."

The phone on Pee Wee's desk rang, and Moon picked it up. "Pee Wee and Zuke's love shack." Moon prided himself on witty little phone greetings. "Moon speaking." There was a woman's voice, but Zuke couldn't hear who it was. "He's right here." Moon scooched his chair over to the side of Zuke's bed. As he handed the phone over, he covered the receiver. "Her ears must have been burning," he whispered. "It's Glory." Zuke took the phone and Moon leaned down so his ear was close to the receiver. He still had cereal breath. Zuke shook his head *no* and motioned for him to move away. "C'mon," Moon whispered. "I ran from my date."

"Just a minute," Zuke said into the phone. "Out," he said to Moon, who made a clucking noise with his tongue, put Pee Wee's chair back, and clutched his heart as if he'd been shot. On his way out the door, Moon announced in his best Arnold Schwarzenegger voice, "I'll be back."

"Hey," Zuke said, talking softly into the phone. It was a rare treat for him, lying in bed, almost time to go to sleep, to get to talk to Abby. Zuke remembered Billy Crystal's speech to Meg Ryan in *When Harry Met Sally*, when at the end of the flick he tells her that part of the reason he loves her is that she is the last person he wants to talk to at the end of a day. Zuke always imagined that would be how he would feel toward anyone he loved. The pendulum in Zuke's rib cage had swung as far as it would go toward Marie; now it began to come back the other way.

"I learned something tonight," Abby said.

"What's that?"

"What it feels like to be you. All this time I've been thinking about me, I've never thought about what it feels like to be you, seeing me with Brett. Marie—she's beautiful. I've always thought she seemed so smart and nice. Everyone thinks she's great. I think she's great, and I feel terrible, as if I've lost you."

Zuke thought he must have been crazy to think of transferring. He'd had a great date with Marie and now here was Abby, seemingly completely transformed and worried about losing him. Was getting people to like you as simple as supply and demand economics?

"Have I lost you?" Abby asked. She was used to Zuke speaking up against such speculation on her part.

Zuke looked over to the wall above his desk where his *Say Anything* poster hung, Cusack's character holding the boom box over his head. That's right where Zuke was, in the very spot Dobler was in the photograph: on the edge of love, ready to topple forward into it with Abby or Marie, or else backwards, down into a dark pit of loneliness. Unlike Dobler, Zuke didn't know which direction led to what. Which of the girls was most likely to stay with him? Wouldn't he be thrilled with either one of them? Zuke asked Abby,

"You still think you're going to break up with Cheese?" Abby didn't answer right away. It seemed like given what she'd just asked then she'd be sure she wanted to break up with Cheese, right?

"Yes," Abby eventually said, her voice going up almost as if she was asking a question. It wasn't an answer that gave Zuke confidence that she would actually do it. "It's just so much to deal with," Abby added. "I feel like a lame-duck girlfriend. How should I act around him? And then today, you know, with all that happened, he seemed pretty decent. He always acts like he doesn't care, but he cared today, when I was in danger, when I almost got hurt. What I need to know is if you're sure you want me to go through with it."

Zuke couldn't imagine telling Abby he wasn't sure, not after the past year, but he also couldn't imagine facing Marie and telling her that he wanted anything besides another date.

"Zuke?"

He had to give an answer and so he gave one that would protect his interests: "Yes, I want you to go through with it." Zuke noticed he felt a little more sure of himself saying it out loud. Maybe in relationships what a person has to do is to make a decision and bulldoze everything else out of the way. "If you break up with Cheese tomorrow," Zuke proclaimed, "I want to see if we can make it as a couple."

"All right," Abby said, "You had me worried. I just wanted to check. It was hard seeing you out with her. I'm exhausted. I think I can finally go to sleep. I'll call you tomorrow."

"Between seven and nine," Zuke said.

"Yes." The two said good night and Zuke hung up the phone. He felt as if his life was in total limbo, but he would have his answer in less than twenty-four hours. There was a way, Zuke thought, that he wouldn't have to decide anything. If Abby broke up with Cheese then he would be with her and he would just have to explain to Marie about the history of his last year. If, however, Abby wasn't able to follow through on her breakup plans, then Zuke wouldn't have anything to explain to Marie. He would just have to ask her out for a second date.

Zuke went over and sat at his desk. He was very not sleepy. All he had to do now was let go of the rudder of his romantic life and see where the current of the next twenty-four hours took him. He knew he was in danger of going a little crazy over thinking all that could happen. Sometimes his craziness, especially late at night, caused him to entertain notions that could muck everything up. He was prone to writing a dumb letter that he wasn't smart enough NOT to mail in the morning or even call Abby back up with some random question that would throw everything out of whack when it looked like things would go fine.

Back in high school, Zuke's way of dealing with such a circumstance—the circumstance of an impatient mind about to drive him crazy—was that he'd go down to the town park, often late at night, and shoot free throws. At first, he wouldn't be able to concentrate, but eventually he was always able to lose himself in the craft of what it was to shoot a basketball: the rhythmic repeated bounces, the placement of the ball into his shooting pocket, the feel of his fingertips over the grooves, the concentration needed to pick out the paint chip on the front of the orange rim, and then the soothing swish of the net as ten in a row led to twenty, which on some nights led to ninety-three out of one hundred.

The craft of an action could form a bridge over a cliff of edgy insanity, but free throws weren't an option tonight. It was winter, Zuke had no keys to the gym, and his shooting-hand wrist was broken. Zuke thought of the assignment he had due the following Tuesday in Professor Moore's expository writing class. It would make perfect sense to try and get some work done on that. By Monday, there was the possibility that he'd be in his first day as Abby's boyfriend or else asking Marie out for their second date. Zuke didn't want to be stuck in the library writing when he could be out with one of those young ladies. If on Monday Zuke was suddenly faced with no romantic options, then he would be pretty depressed and not feeling like working on the assignment. The thing to do—the craft that could also save him—was to fall down into the work of completing his assignment.

Although Professor Moore had given her students complete freedom to write about whatever they wanted, Zuke felt dread for his "A Chip Off the Bloc" political essay. Rather than choose his own subjects, Zuke went to his dad for help, who always steered his son toward politically themed current event topics. It wasn't Zuke's dad's fault that he did this. He was only obliging his son's request for help. That Zuke was bored with his own work was his own fault.

Professor Moore was always telling her students to write about something they were interested in. What was Zuke interested in? Well, there was basketball, a topic Zuke had long grown sick of. What was on his mind, of course, was whether or not Abby was actually going to break up with Cheese, and he was also curious about Marie, if she would be interested in him as she started to think back on the night. These were not, Zuke thought, topics that would work.

Abby was in Zuke's expository writing class. He couldn't very well sit there and read a paper containing Abby right there in front of her. Zuke would be embarrassed and besides, it would be totally unfair to Abby to expose her private life to their classmates. Zuke remembered how for one little instant on the TWIRP date, he'd had the thought to write something that might interest a classmate, particularly interest people such as Abby or Marie. Then Zuke thought of how Abby had seemed maybe a little (or a lot) jealous of Marie. The emotion was something Zuke thought might have surfaced the year before when he had kind of randomly ended up having a couple other "dates." Upon learning of this, Abby hadn't even shown the slightest sign of envy, and had in fact prompted Zuke to tell the story of one particular night to her friends.

Professor Moore had instructed her students to write something with some sort of publication in mind. For his "Chip off the Bloc" essay, Zuke had been imagining a publication such as *Time* or *Newsweek*, but now, with this "bad date" story, he was thinking of something along the lines of *Reader's Digest*. There was something new about this assignment, Zuke realized. Previously, he'd always written for his teacher. This meant he was writing for a person who'd given the assignment, a person who already knew him, and had something in particular they were looking for. But now, imagining all the people who might flip through a magazine and see what was there that was interesting, Zuke could see that to tell the story of his date he would have to explain who he was, who he went out with, and the context of the date within the community of Pison College. Zuke, for once, did not feel bored. He felt excited to put down into words the story he'd already told quite a few times. With many instances of going back, starting over, and changing words, this is what Zuke finally wrote:

The Royal Castle

On a dare from my friend Cowboy, I crossed over from the geeky side of the cafeteria and asked out this girl me and my college buddies call Ratio. We have this elaborate rating system for the women on campus—it takes in a lot more qualities than just looks—and Ratio makes everyone's top five. I think it's easier to ask someone out I don't see in the normal course of my day—say in Biology lab—because someone like that would just remind me with her presence that she once told me no.

When I crossed the cafeteria to ask this girl "Ratio" out, it was early in the fall semester and occasionally still very hot outside. She wore a bright yellow dress—I think it was linen with frilly white trim—and she was very tan. As it turned out, she's from West Palm Beach, a bit of information I didn't know yet. Her hemline really pushed school guidelines, which state that any skirt or dress (shorts are prohibited) must reach the top of the knee, something my buddies and I had already discussed regarding Ratio's attire. At our school, the serving line squares around the seating area so it's almost like one has to walk the runway of a fashion show to obtain a meal. Or you could think

about it like a line outside a popular club
where people are going to be let in or kept
out based on the way they look. One of my
friends is a resident assistant, and he's
actually asked girls to go back to their rooms
and change into more conservative clothes.
It's embarrassing when he does that, and I'm
trying to get him to stop.

Ratio has frizzy, but a nice kind
of frizzy, blond hair, carefully plucked
eyebrows, bright white straight teeth, and
it seems like her lips are always shiny with
gloss. She's a smaller girl, sort of like a
gymnast, but I imagine too curvy to be much
good on the uneven parallel bars. Ratio is
a cute rather than beautiful girl, more say
in the spirit of Elizabeth Shue in *The Karate
Kid* than Robin Wright in *The Princess Bride*.
Both, supremely desirable but in different
ways, right?

Once, when Ratio went walking by, I
heard this administrator who is always leading
chapel say something about the beauty of God's
creation. He's a regular up at the pulpit for
chapel and always saying that some women can't
hide the body God gave them, even if they were
to dress in a burlap sack. I guess this is
true, but if you ask me, it's kind of creepy
to know an old church guy like that is even
mentally in touch with the female students'
bodies.

When I got to the table where the
girls were, there was this really great and
terrifying instant that they all stopped
talking and looked at me. For some reason,
right then, I noticed Ratio had on gold-
hoop earrings, each with a heart dangling,
twinkling once in awhile under the cafeteria
lights like a tiny star. Those hearts gave
me hope, as if a girl who wore something like

that on her ears must surely be open to the
idea that love can strike as swiftly as a bolt
of lightning in a sudden storm or from a boy
taking a chance by walking across the floor
of a cafeteria. It sounds like I'm arguing
for some sort of love storm; maybe I am, but
what's my supporting evidence?

Thankfully, before I said anything, I
reminded myself not to use the nickname Ratio.
"Hi, I'm Eric. Would you like to go out with
me next weekend?" That was all I said, and
it wasn't nearly as difficult to get that out
as I'd imagined it would be. To everyone's
surprise—her friends at the table, me, and
maybe even her—she said yes; real easy like.
Just a smile and a yes, and she told me her
number was in the campus directory. Was mine
in there? It wasn't, so she said the burden
was on me to call her. That was a funny word
choice—burden—and her friends all smiled like
I was some kind of romantic figure, which is
just what I wanted to be. The world never
seemed so good as when I walked back over to
our table where Cowboy had sat looking forward
to me making an idiot of myself.

Ratio and I "went out" several times, if
you'd even call it going out. Mostly, she'd
randomly call me and ask me what I was doing
or else I'd be coming out of the library at
closing time and there she'd be hanging out in
the quad with a bunch of guys. It was all an
experience unlike any I've had before, mostly
because she talked constantly of men that
were interested in her and whether or not she
should go out with them. This I didn't know
what to do with. Should I seem offended so
that she would know I was interested, or would
it be better to pretend I didn't care so that
I might draw her in with a strategy founded
upon aloofness? On one of these random nights

she called me, we ended up driving all the way
to Chicago, where we got on Lakeshore Drive,
turned around at Lincoln Park, and then came
all the way home. For the whole trip, she
never stopped telling me about this boy Tommy
Keller who she used to date but was now in the
Army. Ratio often made me feel as if I were
her gay friend.

I asked Ratio to go to the Christmas
Banquet with me—this was the year they had it
in the Sears Tower—and when she agreed to go,
I got tickets to see *Les Miserables* at the
Roosevelt Auditorium at a cost quite beyond
what I could afford. As they say, I slapped
the tickets on the credit card, no price too
great for love. A week before the banquet,
the basketball team added a junior varsity
game to the schedule for the same night as my
date with Ratio. If you're like I was before
I started sitting at the end of a small-
college basketball team's bench, you didn't
even know there was such a thing as a jayvee
team. But schools have them, practically
no one comes to the games, usually not even
parents, except for mine who come to just
about all of them.

I told Ratio I was very sorry about the
new game, that I couldn't attend the banquet,
and that she ought to try to find another date.
However, she insisted that we do something
else when I got back from the game, which was
over at St. Joseph's College, just across the
state line into Indiana. This was a mystery
to me, that we kept getting together. We
never seemed to have much fun, she constantly
talked about other guys, but I thought it was
really decent of her to stick with me for the
night of the Christmas Banquet. But still,
I was in sort of a bind: last second, I had
to find something for Ratio and me to do that

would start around nine o'clock. In one of
those newspapers that have all the 900 numbers
in the back, I found this place called the
Royal Castle, which advertised a ten course
meal with skit comedy. This I imagined would
be like going to *Saturday Night Live*, but with
food. The tickets were expensive, which I
thought served as a sort of guarantee that the
night would be grand.

The Monday before the Saturday of the
date, I developed a small pimple on the side
of my face. With the nail of each of my
thumbs, I tried to pop my pimple, but it was
one of those failed attempts where nothing
comes out and you're left with a larger,
redder, and more painful blemish. The next
day it was infected and by Friday in such
bad shape that I went to the doctor. If
that sounds peculiar to you—someone going
to the doctor for a pimple—don't worry that
you're hearing the story of a freak; it was
peculiar for me too; my first time doing such
a thing. The doctor diagnosed my face as
having a carbuncle, something I'd describe as
a medieval infection, at least one big step up
from a boil. The diagnosis sounded to me like
the side of my face was a ship's hull, but the
word had been carbuncle and not barnacle as my
mind had first perceived it. Whatever I was
supposed to call it, the thing was so tender
in the days that preceded the banquet, that I
was unable to shave. Stubbly hairs poked from
within and around the quarter-size plateau on
the right side of my face, just up from the
line of my jaw.

Everything about the way Ratio
approached the night was as if she were still
going to *Les Mis* and the Christmas banquet
rather than the last-second substitute I had
arranged. This meant that she had mentally

and physically prepared for an elegant
evening: one which might feature candlelight,
classical music, a limousine, gloved hands at
the theater, and possibly a carriage ride.
She'd told me she was going out shopping the
afternoon of my away game, and when she came
out into the lobby of the residence hall, she
was wearing a black jacket with white trim
that had loose-fitting sleeves. It seemed
like something Prince or one of his backup
singers would wear. She wore the coat over
a strapless black dress that fit her as tight
as a stocking. Ratio looked great, so great
that my hands shook on the steering wheel all
the way up to Chicago. I wore the only suit
I had, which was a navy blue one with light
pinstripes and a bright green tie meant to
match my eyes. Ratio looked like a rock star,
and I looked like I was on my way to my first
middle school dance.

The address of the castle was Homewood,
a suburb of Chicago I didn't know anything
about. When we arrived, I felt afraid to get
out of the car. After a twenty-five dollar
parking fee that felt more like protection
money, we rolled up into the Royal Castle
lot, which was surrounded by a fifteen foot
high fence with barbed-wire twisting over the
top as if we'd arrived at Guantanamo Bay—not
that I've ever been there. Two intimidating
looking men—mostly for their leather,
piercings, and tattoos—guided us through the
maze of the nearly full parking lot. Ratio
told me the place didn't pass the car test, a
method she has for gauging the quality of a
neighborhood: BMWs and the like rated high
optimism, Accords meant the area was fine, and
run down Lincolns or Chevys signaled trouble.
Perhaps Ratio should have applied the car test
to me before she agreed to our date. I parked

my grandma's hand-me-down red Chevette next
to a Caprice that had orangish flames fanning
out on its side and a giant piece of cardboard
duct-taped into one of the rear windows.

The city block was made up of three-
story brick buildings side-to-side, the ground
floors rented out for shops, and the upper
ones as apartments. Somehow, maybe it was a
wooden façade, the building was lined with
parapets, all of which had flags flying. As we
entered through the large wooden doors meant
to look like the entrance to a castle, I was
immediately able to see why the tickets had
cost over fifty bucks each: it was all you
could drink, something that didn't sit well
with Ratio, whose parents didn't drink, and
who had herself never drunk a drop of alcohol.
I don't drink either, but not for religious
reasons; it's just that if I got caught I'd
lose my basketball scholarship. Ratio didn't
approve of those who consumed alcohol, an
aspect of her belief system that meant she
didn't approve of anyone in the Royal Castle.
This, I was gathering, was not so easy to hide
from our fellow restaurant patrons.

The place was packed and set up in a
way that for me invoked Hrothgar and his mead
hall, featuring long family-style tables with
benches to match. We were in the middle of
what seemed like a Viking party when Ratio
had imagined softly lit nooks in a stylish
restaurant. Nearly everyone had come dressed
as if for a night at the bowling alley, a
characteristic of the crowd that caused many
of the patrons to stare at us and wonder just
who we thought we were. Although I attempted
to steer her otherwise, Ratio chose to sit on
the carbuncle side of my face.

Much of what happened the night I
visited the Royal Castle I've been able to

block out as some sort of psychological self
defense strategy, but I do remember what our
waitress said when she first approached our
table dressed as if she might work a second
job as a dominatrix in a dungeon club: "Hello
you two. I'll be your wench for the evening.
Would you like for your first pitcher to be
Miller or Bud?" Skit comedy was already
underway, a tasteless rendition of a Mexican
Christmas. Hubcaps hung on the tree.

The first course of the meal was soup,
an entrée we were expected to consume sans
silverware. On Ratio's first attempt with the
bread—you should have seen her face ripping
off a chunk—one of her fancy black cuffs
drooped into the soup then dripped down the
front of her chest. When I tried to wipe it
off, she thought I was taking a cheap shot at
her breasts. As it turned out, Ratio wasn't
the sort of girl to try and make the best of
a bad situation—there was no buck up little
camper in her spirit—but on the night of the
Royal Castle, I could've been with Happy the
dwarf's twin sister, and it wouldn't have made
any difference.

On the way home, I didn't really try
and defend my choice; the evening had gone
poorly enough that I just wanted to get back
to campus, let Ratio out of the car, and try
to forget about it all. She had been a big
opportunity for me, probably the only time in
my life I'd get to go out with such a girl,
and I had blown it. When I stopped my car in
front of her residence hall, I told her I was
sorry for how the night went. She lowered her
head and placed her thumb and forefinger on the
bridge of her nose as if she had a terrific
migraine. Without expectation, and without
a thought of asking her if I would ever see
her again, I watched her struggle to get the

passenger door open. It was rusty or else something else was wrong with it and it took quite a bit of force to get it open or shut. After what had happened with the soup on her chest, I was too afraid to reach over and try to help. When she got out of the car, Ratio leaned down but didn't look to where I was.

"It's not your fault," she said, more to the roof than to me, and then she stepped back and slammed the door with explosive energy. I'm not ready to certify that this was in anger. As I said, the door was stiff, and she'd been in the car enough to know that it took all she had to get it shut.

I watched Ratio go, wrapped as neatly as a new dress shirt in her tight black dress, and she tugged her jacket a little tighter as she walked away from me. Watching the glass doors of the residence hall close behind her, my gut felt the hollowness of solitude.

The following Monday, I went back to the doctor. He lanced my carbuncle, which gave birth to a dull white pearl he teased out, mucus and all, with his latex-gloved fingers. Later, I heard Ratio transferred to Wheaton College—that's where Billy Graham went—and I can't help feeling our night together, her final Christmas Banquet experience, might have been one of the reasons why. When I remember our date, I wonder if I'm bound to repeat this cycle again and again. I think it's got something to do with me needing to ask out girls I know. I've got to stop putting so much hope into visions of golden hearts hanging from the earlobes of pretty girls.

With the completion of the last sentence, Zuke pushed himself away from his desk, his right wrist sore from the position required to accommodate the cast. He stared at the gray keyboard of the word processor as if it were one of those pianos made to play itself, and he'd just discovered how it worked. Usually when he wrote, the words came slowly: three sentences, read what he'd just written, squeeze one more thought out of his brain, check notes, sit and stare, and then repeat an idea he'd already stated but in different words. Once when Zuke was in high school, a preacher from the local Methodist church had been a substitute teacher and given him the only piece of writing instruction he ever could remember receiving: say what you're going to say, say it, and then say it again. It was communicative advice Zuke followed religiously up until this "Royal Castle" paper. Already on the fourth page, for the first time, Zuke had exceeded Moore's minimum page requirement. What he'd just written didn't have anything in common with the five paragraph essays some of his professors encouraged.

From down the hall, there was laughter and the slam of a door. Zuke looked at the red numbers of his digital clock; it was 12:30 a.m. He'd written an hour and barely noticed. Suddenly he felt tired but relaxed. Zuke took his contacts out and plunked them into his case. Still dressed in his clothes from his date with Marie, Zuke turned off the light on his desk, rose from his seat, eased into the bottom bunk, and laid his broken wrist across his chest. Zuke thought briefly about Marie and Abby but his mind had been emptied, as if it had completed a long run and was now too tired to think another step. Zuke went right to sleep.

Sometime in the night, Zuke heard Pee Wee come into the room, and with a little cough, not saying anything, he gingerly slipped up on the end of the bunk bed and lay down with such defeat that Zuke thought of Mulligan, thought maybe Pee Wee had gotten into it with Mulligan again and been beaten up. Overhead, Pee Wee coughed as if he might be gagging on something. Zuke, who was practically blind without his contacts in, reached for his glasses so he could see the clock on his desk; it was 2:37 a.m. "Are you okay?" he asked, and leaned out from the side of bed to look up to the top bunk, where Pee Wee had just leaned over to vomit. A splash of it hit Zuke in the face and ran across his cheekbones and onto his neck as if he'd been hit with a runny cream pie. From the sound Pee Wee made and the smell of alcohol that filled Zuke's nose, he knew right away what had happened. Zuke didn't feel sick himself, just disgusted at first, and then worried for his own health. At Pison, the acronym AIDS was thrown like a dart by some at the college as a consequence for sexual activity. Even before coming to college, Zuke had conducted his own nervous study of the disease with fear fueled by his own sexual history. He wasn't exactly sure which acts might transmit what, but before Zuke had dated Colleen, her boyfriends had always been older, young men who were known for porking a lot of girls. Pee Wee had likely been sexually active and surely vomit was a means of transmission for the disease. There was a knock at the door.

Zuke got out of bed and grabbed a towel from a hook on his wardrobe, and as he wiped his face and opened the door, he found his R.A. standing there, a guy named Warren who thought he looked like Tom Cruise and was often wearing Ray Bans to enhance this feature of his appearance. Warren—sans sunglasses—looked suspicious and angry at first, but then a look of puzzlement swept over his face when he noticed the fresh cast on Zuke's arm and the brown and clumpy liquid that still covered much of his face, neck, and shirt. "What's happened?" Warren asked, leaning forward and sniffing like a bloodhound for alcohol. Along with women, booze was what the R.A.'s were most ready to prosecute.

"Pee Wee's sick," Zuke said, using the nickname everyone used for his roommate. "He just threw up on me. I think he's got the flu." Zuke swallowed hard and wiped some vomit from his neck. "I suppose now I'm going to have the flu." Warren jumped from Zuke back into the brightly lit hall.

"Oh," he said. "Sorry to hear that." Warren was already returning to his room, and his voice switched from one of a concerned big brother to a big brother who didn't want to do anything other than go back to his room and go to sleep. "Anything I can do?" Zuke knew his answer was supposed to be no.

"I don't think so," Zuke said. "Thanks for checking on us." Zuke retreated into his room and closed the door. Next, he reached over and flipped the switch for the room lights.

"Not the inferno," Pee Wee said. His voice was a whisper, but a smile spread onto his face. The inferno was what they called the overhead light because it was so bright. "I'm drunk, Roomie," Pee Wee said cheerfully.

"This is without a doubt, the most disgusting thing that has ever happened to me." Zuke took off his t-shirt, dropped it into one of the little plastic bags he saved from Walgreens, and deposited it into the garbage. "You better not have just given me some stupid disease."

"Disease? What are you talking about?"

"I don't know; how about AIDS?"

"Blood and sexual intercourse."

"What?" asked Zuke.

"Just learned it in science class," Pee Wee said. "The only ways AIDS is transmitted: blood and sexual intercourse."

"Well then you owe me a new t-shirt," Zuke said as he used the towel that he'd already dirtied to wipe off the hardwood floor next to his bed.

"I'll get you a whole package of shirts," Pee Wee said. "Fruit of the Loom, anything you want." Pee Wee placed one of his pillows over his face to shield it from the light. "Let's just not talk about it right now. I'm not feeling so hot." Zuke finished with the floor, grabbed the soiled towel and a clean one, and went down the hall where he put the plastic bag with the dirty shirt into the garbage chute. Once in the restroom, he rinsed out his vomitous towel, and then took a shower. It was nearly four o'clock when Zuke got back to the room.

"Roomie?" Pee Wee asked. Zuke had felt sure that Pee Wee would have already been asleep.

"Yeah?"

"That was really decent of you tonight—I mean with what you said to Warren." A month before, Zuke would have certainly told Warren exactly what was the matter with his roommate. What in the name of Lloyd Dobler's boom box was going on?

CHAPTER THIRTEEN

Every Sunday morning that Zuke was on campus, he went to Crowe's Café where he bought the *Chicago Tribune* and ate breakfast by himself. It was his favorite activity of the week. The rest of the Fab, along with most of the students at Pison, went to church, something Zuke felt he got enough of during the mandatory chapel services. Zuke sat down in his customary last seat at the counter trying to not think about Abby and Marie. Despite the interruption in his sleep the Pee Wee vomiting incident had imposed, Zuke woke earlier than usual and hadn't been able to go back to sleep. He'd woke thinking especially about Marie. It was complete proof to Zuke that the mind got plenty done when a person slept. It was as if he had another self, a self that had sorted out something Zuke had missed, and that self rapped him on the shoulder and asked, "What about Marie?" Zuke's plan for just riding the current of his life for one day didn't include the possibility that Abby would break up with Cheese and Zuke would feel that Marie was the person he ought to try and date.

The man working the counter came over to Zuke. His name was Dennis, and he had a full head of gray hair, was at least sixty years old, always businesslike, and the only Asian off the campus of the college that Zuke had ever seen in Beau Fleuve. Dennis glanced at Zuke's cast but didn't say anything about it. Instead, he greeted Zuke good morning and asked him if he wanted the usual, which meant a pecan waffle, two fried eggs, and bacon.

"Yes, sir," Zuke said. Dennis set a cup of coffee down and went to turn in the order. It was nine o'clock, no one else was at the counter, there were only a couple of booths with solitary diners, and one group of thirtysomethings still dressed for the bars and capping off a night of drinking with breakfast.

"So when I finally find him," said a woman wearing a *Frankie Say* t-shirt, "he's sitting on the sidewalk with a homeless guy, playing his guitar, and passing back and forth a two-liter bottle of Orange Crush. God knows what it was mixed with."

To the sound of the group's too-loud laughter, Zuke unfolded the newspaper, glanced at the first page—there was Hussein again and something about *human shields*—on his way to the sports section. Zuke kept telling himself not to worry about something before it even happened. All he had to do at the moment was wait until Abby called, see what she had to say, and then he could decide what to do.

Trying to make himself focus on the newspaper, Zuke read that Mike Tyson had won in the first round, that the Blazers had beaten Jordan's Bulls, and it could be that there was an NCAA Division I football playoff in the works. Zuke looked up from the paper feeling as if something about Crowe's Café was off. Previously, it had been a place of anonymity for Zuke. Sure, Dennis knew who he was, but Dennis was no conversationalist. There was also Wendy, but Zuke had never seen Wendy on a Sunday. She likely kept those free for church. Zuke had just been thinking this business of Crowe's being somehow ruined for him was all in his mind when Wendy came strolling in from the back room with a pink bag slung over her shoulder. She looked a little tired, but laughed when she saw Zuke.

"It's your stalker," she said with a smile, "or else you're clever enough to get here first." It was an eerie thing for her to say and Zuke thought of his Abby Plan. Surely, that could have bordered on stalking. Funny, Zuke thought, it's stalking only if the interest turns out to be unreciprocated.

"I was just thinking that you probably didn't work Sundays," Zuke said.

"I don't." Wendy came round the counter and put her bag in a cubby near the register. "Usually. The tips stink. Everybody blows their money over the weekend and tries to save it back by stiffing the wait staff." She situated herself behind the counter and picked up an apron which she began to unfold and then tie around her waist.

"Hey Zuke!" a familiar voice yelled from through the silver-framed window that led back into the kitchen. It was Mulligan, and he placed Zuke's food up on the shelf. "I didn't know you came in here."

His head was so big that Zuke could only see his eyes and nose, but he still knew it was him. Crowe's was forever changed, Zuke thought, smiling at Mulligan. "I'm here every Sunday and usually another time or two in addition to that." Dennis set breakfast down in front of Zuke—the plate of food that Mulligan had evidently just cooked—and Zuke held it up and asked him if he'd spit in it. It was an allusion to a film Zuke had loaned Mulligan the first week of school.

"*Weird Science!*" Mulligan said, excited to have got the question right. He was a man who probably endured semester-long stretches of mis-answered questions. Wendy studied the exchange, probably still trying to gauge what sort of person Mulligan was. Dennis laid an order down on the silver ledge by Mulligan's face and tapped it with his fingers.

"Shit," Mulligan said. He'd made scrambled eggs for someone who'd wanted sunny side up. His face disappeared from the little window behind the counter so that he could cook up some more eggs. Wendy idled closer to Zuke.

"He seems almost normal," Wendy whispered, "when he's talking to you."

"You know he's on the football team, a pretty good player. Haven't I seen you there?"

"Aww," Wendy said, smiling. "I noticed you too."

"But not the guy sacking the quarterback?"

"Like you can recognize those guys with their helmets on."

Zuke saw Mulligan look through the window to where he and Wendy were. He certainly did seem to be captivated by her, but who could blame him?

The door to Crowe's Café opened again; Marie walked in wearing a baggy navy sweater, tight jeans, and a pair of brown cowboy boots. Crap, thought Zuke, I'm not ready for this.

Marie wasn't wearing any make up, and Zuke thought it a good sign that she was the kind of girl who could wake up, throw on some clothes and get out and about. Marie eyed Wendy suspiciously, who held her hands up as if she were being robbed.

"I swear I didn't know," she said. "Tell her Zuke."

"She didn't know I'd be here," Zuke said. "Sundays depress me. I come here to cheer myself up."

Marie looked around the café and laughed. "This does the trick?" With the partiers from the night before now eating, Crowe's was especially quiet. The walls were covered with either automobile memorabilia or pictures of old Beau Fleuve, mostly black and whites. The jukebox was turned off and the radio wasn't on. Marie set a Walgreens Drug Store plastic bag down on the counter and nodded to Wendy.

"Female problems," Wendy explained. She picked up the bag, nodded thanks to Marie, and then wrinkled her nose at Zuke. She headed back to the doors that led to where the kitchen was, back to where Mulligan worked. Zuke liked how she'd cut right through to the contents of the bag. Marie sat down on the stool next to Zuke, took a deep breath, shrugged her shoulders, and pointed to his plate. "Can I have a stick?"

"Sure," Zuke said. "But I'm not sure *stick* is what you'd call it." He laughed. He felt at ease around Marie but wondered what it was about her that made him feel that way.

"You wouldn't call it a slab," Marie said, and munched her first bite.

"Not a slab," Zuke said, looking thoughtful, while the two stared straight ahead, where the fiery hood of a Nova hung on the wall. Zuke carved up his pecan waffle and asked Marie if she wanted some. When she agreed, Dennis brought over an extra plate. He was like that character Radar on the television show *MASH*; he had what you needed right before you realized you needed it. Zuke marveled at how twenty-four hours before he'd never talked to Marie—and now here they were, almost like a couple, sharing his breakfast. Zuke was always thinking thoughts such as those, thoughts about what it was that couples did. Wendy came out of the back carrying a pot of coffee, and she shook her shoulders as if she'd just seen a tarantula crawling across the kitchen floor. After a round of refills for the bar goers, she swept up to the counter and said, "I'm off at four. We should all do something tonight."

"Wendy," Marie said, shaking her head. "Give the guy a break. That's embarrassing." She looked at Zuke, who felt a shiver in his chest that fanned out like a peacock's tail feathers. He couldn't do anything tonight; at least if he was really going to see Glory between six and eight.

"I need to explain something," Zuke said, his eyes moving from Marie's, then to Wendy's, where he thought she might give him some idea of what she knew. Zuke's plan of riding the current, of not thinking of Marie until he heard what Abby had to say—that wouldn't fly now. Here was Marie, and he might as well tell the truth. With no clear cut line of action, he might as well go down explaining things as they really were.

"Uh, oh," Wendy said. "You're about to say something foolish." The door to the diner opened and a couple came in. "I don't want to hear it," she said, and moved away, grabbing two menus as she went.

"You don't need to explain anything," Marie said, looking at Zuke, who sat thinking that he liked how the two little creases formed above her lips and out from her nose. He thought she must smile quite a bit. "Sure," Marie said, "I had a good time; I know I shouldn't have kissed you and that you went on the date because Cowboy and Wendy pushed you into it." She looked down and took a bite of waffle. "I just got carried away, that's all." She looked back up to Zuke. "Can't a girl get carried away once in awhile?" Zuke forced a smile, but he felt bad; in fact, he'd never really been in position to tell a girl something relationally awkward. Sure, he'd told girls that he didn't want to date them, but that had almost always been through a friend who asked a friend if he would be interested. Here he was for once on the other side of an almost break up, in a spot feeling as if he couldn't have asked for a more promising first date, and it all felt ugly. With his good hand, Zuke reached up and massaged his temple.

"You know that girl we ran into with the basketball player?" Zuke asked.

"Abby Grant and her boyfriend Brett?"

Zuke explained the whole thing, starting with the composition class sighting the year before, and making use of some revision strategies with regards to the part where he chose his major.

"All right," Marie said, the tone of her voice hooked with a degree of skepticism. She looked away from Zuke, disappointed, but pressed on. "So you'll see how it goes with ole Glory and then maybe give me a call? I'm the back up plan?"

"You're not the back up," Zuke said hurriedly. He sighed. Marie wasn't a second choice at all. Zuke had tried not to think of all his life at once and instead broke it up into segments: first on the list was his Sunday night meeting with Abby. Maybe she would never call him, maybe she would stay with Cheese, or maybe something else he hadn't even thought of would happen. Zuke liked to let his thoughts sit like fruit on a window ledge so he could see how they ripened. But now here sat Marie, out of order compared to the mental list of thoughts he had to tackle. Soundless ripples sped across the dark water of his thoughts. He had to say something. "You and I seem better than Abby," he began without knowing where that sentence was supposed to take him. "What I keep thinking about is…" Zuke stopped and smelled danger as he spoke his thoughts to see what they would be. "I'm a finisher," he tried again, thinking of how he'd nearly quit the cross country team in high school. "I've got this whole principle of finishing what I start before I go on to the next thing. I think people can really miss out on something just because they quit about the time they're going to reap the benefits."

"Reap the benefits?" Marie jumped on the end of Zuke's sentence as if it were a springboard away from him. She sounded disgusted and risked only a glance at Zuke before she returned her disappointed gaze to the flames painted on the hood of the Nova. "That's what a relationship is to you? Reaping? I'm not sure you're who I thought you were."

"Bad analogy," Zuke said. "This is all going wrong." Marie's body language was closed off, her shoulders square to the counter, her gaze down, and she looked as if she might get up to leave at any second. "Let me just say this," Zuke said, with a halting voice, one that inched toward desperation. "It might be a pretty messed up way of thinking, and I probably need to reconsider my whole approach, but I ran cross country in high school, and I was terrible, probably the worst runner in the history of the school."

Marie likely thought this an odd turn in the conversation, but she did look up at Zuke as he told her about how the staff at the meets would sometimes tear down the finish line before he even got there. She couldn't help but laugh at that, a laugh which signaled to Zuke that maybe he and Marie could still work out, that maybe she still liked him. For Zuke, it was so important to be liked. "When I was a sophomore," he continued, "the team went to the state finals, and I traveled with them every weekend, didn't run, and I felt embarrassed. I wanted to quit, but I decided that I'd been through the worst part, the coming in last part, the people laughing at me part, and I figured that if I worked hard, I'd actually be on the varsity. So in that sense, I didn't want to quit right before I *reaped the benefits*."

Upon saying this, Zuke could now see that he'd always thought of himself as having been right to stay on the team, justified because in his final two years he had indeed run well enough to make the varsity. But what were these benefits that Zuke had been referencing? All the miles he'd run? No, Zuke had seen sticking with cross country as a good thing because he'd eventually ended up dating Colleen. "So I don't know what kind of *reaping* you were thinking about..."

Marie turned and narrowed her eyes at Zuke and spoke to him in an even, nearly emotionless, tone. "No matter how you put it, you're telling me that you don't want to see me right now, and for as excited as I was at the prospect of what it looked like we could be, that isn't good news." Zuke nodded his head and sighed. The possibility of two girls was nearly as exasperating as none. Marie reached over and took Zuke's last piece of bacon.

At the far end of the counter, Wendy had been talking to Dennis, who was a good four inches shorter than she was, which allowed her to steal quick looks directly over his head down to Zuke and Marie. Through the window behind Wendy, a bright sun shone which made it hard for Zuke to see her, but he thought he detected a look of dissatisfaction in her gaze, as if she had believed him an honest man but caught him plagiarizing his expository writing assignment.

Somewhere in the kitchen, silverware clanged to the floor and Mulligan could be heard swearing. There was the smell of bacon and coffee, and through the door came two more waitresses, neither of whom Zuke knew, for the post-church rush that fills nearly every diner in the Midwest on Sundays from 10-2. Somewhere, someone turned on the radio, which played a too-happy song for Sunday morning: "The Locomotion." Marie laughed and shook her head. "I hate that song," she said, as if some soundtrack God regularly made ironic choices just to spite her. "When it comes to you," she said, "I think this is it for me." She stared into Zuke's eyes for a second, as if her words might need time to penetrate Zuke's skull.

As soon as the expression had changed on Marie's face, even before she spoke her first word, Zuke believed he'd made a mistake, and he felt that delicate lever of human nature that makes people want what they can't have slam forward inside him as if it were the throttle on a train.

"Some day," Marie said, "I may want to rethink my approach too, but I also have a way I think love grows: it starts like you and I started, a first date that seems easy, with even feelings and steady enjoyment, with laughs and real conversation. There aren't games." She hesitated. "Not that you're playing one now. I know you're confused, but I believe, at least at the start, there shouldn't be so much drama. Just one good but not great date that leads to the next one, and the okay days start to pile on top of one another like a steady snow, one of those where you barely realize what's happening, but by afternoon there's a foot of that pure white stuff on the ground."

Who talks like that? Zuke wondered with admiration for Marie as she stepped off her stool. Zuke felt her leaving, not just physically, but leaving in a way much different than she had the night before, leaving Zuke with the knowledge that he'd been handed rare company only to say that he wasn't sure he wanted to keep it. "Good luck tonight," Marie said and bent down again to catch Zuke with a surprise kiss, this one landing on his forehead, something that made him feel silly and much younger than Marie. This time Zuke didn't say anything when she walked away, speeding up with each step, as if she couldn't put her night with him behind her fast enough. She touched Wendy's shoulder as she went past her on the way out the door.

CHAPTER FOURTEEN

The weekly meetings of the Brothers in Pursuit were held on Sunday nights at 8:00 p.m. on a rotating basis in the members' dorm rooms. Because Zuke thought it was possible for Abby to call anytime, he'd asked to have the schedule rearranged so that everyone would come to his room. Sitting and waiting for Cowboy to call the meeting to order, Zuke realized that he didn't really believe that Abby would call, or that if she did, it would be to tell him that she'd changed her mind, that she had decided that Cheese was the best course of action.

Ultimately, if Zuke were to peel off the golden layer of optimism he sprayed onto his personality, he would find a dark belief about himself; that he felt he was destined to inhale brief bursts of happiness as potential girlfriends glided past. These would be women who would pause, allow him a whiff of love cocaine as they considered him, and move on filled with the dream of finding someone better. Ever since Zuke's high school girlfriend had ended their relationship, an event followed by not playing on his college basketball team, Zuke tried to live with low expectations, actually not quite so low as the valley of depression, but more on a plateau of even-temperedness.

"All rise," Cowboy said as if he were a judge on *Divorce Court.* Like everyone else in the room, he wore the shrunken boxer shorts they had worn for the Pisonmania wrestling match. The only other items anyone wore were the black plastic medieval children's helmets they'd all purchased one night at Toys R Us. Helmets and boxers, that's what the Brothers in Pursuit wore to the meetings.

"Mmm, hnnn," Moon said, laughing at Flabby's boxers which pinched his thighs as if the legs had been fitted with rubber bands.

"The dang things shrink," Flabby said. The elastic around his waist was stretched to the max. It seemed as if Flabby were to clench the muscles in his butt cheeks—and there was a lot of muscle there to be clenched—that he would burst free of the flimsy fabric.

Like a drill sergeant drawing out his enunciation, Cowboy said, "Attention." At first, the Brothers had taken turns leading the meetings, but Moon and Cowboy enjoyed it so much that everyone else had agreed to let them do it. While Zuke turned to his desk and fumbled with a cassette, the rest of the Brothers faced the door and lined up reverently cradling their helmets as if they were football players waiting for the national anthem. With their helmets on their hips and their right hands over their hearts, the Brothers in Pursuit stared toward the back of Zuke's door, which was covered with the following: the phrase "*Adelphoi en Diogmi* " made from letters cut out of bright red construction paper, the symbol of the Christian fish, Rodin's *The Poet,* and in place of the sign that would generally mark a women's restroom, Zuke had placed a poster of a bikini clad Heather Locklear. His morning talk with Marie had put him in the dumps, he was stricken with the feeling that Abby would not call, and so he was taking out his frustrations by flouting the Pison conduct guidelines, once again considering a transfer.

"Not funny," Moon said about the poster. "Hope that's worth twenty-five dollars to you." Zuke pressed the play button on his silver boom box to begin the Brothers' anthem: Cyndi Lauper's "True Colors." For all of Lauper's out of control hair, wild dress, and general outlandish appearance, when her voice was able to stand on its own and ask listeners to take courage, it seemed as if the writers Billy Steinberg and Tom Kelly had known even better than the Brothers themselves the reasons for which they'd decided to come together on Sunday nights after church. Their anthem, chosen mostly because it matched the title of the board game the men played during meetings, had been a surprising source of inspiration. As they all stared at the symbols on the door—that is if you're willing to grant Heather Locklear that sort of status—they once again considered their individual pursuits of God, knowledge, compassion, and women.

When the song ended, with everyone still standing at attention and holding their helmets, Cowboy made an announcement: "I call to order this forty-third meeting of the Brothers in Pursuit. First order of business is Cowboy's absence last week. Cowboy, where were you?" It was a question Cowboy asked of himself, and when he answered it, he did so using a slightly different voice. "Went to the Bradley / Southern Illinois game with my dad and brothers." He took an extra long pause, going for the effect of switching personas. "Brothers, your vote is pass, jockstrap, or naked."

"Naked," Flabby said, deadpan, straight-faced and serious even though he must have laughed on the inside. "Are we having Sunday night meetings or not? I could be at *Pretty Woman* with my girlfriend." Moon cleared his throat. At Pison, there wasn't even a level of discipline that involved a fine for the movies; anyone caught there was to be reported straight to Dean Parrot.

"Just kidding," Flabby said.

"Naked?" The Dini asked, wrinkling his nose at his roommate. "I'm not staying if that's how it turns out."

"Your vote?" Cowboy asked.

"Pass," The Dini said, a vote which meant he excused Cowboy's absence without penalty. "Aren't you boys all about sports?"

"Jockstrap," Zuke said.

"Jockstrap," Moon said.

"Jockstrap it is," Cowboy said, clearly happy at the result. All the brothers were allowed a vote on each motion, even if the motion was in regard to their own fate. "All agree?"

"Aye, Aye," everyone agreed. Cowboy took off his boxer shorts, where in preparation of his anticipated penalty for missing the previous week's meeting, he had already put on a jockstrap, a dingy white garment with squiggly bands hairing out from where age had frayed it. Left over from the year before when he had been on the basketball team, printed in all capital letters with a black magic marker, was the word COWBOY. All the players labeled their practice gear so it could be returned to them after the managers washed it. Cowboy grinned and rubbed his mostly hairless, milky-white upper thighs.

"That jock strap from middle school?" Flabby asked.

"Who is the penalty supposed to punish?" The Dini questioned, looking away from Cowboy toward the window. "Him or us?" There was a knock at the door and Zuke asked who it was.

"Warren," the R.A. from the night before answered loudly. "Open up." Zuke cracked the door and asked him what he needed. "Move away please; I have reason to suspect a violation. I want to inspect the room." The phrase was straight out of the R.A. training manual. Possibly the sound of the music and the crowd of five that had assembled in the room had caused Warren to re-suspect Pee Wee of foul play. But there was no Pee Wee in the room.

"Sorry Moon," Warren said when he came in. "I didn't know you were in here." Warren looked around the room at the Brothers in their boxer shorts and when his eyes fell on Cowboy he said, "I don't even want to know." Cowboy moved his helmet over his crotch. "When am I going to remember to stop looking in on you guys on Sunday nights?" He stepped back and closed the door.

"Let's take a seat and give report," Cowboy instructed. They all sat cross legged on the floor, in the middle of the room, which was covered by a mauve carpet remnant. To give report meant that each Brother told the others how he did the past week with regards to the four pursuits. For the first time in awhile, in the category of the pursuit of women, there would be news.

"Excuse me Mr. Moon," The Dini said, gesturing with his left hand while he made a face as if an effluvium of toilet smell had exploded into his nose. "Could you move the fabric of your boxer shorts over a little? I can see your stuff." He laughed to himself. "It's not too pleasant."

Moon squirmed around trying to adjust himself.

"Oh lord," The Dini said, "the other way."

A flood of crimson broke out onto Moon's face and everyone looked from him to The Dini, thoughts going to his sexuality, that he might or might not be gay. Zuke was the only one The Dini had said anything to. "And I know what y'all are thinking, but you need to get over yourselves. I don't want to see your ball sacks anymore than those women on the other side of campus do."

Flabby laughed; Zuke realized he hadn't ever thought about how ugly a ball sack was while Moon, who seemed the most likely candidate to speak against homosexuality, said, "Fair enough." He fumbled with the box to the game and his hands visibly shook. Cowboy looked at the floor, Flabby to Zuke who looked at The Dini who looked back at him. Out in the hall, the massive door that led to the stairs banged open and shut. There was wild laughter and the sounds of a chase, almost like a game of tag. "You faggot!" someone yelled. Cowboy rose his shoulders a little, a half shrug, and asked The Dini, "Want to talk about it?"

"Everyone," The Dini said, his posture straightening if that were possible. "I feel gay, whatever that means, but I'm not sure I'm going to do anything about it." Flabby looked like a proud father, proud that The Dini had been willing to disclose that much; Zuke pursed his lips and nodded, worried that Moon would suggest an on the spot prayer.

"Want to forget the reports and just start the game?" Moon asked as he unfolded the board.

"No you don't," Cowboy said, his voice a little hard. "This is what we've come together for, isn't it?" He looked at each of them. "To talk about what matters?"

"Thanks," The Dini said, "but I don't really want to have a press conference. Now you guys know—probably you already knew, or at least suspected—and so maybe you won't want me to come to the meetings anymore, or maybe you won't want to be my friends…"

"Dini…" Flabby said.

"Dude," Moon said. "I'll always want to be your friend."

The Dini held up his hands as if he were a coach trying to settle his team down against a full court press. "I appreciate y'all, but don't go there. This emotion does not become you. Didn't the Los Angeles Reds or somebody play ball today?" He looked around the circle. "Go ahead," he said, his fingers fluttering as if he were scattering away pesky kids. "Talk to each other. This is making me uncomfortable."

From the spot on the corner of Zuke's desk, just a few feet away from where he sat, the telephone rang. Zuke jumped as if his boxers had been invaded by a brigade of red ants. "It's probably my mom," Zuke said. His chest felt as if it were in full arrest. "I'll call her back after."

"Eric Stanley Zaucha," The Dini said, "you answer that telephone right now." With the hairs on his neck and arms prickling to life, Zuke's mouth went dry; he picked up the receiver and said hello the best he could. Had Glory really called? The rest of the Brothers silenced and listened hard.

"It's me," Abby said. "I'm back. Can you come over?"

"When?"

"Right now."

"I'll be there in a sec." As Zuke placed the phone back on its charger, he felt confused as to whether he'd read any indication in Glory's voice related to the sort of news he was about to receive. *I'm back; come over*—it was such neutral language. A bad sign or had she just had a long night? A break up, especially one within the long term relationship she'd had with Cheese, could be terrible. Zuke couldn't imagine telling Cheese something he didn't want to hear.

The Brothers rose from their spots on the floor—obviously they'd planned for what they would do if Abby called—and they all began to sing, as if in church: "Glory, Glory, Hallelujah..." Zuke took his pants off the chair and pulled them on over his boxers. The Fab members began to position themselves as if forming a tunnel for starting line ups, all the while singing and clapping. "Glory, Glory, Hallelujah..." Zuke wriggled into his polo shirt and fell into the spirit of it all, forgetting that he'd thought Abby would never call, forgetting even for at least a few seconds the bad scene with Marie.

Zuke smiled even though he wanted to look grave, a young man who always expected the worst when it came to love. He ran out of the room as if he had five minutes to cash in a winning lottery ticket, this one at the women's residence hall.

Outside it was colder, in the upper thirties, and Zuke hadn't thought to put on a coat. With his hands thrust into his pant pockets, he walked down the sidewalk, toward the Tree of Knowledge and Barrett Hall, the building where Abby lived, the building which carried Marie's family name. He involuntarily shivered and the shadow of The Tree of Knowledge, cast by the power of the women's residence hall security lights, reached out to Zuke, black and unnoticed, as he hurried through the quadrangle. Zuke couldn't help but climb up off the plateau of even-temperedness and for once believe that it was possible for Abby to choose him. It wouldn't be that bad for Marie, Zuke thought, surely she must get asked out nearly every day and it wouldn't be long until she was fine.

Zuke laughed at himself, at his own ignorant arrogance. Who was he kidding? Marie was fine now. Finally his life could begin. Ever since he and Colleen had broken up, he felt as if someone had lopped out a scoop of his spirit, but now if Abby had been able to follow through, he could be happy. The laughter of a woman sounded from across the quadrangle over by Ludwig, and Zuke looked to see a couple, the woman's arm cradled around the man's, as if he were an usher at a wedding.

The lobby of Barrett looked like a small and square greenhouse, that is if it weren't for the six cushy chairs, three to a side, which lined each wall just inside the entrance. Abby was already there, waiting alone—it was too cold near the door for anyone to really sit there for any length of time—and she wore a long green coat, one Zuke had not seen, maybe one she'd brought from home. She sat up straight, hands folded in her lap, as if she were waiting patiently for a bus or to see a doctor. As Zuke tugged on the silver handle of the door to enter the lobby, he thought to himself that he must prepare himself for whatever condition Abby might be in: confused, sad, or maybe just exhausted. Dare he hope she be excited to begin with him?

Zuke still had two full steps to really reach her, and then he saw it, on her left hand, a glassy drill bit of a diamond ring that zipped a neat hole through his heart. He looked at it and then—because he was unable to raise his eyes up to meet hers—Zuke said to the muddy doormat on the floor, "Nice ring." Suddenly, he felt embarrassed, even ashamed that he'd thought it possible that Abby would ever choose him over Cheese. Zuke turned and went right back out into the cold, heading for he didn't know where.

"Zuke, wait!" Abby followed Zuke back outside, and she ran up to him. "C'mere," she said, grabbing his arm and pulling him out of the light that illuminated the entrance and over to a darker place, where there was a bench up near the wall of the building. Through the window was Professor Moore's apartment. She was the resident director of Barrett Hall. Abby and Zuke sat down and Abby shook her head looking at him. "Oh God," she said, "Are you okay? I'm so sorry."

Zuke felt numb, maybe even distant, the way he felt when the movie was bad and he didn't even care what happened to the main character. This out-of-body sensation was how he always felt at receiving bad news. When his grandfather had died, his outward appearance hadn't changed any more than if he'd been told the restaurant was out of whatever he had ordered. It wasn't until time passed that Zuke got down or even felt panic at what his life had become. "I don't get," Zuke said, "how you go from planning to break up with Cheese to promising to marry him." There was a hint of something important in that statement, that love tipped on such delicate scales that an ounce here or there meant a life shared or lives separated. When Zuke looked to Abby, he thought she appeared frightened, not as if Zuke would harm her, but as if she were a child and heading off to her first day of school. "What happened?"

Abby looked down and bit her lower lip. "My whole life," she said, "I dreamed of marrying Brett." She took Zuke's hands and looked back up into his eyes. "You know, I remember being a little girl and acting out Cinderella with my baby dolls and whenever it got to the part where I imagined the prince at the ball, every time the clock struck midnight, it was always Brett in my mind left examining the glass slipper."

This made sense to Zuke; in fact, it was just what he'd feared. "Right," Zuke said. "I knew it already, I think, that you couldn't do it."

"I don't know," Abby said. "I used to think that there was one person in the world for me. I thought that God would pick a man, and he'd be the father of my children, and all I had to do was be open and follow His will. But then you came along, and now I don't believe in one person for each person anymore. I think we've all got little circles of people who we could be happy with. The thing is, what any person has to do is commit and work at it. I haven't been happy with Brett, and I think part of that feeling comes from my always comparing the two of you. If I had a complaint about him, it would have been his lack of commitment. I was never sure how serious he was and so when he showed up Sunday with the ring, he was offering me the dream I've had ever since I can remember: to be his wife. I think my problems with Brett came from the way I was always looking outside the relationship. I think he sensed that more than I realized, and it freaked him out." A few gentle tears crawled out of the corners of Abby's eyes and ran along her cheekbones and trickled down onto her neck.

Zuke shrugged his shoulders. "I don't know what to say. I understand, I guess."

"I can't bear to think that you're going to hate me. I feel like with time, that you and I could marry and be happy, but Brett and I have all that history. I wanted a soul mate, I wanted a prince charming, but I can't feel that. I don't think those things exist. There's you and there's Brett and I've decided. I feel awful."

Zuke rose. He couldn't listen to this. He didn't want to face this. He felt he loved Abby, but he could hear her. He thought she was right. Hadn't he just glimpsed what she was saying when it came to himself, that he could see how Marie or Abby might make for great girlfriends. "I understand," Zuke said again, this time more like he meant it. "I feel like I had a great chance and missed it, but I'm glad to hurt—you know—it's being alive: loving people, taking chances, and getting hurt. It happens. It will happen again."

Abby stood to join Zuke, and he thought of the golden locket that he'd given her as a birthday present. He hoped that maybe for at least tonight she would have worn it. Perhaps she would tuck it away in some corner of her life so that once a year—maybe—she would hold it and think of what they almost were. "Good luck." Zuke forced a smile. "Congratulations. You should be happy. You're engaged."

"I know," Abby said. She looked as if she'd just pulled an all nighter. "I've been waiting for this my whole life, and all I feel like doing is throwing up."

Zuke laughed. "Married," he said, grinning. "Holy crap. You make me feel like a little kid."

"What do you mean?" Abby was composing herself. There had only been a few tears. She looked bemused at Zuke's comment.

"I don't know, like, I've been trying to get you to go out on a date and you've been thinking about getting married. I felt like I was really in the middle of a big deal but a first date seems like such a little deal compared to getting married."

"You shouldn't think that," Abby said. "When I thought I was going to break up with Brett it was because I wanted to marry you."

This was a shock to Zuke. "Wow." He looked at Abby's face and thought of the way that his life had almost become a life where it was Abby's face he would see for sixty years or more. Just a few words—sometimes only yes or no—and the entire arc of a life changes. "That's amazing. I can't believe it."

"Well, it's true. And I didn't know what to decide. I thought by deciding nothing I could lose you both and probably only end up hurting you more than I already have. You should give yourself more credit. I don't know for sure, but if you could have believed in us more, believed more that you deserved to be with me, then maybe things would have been different."

Off toward the lobby, Zuke saw Cheese coming up the sidewalk. He gave Zuke a quick wave that was practically sheepish, maybe even humbled. He didn't come over but instead thrust his hands into his pockets and went inside the lobby to wait for Abby.

"I told him about us," Abby said, looking Cheese's way too, "that I had planned to break up with him and start dating you."

Zuke could already see that Cheese's reaction wasn't the angry one he might have expected. "What did he say?"

"He said that you're a good guy, that he could understand why somebody would leave him for you. He said he was always jealous of us and that he wanted to know more about what I was working on. He said he wants to read books."

Zuke laughed again.

"I know, right? We'll see how long that lasts. He doesn't have to read books for us to work. I think the more insecure he got the more brashly he tried to carry himself." Abby gave Zuke a playful elbow. "So you're going to be okay? You seem okay."

"Ahhh, crap," Zuke said. He massaged his temples hard and started to think about life beyond the moment: there would be a humiliating return to the Brothers, the night that would follow after during which Zuke would surely review all the moments he could have done or said something different, something that would have turned the love tide his way. Oh, Zuke thought, and after that there would be an entire spring semester during which he would see Abby class after class. The two had signed up for identical schedules. Zuke wondered if maybe he could make a few changes.

"I guess I'll see you tomorrow for *MacBeth*," Abby said.

"Oh, right. I totally forgot about that." The English Honor Society had a trip up to Chicago planned for the following day.

"Should I just skip it?" Abby asked. "I'm sure Professor Moore would understand."

"Don't worry about it." Zuke waved his hand. "Might as well start facing it all tomorrow." Zuke looked into the lobby where he caught Cheese staring at them. It felt strange to see Cheese looking anxious all because of his presence. "See you tomorrow," Zuke said, and he began to trudge away toward he didn't know what.

Abby took a deep breath. "See you tomorrow."

Zuke walked toward the student parking lot with the intent of driving, an act along with shooting free throws, he had often found refuge. It was something he'd learned to do from Lloyd Dobler, who after being dumped by his love interest in *Say Anything*, begins to engage in round-the-clock driving, mostly in the rain, all the while inspecting significant geographical landmarks of the relationship as he talks into a portable tape recorder.

At the moment, Zuke didn't feel as suicidal as Dobler had seemed to feel or even as desperate as he himself had felt when Colleen had broken up with him. That night, Zuke had taken his Chevette out on the "S" curves near the river and fantasized about driving his little car into a telephone pole or maybe off the high bank down into the river. He'd scared himself that night, gunning the engine and getting a little too close to his fantasy. Zuke realized he could just drive home—it was only two hours away—or maybe even all the way to Ball State, where he could see his buddy Road Dog and maybe even visit Colleen Flannery. He did, after all, believe he had her address somewhere. What if he just knocked on her door and said he'd missed her?

Zuke had nearly decided to do this very thing—why not?—it would be sort of an adventure, but fidgeting in his pocket he realized he didn't have his keys. He had to go back to his dorm room. What in the world was he going to tell the Brothers?

When Zuke reached the door to his room, he paused, where the hall was empty and he could hear the sound of laughing as his friends played the board game True Colors. He probably hadn't even been gone thirty minutes, and he'd briefly considered going down the hall to wait and let some more time pass. But what would he do? He was going to have to eventually tell his friends what had happened so he might as well get it over with.

"What'd you forget?" Cowboy asked when Zuke entered the room. None of the Brothers even looked up; they were all engrossed as Moon tallied the colored tiles he'd just dumped out onto the playing surface. True Colors was a game that asked hypothetical questions such as these: Which of the players is most likely to stare at him/herself? Who among the players would be your sexy dream date? It was a game for friends and the objective was to predict how many votes you'd receive, thus revealing how in harmony you were with the way the rest of the players saw you.

"She got engaged." Zuke said as he walked behind The Dini and sat down on the edge of the bed.

"I'm sorry Zuke," The Dini said, putting his voting cards from the game down.

"To a guy named Cheese," Flabby added, as if he hadn't thought it possible for someone to say yes to such a name. "Well, I'll be."

The reality of marriage—that is that someone they knew actually planned to commit to the act—popped up like a surprise answer on a magic eight ball. It's one thing to think *someday I'll get married and have a family*, but quite another to reserve a reception hall, decide on whether or not to have a carving station, and actually look a real-life future spouse in the eye. It's the difference between fantasy and reality, the difference between love in the movies and love as experienced by real people.

"2:4," Cowboy said, matter-of-factly as he stood up. The numbers were a well-known code to the Brothers in Pursuit.

Zuke shook his head. "Guys," he began to protest, "I don't think...."

"2:4," The Dini said with conviction. "I need it too."

"All in favor?" Flabby asked.

"Aye, Aye!" everyone responded, except for Zuke, who smiled involuntarily as a laugh escaped his lips. He twisted his right ear lobe to scratch it and then held out his hands as if to say he surrendered. Still clad in only tight and short boxers, The Dini exited Zuke's room and headed down the hall. 2:4 was an event only held in Moon and Cowboy's room. The other Brothers followed. Although he was no longer clad in his boxer shorts, Zuke grabbed his helmet on the way out.

"Nice," Mulligan said, as he shook his head in disbelief at the sight of the Fab, who carried their helmets as if marching to battle, a battle they would fight with 80% of their flesh exposed. Pee Wee stood next to Mulligan, hanging out near the bathroom right across from Moon and Cowboy's room.

"Glad you like it," Flabby said.

"What's the matter?" Pee Wee asked The Dini.

"2:4," The Dini responded. "Drums?"

"What happened?" Pee Wee wanted to know as Cowboy arrived and unlocked the door.

"Glory's engaged," The Dini said.

"Oh no, Roomie." Pee Wee began to follow Zuke into Moon and Cowboy's room.

"What you want with those queers, Pee Wee?" Mulligan asked. "I thought we were going to," he looked at Resident Assistant Moon, "you know."

"Forget it," Pee Wee said.

Mulligan shrugged his shoulders. "Your funeral." The Dini entered the room, closed the door, and locked it.

Inside, Cowboy was in the process of covering his bed with two old beach towels, one green from Hilton Head and another a red one from Cedar Point. 2:4 called for three members of The Fab to stand on Cowboy's bed, and the towels were there to protect his sheets from dried skin, toe jam, or the other destroyers of sterility that Cowboy sensed, real or imagined. On a different day, Mulligan had come into the room sweaty from football practice and run Cowboy's pillow between his thighs before anyone had thought to stop him. It was what Cowboy always suspected had happened whenever he came into the room and detected any irregularity among his linens. Generally his bed was a "no touch" zone, but when he had time to put the towels down, he made allowances for 2:4.

"I've got sax," Flabby said, stepping up onto Cowboy's bed and putting his bare foot under the towel that Cowboy had just laid down. Pee Wee turned the desk chair around and assumed his seat to play the imaginary drums.

"Can I at least be trumpet?" Zuke asked. "It's my sorrow we're combating here."

"You know the rules," Moon said while Cowboy made a sad face at Flabby's giant foot. The rules, as created by a unanimous vote of the Brothers, stated that if 2:4 was initiated to lift the spirits of one particular member, said member must assume the role of lead vocals.

"I'm guitar," Cowboy said, "and don't forget the microphone. I spent two bucks on it."

"Want us to chip in?" Flabby asked sarcastically.

"I'm just saying that I bought it; we ought to use it."

The Dini and Moon joined Flabby standing on the bed. They

were generally trumpet and trombone respectively. Zuke went and stood by the window, his shoulders slumped and his feet shuffled across the carpet. Zuke hadn't yet begun to bring energy to the ceremony. Cowboy opened the bottom drawer of his chest of drawers and pulled out a frizzy blonde wig. He wouldn't dress like a woman for a skit, but he did believe in the patriotism inherent in playing a mean air guitar. Using his open drawer as a first step, he carefully scaled the shoulder-high piece of furniture between his bed and the window. The ceilings in Chapman Hall were at least fifteen feet high.

"C'mon Zuke," Moon said, holding the remote to his stereo. "Up on the desk." Zuke reached into Cowboy's left hand drawer and pulled out a plastic microphone, again from Toys R Us, and then he mounted the desk. Cowboy had grabbed a broom which would serve as his guitar while Moon, The Dini, and Flabby would all play "air" horns.

"Wait, Wait, Wait," The Dini said urgently as he hopped down off the bed. "Don't forget the lights." Pee Wee turned his chair away from his imaginary drums in the center of the room, and Zuke passed him Cowboy's neon green desk lamp. The Dini flipped off the inferno and Pee Wee shined the lamp on Cowboy as if it were a spotlight.

"Here we go," Moon said as he thumbed a few buttons on his stereo remote. The green digital numbers on the console lit up with the numbers 2:4. The "2" stood for the second slot in the five-disc changer which contained Chicago's *Greatest Hits Volume II*. Before a lawsuit was threatened, the band had formerly been known as the Chicago Transit Authority, the album was their fifteenth, and several of the group members had once been music students just up the road at DePaul University. The fourth song on the CD was entitled "Alive Again."

With the desk lamp shining on him in the otherwise pitch-dark room, Cowboy struck a guitar pose, leaning back and pointing the tip of the handle to the ceiling while he worked imaginary strings. The rhythm of the music was fast, and Cowboy began to shift his weight quickly from side to side, careful to get his hair rocking in tune with his body. The song gave Cowboy just enough time to showcase his skills before the horns came in. Pee Wee shifted the light to The Dini, Moon, and Flabby, who had arranged themselves by height and begun to execute their carefully choreographed movements which had evolved over the many times the Fab had come together for this uplifting ritual. They stepped from side to side in rhythm, bobbing their invisible horns up and down imitating Chevy Chase and Paul Simon in the "You Can Call Me Al" video. The Dini, who had an ultra-pasty white and hairy chest, sometimes paused to twirl his make-believe trumpet fancily on his hand. Pee Wee scurried around and turned on two more lamps, one by the bed and one by the window. The effect was that they were on stage, and that the imaginary crowd was out in the dark toward the sink by the door.

Despite the swampy expectations Zuke had created with his down and out demeanor, he came in strong with lead vocals, belting them into the plastic, otherwise useless, microphone. His face scrunched into intensity, his eyes narrowed in a squint, and his jaw jutted out toward the unseen crowd. Pee Wee began to work the drums.

Zuke continued the lyrics of what amounted to a three part song sandwiched between solos for the varied instruments. Although Chicago was well known for its love ballads and incorporated instruments such as the flugelhorn, cornet, flute, clarinet, congas, and the bongos, this first hit after the band had suffered the accidental shooting death of its co founder Terry Kath—supposed last words, *don't worry guys, it isn't even loaded*—contained heavy metal segments that were electric for the Brothers to perform. When lead vocals took a break halfway through, Cowboy broke from his usual routine and gave this performance a little bit extra: he jumped from the chest of drawers down onto the bed, knocking Moon up against the wall. He bounced high into the air and then to the floor where he landed on his shins and knees all the while never missing a chord on his broom guitar. He seemed to momentarily leave the sometimes jazzy world of Chicago and become inhabited by the spirit that more commonly possessed Eddie Van Halen.

Zuke jumped from the desk to the floor so that he could work the imaginary crowd. He closed his eyes and belted out the lyrics which forced him to claim over and over that he was alive again. And Zuke felt that he was coming alive, at least for the length of the song.

The Dini broke into an uncontrollable fit of laughing, and Pee Wee put down his drumsticks so he could shake two mentally constructed maracas. It was all a more gruesome and joyful scene than the one acted out in the film *Risky Business*: gruesome for the bare-chested brothers in their tight boxers—no adequate replacement for Tom Cruise in sight—but joyful for the concoction of energy that was born from the mix of the music and the company of good friends. After the climactic ending of the song, which left the Brothers soaked in a sheen of sweat, The Dini, who cupped his hand to his ear, remarked, "Fellas, I do believe they'd like for us to play it again."

CHAPTER FIFTEEN

On Monday afternoon, dime-sized snowflakes fell on the campus of Pison while Zuke hurried out the back entrance of McClain Gymnasium to a purple Pison College van, where six other members of the English Honor Society waited for him so they could leave for Chicago. Zuke had just come from the basketball office where he'd reminded Coach Miller that he had the performance of *MacBeth* to attend. Now that his left arm was in a cast, it mattered even less if Zuke was at practice or not. Zuke went for the front seat on the passenger side; he could almost always count on the spot next to Professor Moore being left open, so strange she was that almost no one ever tried to talk to her. Zuke had decided that he would let Abby be and talk to her only if she spoke to him first.

But Jay Schweitzer was already riding shotgun, and he rolled his window down. "Hey there, Mr. Zuke," he said. "I left you a spot in the back next to your girlfriend." Jay seemed to think well of himself for being so bold to make such a joke. Evidently, Jay hadn't noticed Abby's latest piece of jewelry.

Professor Moore, dressed in a shiny-yellow raincoat that crinkled like a Halloween suit when she moved, leaned over Jay and called to Zuke, "Hurry up. Scotland awaits." By Scotland, she meant one of the settings of Shakespeare's *MacBeth*.

"You owe me," Jay whispered. Heading for the side door to the back of the van, where somewhere inside Abby lurked, Zuke tried to steel himself against any sort of visible personal response. The morning had brought mostly a feeling of lifelessness. Most days waking up had meant looking forward to seeing Abby, but now he was left with little to look forward to at all. The transfer virus was getting stronger inside him.

Zuke moved along the side of the van where he opened the large rolling door as if he'd thrown the curtain to a stage, the English

Honor Society waiting behind. As he stepped up into the van, Zuke smiled at everyone and scanned it for where Abby had chosen to sit. She was in the far back, staring out the window and dressed for the theater in all black: slacks, a turtleneck, and a woolen trench coat. The only empty seat was next to her and when Zuke sat down, she turned and said, "Hi."

Zuke forced a smile, said good morning, and then didn't know what else to say. The silence continued ten minutes up Interstate Fifty-Seven, through what appeared to be the beginnings of a snowstorm. The van, all except for the backseat, was full of chatter. The two girls in front of them, Katie and Emma, discussed the relative attractiveness of Duran Duran. "I like them all when they wear a coat and tie," Katie explained. "Men just look so much more handsome when they dress up." Zuke had on a cream shirt that had a thin violet stripe that ran along the line of his buttons. It was a shirt that Katie had previously described as "having a European Look," a comment which Zuke had liked and thought about as a possible identity for himself (the European look), except that he didn't quite know what that meant, especially since he'd bought the shirt at the Logansport Mall at a store called Maurice's.

So far no one had noticed the change in the dynamic between Abby and Zuke, who by now would have usually fallen into whispers or laughter, glad for the circumstance that didn't require an invention strategy for a reason to be together. Without too much thought—there she sat; it seemed the thing to do—Zuke decided to make a wisecrack that had occurred to him: "I see Professor Moore has borrowed your jacket." Moore was known for her odd choices, as if her internal life was a conflation of *Wuthering Heights* and the comic strip *Calvin and Hobbes,* the latter of which she had once used as a text book when she taught English in Japan for a semester. Zuke picked up conversationally with Abby as if nothing had happened, as if it were the second month of the school year, as if Abby hadn't just gotten engaged on the very night Zuke had hoped she was going to begin dating him.

"Don't get all pissy," she said, smiling, "just because Jay got the seat next to your girlfriend."

"Uh, huh," Zuke said. The return to how they'd been—which surely was full of avoidance issues—did have a peculiar feel, but Zuke felt relief in comparison to how he'd felt on the way over, which was a condition of near paralysis. Abby twisted her legs away from the window toward Zuke, unbuttoned her coat, and held out her arm so he could help her out of her sleeve. And that was it. Somehow, just pretending as if nothing had happened, Zuke— somewhat happily—went back to the way things had been before Abby had become engaged.

Without having given the theater in which *MacBeth* would be performed any thought, Zuke was surprised when Professor Moore turned the van down a quiet tree-lined street, only partly lit, and parked in front of a three story, 1920's, tall and thin stone Victorian. Its steps led up to an ornate wooden door. Moore shut the van off and everyone began to climb out. Zuke felt like he might be at the home of a professional baseball player, maybe in the vicinity of Cowboy's baseball card gift Ryne Sandberg, and he wondered if his teacher hadn't driven to the wrong place. Despite the scatterbrained way her mind randomly fired cannonballs of information, Moore was usually pretty good with directions.

Outside the van, the snow was ankle deep and marked with many sets of half-filled footprints leading around the side of the house.

"You think maybe it's going to snow all night?" Zuke asked. Abby shrugged her shoulders.

"Who cares? Maybe we'll have to stay here. I need a break. My life is such a mess." This wasn't, at least in the way Zuke had ever imagined, what someone who had just gotten engaged should be feeling like. He looked at Abby and raised his eyebrows for her choice of the word *mess*. Zuke thought that maybe in his talk with Marie he'd glimpsed just a bucket full of the swamp of trouble Abby had been paddling around in. It didn't matter what decision Abby had just made; she was bound to have doubted it either way.

"Snow Angel," Professor Moore said. "Snow Angel, Eric." Zuke's teacher had moved to within several inches of him, and her breath smelled like a fortune cookie. She wasn't a great observer of personal space.

"I'm your snow angel?" Zuke asked, hesitant. Jay, who'd produced a black beret for his head upon arrival, laughed. Professor Moore looked embarrassed.

"She's so weird," Katie said, as if Professor Moore wasn't standing right next to her.

"I'm a little old for you, don't you think?" Professor Moore giggled as if she were twenty, joyously fluttering her fingers as if she might try to use them to fly. Many times the English Honor Society had tried to guess her age, guesses which ranged from forty-two to sixty. "I want you and Henry to make snow angels, a picture for the annual. What do you say? Don't be a party pooper."

"Yeah Zuke, don't be a party pooper." Abby took Moore's bear into her arms. It was dressed in a little red bow tie and a black jacket. Dinner had been at a Chinese place—sometimes Zuke thought maybe Moore didn't realize she wasn't Asian—and his professor had brought her bear named Henry into the restaurant and sat him in a booster chair. Zuke had already known about the bear, that Moore treated the stuffed animal as if it were her pet or even her toddler-aged son. Once she'd brought her photo album from her semester abroad to an honor society meeting and there was barely a human being in the book. It was just Henry and China's most famous landmarks. Zuke thought of his professor as a more gregarious Emily Dickinson.

Abby took the bear out into the yard where the snow hadn't been trampled by theater goers. She placed Henry the teddy bear in the snow and began to move his little arms and legs back and forth to create a miniature angel. "C'mon Zuke," Abby said, "Scotland awaits."

"Here, Here," Professor Moore said. She liked Abby, who as president of the English Honor Society spent a lot of time with her. Abby played along enthusiastically with Moore's quirkiness and unusual ideas. They hosted a mini golf fundraiser—complete with a Woolf *Lighthouse* hole and a Faulkner *Barn Burning* one—which had actually been a hit among the students. Of course this had been aided by the literature-themed trivia questions at each hole where a right answer earned a prize donated from an area business.

"I'm going to look for the little boys' room," said Jay, following the footprints around the side of the building. Moore pulled a Polaroid camera out of her bright red bag. Her large round glasses were covered with a film of slush from melted snowflakes. Zuke lay down in the yard; it was cold on his neck, but his coat came down past his butt, and he had on a sock hat. Mostly it would be just the bottom of his pants that would get wet. He gyrated in the necessary fashion and made an angel; Moore snapped a picture, then another as he finished, and a final close up of Henry that cut Zuke out altogether.

"That worked out great," Zuke told Abby, who had come over to retrieve Henry. She held out her hand to help Zuke up, and when he grabbed it, he felt the point of her engagement ring under her leather glove. "That doesn't happen to Jordan," Zuke said softly, to himself.

"What did you say?" Abby asked, letting go of Zuke's hand once he was standing.

"It's just something Pee Wee says. Like if my credit card got declined; I'd say it then."

"I don't get it."

"Well, Jordan's got enough money and fame that I doubt his credit card ever gets declined, and if it did, he'd probably have another way to pay. Soooo," Zuke emphasized, "that never happens to Jordan."

"What made you say it just then?"

"The feeling of your engagement ring on my hand." The line felt a little like a punch, not delivered by Zuke consciously meant to hurt, but it had been a quick and honest response. Zuke couldn't decide if Abby's look was angry, hurt, or thoughtful. He hoped what he said would be the first thrash of a conversation sickle that would allow the two of them to talk more about Abby's engagement and that now—somehow—her life was a mess.

"We better hurry up," Professor Moore said as she and Henry began to hustle around the side of the building. Abby and Zuke followed.

Concrete stairs led down a narrow passageway that made Zuke think of Poe's "The Cask of Amontillado." Briefly, he fantasized that Moore had carted them off to Chicago to arrange for their murders. At the bottom of the steps, Zuke—who trailed Abby— found himself in a theater like he'd never imagined. If he'd taken one more step, he would have been onstage, which was at the lowest point in the room and mooned out into the audience. From where Zuke stood, the seating was only two rows deep. Out toward the middle, Zuke counted six rows. The place couldn't have held more than seventy-five people; it was mostly full.

"These are ours," Professor Moore said, a gleam of excitement in her eyes. "Isn't this wonderful?" Zuke sat down in the chair closest to the door and put his feet up on the edge of the stage.

"Eric!" Professor Moore hissed, frantically motioning for him to put his feet down, a moment Abby enjoyed immensely.

"I can't take you anywhere," Abby said, and slapped her hand on his knee, letting it rest there for a few moments before she removed it. Zuke twisted back to look over the blood red theater, to see the sort of person who came to such an event, but the lights went out before he noticed much. With no windows in the basement, everyone might as well have had their eyes closed for all they could see. Zuke thought of the snow, blindly white in contrast to the darkness he experienced now, and then he heard something rustle from toward the door to his immediate left. A foot stepped on his—so light it might have been a child's—and what felt like a person's leg brushed the back of his hand, which had been on his knee. There was the feeling of flesh on flesh, a sensation that didn't fully register with Zuke until he was also taking in the very scent of the same horrible fart spray that the Mulligan and his boys often applied to the fourth floor carpet of Chapman Hall. The stage creaked as whoever had passed stepped from the concrete surface of the stairs to the wood of the stage. Another person walked by and Abby tried to suppress a laugh.

"Oh my God," she said softly. "What is it?" The feeling was of walking through a cheap funhouse at the fair when the simulated rattails slide across everyone's legs. The stage creaked again and another person went by. Three somethings—they had to be people, right?—passed and probably they all would have tripped had it not been for Professor Moore's reprimand about Zuke's legs. Soft strobe lights flickered to the sound of an otherworldly music, music that pricked at Zuke's eardrums with a high-pitched violin. But what Zuke paid most attention to were the three nude women huddled in the center of the stage. Head to head to head, they all had long dark hair that stretched halfway down their backs, and they were squatting as if readying to empty their bowels.

"They touched my leg," Zuke whispered, as if an actress had brushed against him on her way in to the Oscars. Abby laughed a laugh heard by the entire audience. She and Zuke felt Professor Moore's frown even though they couldn't see her down the row where she sat closer to center stage. The naked women began to dance slowly at first; they were obviously, even to Zuke, accomplished dancers, and the pace of their performance intensified to the rhythm of the music. Under the alternating light and dark of the strobes, the witches—*surely,* Zuke thought, *these are the witches*—seemed to appear and vanish on different parts of the stage. The music was intentionally disharmonious.

Because he didn't want to become aroused by any woman that might have been considered ugly, two decades older than he, or God forbid, a man, Zuke tried to first make sure all the creatures before him were female, and secondly, that they were near his age and good looking. Eventually each witch appeared on the stage very close to Zuke's seat, and he was mostly confident—given no radical surgery, creative tucking, or taping—that the dancers were all female and none of them over thirty years old. Check. Check. He could also see their legs had long gone unshaven and their pits hairy enough to support the construction of a braid or two.

Not attractive, Zuke tried to tell himself as a levee against the mounting confusion inside him: he knew a tight pair of blue jeans and a form fitting sweater would transform any of these women into someone he'd see and begin rating highly to his friends.

On the way home, the snow was so thick that there was no sign of Lake Shore Drive's namesake. Professor Moore half-jokingly said she'd probably get fired for taking the Christian boys and girls of Pison to witness such a spectacle.

"Who's going to tell?" Jay asked. He was still riding shotgun. In the backseat, the rest of the students relived the play.

"What about Banquo?" Abby asked from the back of the van next to Zuke. "Was he supposed to have been stabbed in the crotch? I don't remember that from our reading."

"Bloody naked guy," Katie said, as she turned around in her seat from in front of Zuke. "I think I'm going to stay a virgin." The Pison girls were prone to such a statement, bragging about their virginity as if it were a high school state title in the sixteen hundred meters. In some ways, maybe that's just what it was.

The van, which had only been traveling thirty or so miles per hour, slowed even more and then pulled off to the side of the road. There was only an occasional car that inched by.

"Maybe she's going to wait for a plow," Abby said. But Professor Moore opened the door—the temperature inside the van dropped ten degrees—and then, with the engine still running, she jumped out of the van and into the blizzard.

"Just a minute," she called back to her students as if she was going to run into the drugstore to pick up a prescription. The door slammed behind her as she went and the van grew silent. Zuke squinted past Abby through the large window along the side of the van where he could see Moore button her raincoat. Zuke suddenly realized the intelligence that informed Moore's choice of clothing: not fashionable but functional where underneath her rubber-ducky slicker, Moore's bulky sweater surely kept her warm. She could have been heading out on a Maine lobster boat, free from the sting of wind and water. Just in front of Zuke, Katie shivered as if someone had bitten down on a wooden Popsicle stick, a serious pet peeve of hers.

"Let's just leave her," Emma said, looking around the van as if she'd just issued the ultimate dare. "She's old and crazy, right?"

"She's just so weird," Katie said, laughing. "I can't stand it. How did I ever get involved with the woman?"

"For Banquo?" Abby asked.

"Now this here," Jay yelled from the front seat. "Leaving us? That's something you can get fired for." Outside, at the concrete median meant to divide the lanes of north and south traffic, Professor Moore awkwardly swung her legs to the northbound side. Soon she would be out of sight, off to who knew where.

"All right," Zuke said, getting up and sliding along the edge of the seats, "what are you doing, Moore?"

"You better hurry," Jay said. "That old woman is faster than she looks."

"Am I going to die out here with *you* guys?" Katie asked.

"I see a Bennigans," Zuke said as he opened the door to a cold flare of air. "I think we're going to make it."

"Unless we get hit by a snowplow," Abby called from inside the van. Only Zuke, it appeared, was going to brave the elements.

"Or a tractor trailer," Jay added, as Zuke slammed the driver's side door shut.

Outside, the wind blew the snow, just as thick as ever, straight off the lake into Zuke's face as he checked both ways before he crossed to the other side of Lake Shore Drive, to where Professor Moore had climbed her second waist high median. The temperature had dropped; it couldn't have been much over twenty degrees, and the wind gusted, sending the snow into Zuke's bare cheeks and forehead like tiny needles. Moore was evidently headed for Lake Michigan. A rusty light fell over the shore, cast from intermittent street lights that on better weather days were used by walkers, runners, and bikers who exercised along the waterfront paths. The whole feeling was of a doomsday movie, as if Moore and Zuke plowed forward for survival in a nuclear winter.

The skyline of Chicago, at least when it came to what Zuke could make out, had disappeared. Death loomed in the form of a watery snowstorm and ice ran up on the beach like a fast-moving glacier. Not that anyone was in grave danger, but Zuke thought that if he scrambled into the lake and began to swim firm strokes for

Benton Harbor, Michigan on the other side, it wouldn't take him long to be in inescapable trouble.   Twenty or so yards offshore, frothy whitecaps rose and fell to the whistle of the wind and the crash of waves.

A voice from right behind him, it was Abby, yelled something Zuke couldn't hear. She'd come out of the van and followed him to this spot, just on the beach side of the concrete median, where it was apparent she would go no further. She stood, arms folded, leaning against the concrete, appearing more fragile out here in the wind and cold, as if she belonged on hardwood gym floors, inside locker rooms, and anyplace where there was climate control. Zuke smiled. He was glad to see her, and then he covered the remaining distance between him and the lake.

When Zuke reached Professor Moore, she had knelt down at the spot where the water deposited the ice onto the shore, a space about as wide as the free throw lane, and she had her arms, coat, and sweater all down into the water digging under the ice with her hands. There could have been a lost child under there given the frantic way she thrashed in the water. Finally, she pulled out a gray and skull-sized stone, round and smooth, which she held up toward Zuke as if she were Hamlet and breaking from a suicidal soliloquy. Moore's arms shook with the weight of the rock. She was such a thin woman that sometimes her students compared her body to one of a praying mantis. Water dripped from her sleeves and some of it had already frozen into tiny icicles. She began to recite what Zuke thought was poetry; in the spirit of *MacBeth* she could have been a witch herself invoking an incantation, but Zuke couldn't make out many of the words. He heard *rock,* he heard *waves,* and he heard *storm*—appropriate enough, Zuke thought.

"Take it, Eric," Moore said, dropping to her knees just as a wave rose up and crashed into her back. Zuke had misheard what Moore said as *take me* and so as his professor hunched down under the force of a wave as if bracing herself for a tornado, he reached down, put his hands under her armpits and lifted her to the soles of her yellow rain boots.

"The stone," Moore yelled. "Take the stone, you fool!" Zuke felt as if he were in his own tempestuous Shakespearean scene. Moore's rock was too heavy to palm, and so Zuke took it and curled his arm around it as if it were a shot put. He extended his free hand—the casted one—to Moore, who was soaked to the bone and shivering. She accepted it and allowed herself to be helped. Somehow, Moore straightened and put her arm around Zuke.

"Isn't this glorious?" she screamed, a rapt smile on her face as she breathed deeply, turned her face to the dark skies, and let the icy rain beat her flesh.

"Let's go back to the van," Zuke said.

Moore ignored him. "Let this rock commemorate our time together in the English Honor Society." Zuke wondered why it might be coming to an end; he wouldn't graduate for two more years. Then he thought again of his own undeveloped plan for leaving. "It will make a fine paperweight," Moore said, almost as an aside to Zuke not meant for the ears of the water and snow. The wind howled a raucous approval.

"Let's get back to the others," Zuke said as he led Moore toward the van, the way he might have helped his own grandmother cross a busy city street. Abby, collar raised, head down against the wind, walked up to them as they returned to Lake Shore Drive. She looked at Zuke's rock and shook her head in amusement. Abby took up with Professor Moore on the other side, who hooked her hand onto Abby's wrist.

"This never happens to Jordan," she said, beaming that she'd thought to use the expression.

Zuke laughed. "How about I drive?" he asked, and Professor Moore nodded an assent, her wild enthusiasm sloshing away like rain in a storm gutter. Moments ago, she had been exploding with life, seemingly wanting the environment to eat her, but now here she was, gone, and retreating back into that mental mansion she'd built inside her head. Like an exhausted child long past bedtime, Professor Moore accepted Abby's lead to the backseat. Zuke stepped up into the driver's side of the van and sat down next to Jay. "Look what I've got," he said, holding out the rock that Professor Moore had given him. It was still as cold as a block of ice.

"Oh boy," Jay said. "If I'd have known that's what you were doing, I would have come too."

CHAPTER SIXTEEN

The English honor society made it back to campus just before midnight. Other cars on the road hadn't been so lucky—there were at least forty of them in the ditch, something Zuke knew because Jay counted out each snowbound vehicle as they passed it on the road. Driving, Zuke had felt nervously responsible for the lives of those in the van, but he also felt sleepy, which made him more uneasy, and so as he parked the van along the frosty chain-link fence behind McClain Gymnasium, he felt relief at the end of what had been such a long day. But just in the way all that snow that had fallen to the ground was laid out before him, a certain degree of restlessness also still blanketed Zuke's emotions, a covering he couldn't peel off as easily as he hoped to peel off his wet dress socks. As everyone climbed out of the van, Zuke felt in the presence of Abby the way he'd felt for the past year: almost with her but waiting for her to break up with Cheese. A snowball came from toward Burke Administration and thumped into the side of the van. Off in the distance were the squeals of what was probably a snowball fight.

"I'm going to make sure Prof doesn't take a tumble in all this snow," Abby said. Professor Moore stood next to Abby, looking as if she were herself again, a little dreamy and pretty happy. It would be awkward for Zuke to walk to the residence hall with them, and so Zuke was sort of stuck in just saying goodnight and left hoping that maybe the two of them could talk in the next few days about her decision. Zuke alternately felt like making himself move on, possibly seeing what Wendy thought his chances with Marie might be, or taking the completely opposite approach and throwing on a full court press to turn Abby back over to him.

"All right," Zuke said, looking at both women, "you ladies be careful, and I guess I'll see you tomorrow in class." Zuke couldn't read any of Abby's thoughts in her expression.

"Night, night," Abby said. "See you tomorrow." Zuke turned and began to trudge through the snow back to Chapman Hall. He wondered if maybe Abby wouldn't call him again and then for some reason, Marie came shimmering onto the screen of Zuke's thoughts. It was as if someone had slid a VCR tape into the back of his head because now he could suddenly see her: the way she'd looked at the moment she'd leaned over and given him a surprise kiss, and also the disappointment he'd recognized similar to so many of his own disappointments when he'd told Marie about Abby and her stated desire to break up with Cheese. Of course all that had caused Marie to feel as if she was Zuke's second choice. Who in the world would want to be a second choice? Might it be true, Zuke hypothesized, that to be loved at least means being somebody else's first choice?

Whap! A firmly packed snowball struck Zuke squarely in the back. "Get 'em," a voice yelled, and about ten people came from toward Ludwig Center sprinting in his direction and firing snowballs as they came.

If only for Zuke's friends and their t-shirts, he was well known on campus—even if it was a mascot's status—and this made him a treasured target of the masked snowballing marauders. A tightly packed baseball of snow hit Zuke's arm, another the back of his head, while more whizzed all around him cutting into the snow. "Zuke," a female voice yelled. "You're going down." He was just able to make out Lucy the Denny's waitress before he felt a hunk of ice graze his chin. She was dressed in a snowsuit as if she'd come from a snowmobiling vacation in the Upper Peninsula. Another snowball hit him in the neck, and he felt the icy lava trickle down his back toward his waistline. Zuke ran the best he could in the deep snow, all the while being hit with snowballs, until he came to the back door of Chapman, through which he went down the stairs into the basement.

Inside, Zuke felt the solemnity of a storm cellar. He heard one last snowball splay onto the giant metal door through which he'd entered. In contrast to the way Zuke felt, which was that all his energy for basketball and love had been in vain, the rest of the campus was alive with snowstorm energy, the first such storm of the season.

When Zuke reached the fourth floor, it was quiet; probably everyone was in bed or out in the snow. Walking past The Dini and Flabby's room, Zuke noticed a light was on and the door cracked just a little. He tapped on it lightly with the back of his hand and the door inched forward just a little.

"It's open," a shaky voice from inside said. Zuke recognized it as The Dini's, and as Zuke pushed the door open, he felt fear for whatever terrible news The Dini might have just received. It felt like a moment that perhaps The Dini had learned of a death in the family or some terrible accident.

Inside, Zuke found The Dini sitting in his desk chair. Flabby wasn't there. The Dini's room was much different than anyone else's who lived in the hall, namely because it was completely devoid of posters. The Dini had hung pieces of art on all the walls, mostly abstract, some by his art-major friends at Pison, framed and unframed. In the area around his desk, he'd arranged elaborate collages, which featured as different themes, his family, the members of his church, his friends, and those he performed with. Zuke saw a picture from the year before with The Dini and Ratio hugging one another in one of the booths in the basement of the cafeteria.

The Dini took a handkerchief from his bedside table—it was monogrammed P. L. T. in gold cursive—and he blew his nose. Then he wiped his eyes as if he had something in them, but everything about The Dini seemed as if he'd been crying. "Hey Dude," he said, trying to shake off whatever it was that had been bothering him.

"You must really be out of it," Zuke said. The Dini looked for an explanation. "You just called me Dude."

"Oh, Lord Jesus," The Dini said. "Dude, I'm turning into Moon." He laughed and launched into an impression of their friend: "Dude, do you think it's possible to like, Dude, you know Dude, go get a hot chocolate or a brownie or a Gutbuster?"

"Seriously," Zuke asked, "or are you just in character?"

"For real, Dude. I want to go. The Dini is feeling a little overwhelmed tonight." Zuke paused; he'd been hoping his day was over. Could he go another lap in the snow? "C'mon Dude," The

Dini pleaded. "What do you say?"

After clearing Zuke's car of what seemed like at least a foot of snow, The Dini and Zuke were on their way. Although there was a curfew at Pison—it was one o'clock during the week—the men only had to sign in if they were late. The women, on the other hand, faced steeper consequences, although those consequences were unclear. They didn't—as a rule—break curfew.

Out on the roads, conditions were rapidly improving. There were only flurries now and Chicago certainly rests on that northern line near the country's border where the greatest snow removers do their thing. The roads had already been given at least a once over by the fleets of plows that would work through the night.

The Dini tuned the radio to the Pison station. He was a loyal listener, partially because sometimes they played recordings of his performances from various churches, but also because he found the Christian music uplifting. The man's voice on the radio announced that Beau Fleuve had received eight inches of snow. A long list of school closings followed the news.

The road to Crowe's Café went past the Kankakee River Cemetery, which stretched for about a mile along Shermer Boulevard. Upon the sight of two cars parked off to the side of the road, Zuke slowed thinking that he recognized one of the vehicles. "That might be Wendy's Monte Carlo." Zuke wasn't completely sure because he could only make out what was visible in the edges of his headlights. The windows on both cars had just a light dusting of snow so neither had been there too long. The hood of the car, not the Monte Carlo, was up. Zuke couldn't make out what sort of car it was because most of it was blocked by the other. There was a jogging trail along the river and sometimes the more amorous Pison students used the place as a make out spot. That the car might be Wendy's caused The Dini to giggle.

"I hope Cowboy isn't sacrificing his Christian morals," The Dini said. "I'd hate to see Cowboy become President and me have to tell *The Enquirer* that he used to take his woman to the cemetery to get it on. How completely morbid."

"Wasn't Cowboy in bed?" Zuke knew his friend, who often complained about the noise on the hall that kept him up at night, was very unlikely to be up after midnight with classes the next day.

"Good point."

Snow crunched under the tires of Zuke's Chevette as he pulled in behind the white Monte Carlo, and he could see a red racing stripe just visible in the headlights, something that made him more certain that the car was Wendy's. The other car appeared to be a silver Mustang and Zuke immediately thought of Mulligan. Then he saw it: a purple and gold *Pison Football* sticker on the lower right hand corner of the Mustang's rear bumper. Had Mulligan experienced car trouble and Wendy stopped to help?

"Damn it," Zuke said. He didn't like the idea of those two out here by themselves. Zuke brought his red Chevette right up behind the Mustang and stopped.

"What?" The Dini asked, his voice serious—the faux Southern accent gone from his speech.

"I think that's Mulligan's Mustang."

"Well, the hood is up. Maybe Wendy stopped to help."

"Right. Where are they?" The Dini and Zuke got of the Chevette and began to look around. Zuke saw fresh footprints in the snow that led off toward the tracks and the cemetery. The wind stirred the snow up and it created what amounted to an icy fog that clung close to the ground. It was hard to see.

Zuke walked over to where the footprints led up the little ridge to the railroad tracks and out of sight. What could they have been doing? Zuke looked across the street to where there was a gas station, a dry cleaners, and an ice cream stand, all of them dimly lit. The businesses were of course closed, at least for the night and the ice cream stand for the winter. Zuke was just starting to slowly follow the tracks toward the cemetery when, like a power saw fired in a library, a cold scream cut the wintry air. The tracks in the snow pointed out the direction from where the scream had erupted.

"Call the police," Zuke said. He didn't know what was going on but this was Wendy's car, and he'd just heard a scream, one that might have been hers. Zuke, who'd never been in a fight and in junior high was such a timid kid that it used to be that he'd walked two blocks out of his way just to avoid the home of a classmate who picked on him. Charging into the darkness, Zuke's only thoughts were of finding Wendy.

The famous football coach Vince Lombardi had once famously pronounced that fatigue makes cowards of us all, but here in the aftermath of a severe winter storm, Zuke learned something else: love can make a warrior of us all. Not just love of the romantic sort, but the sort of Biblical love that asks for patience and compassion. Zuke didn't feel afraid, he didn't feel concerned for his safety, he only felt the panic of what might be happening to his friend over on the other side of the hill.

"Eric!" The Dini hollered. "You think Wendy's in trouble? Call the police? Are you sure?"

Zuke was frantic and immediately began to stumble in the deep snow as he dug around in his pockets for his car keys. "Call the police! You know where you are. Give them directions." Finally, Zuke had the keys and he stopped so that he could throw them back to The Dini. With the precision he'd only previously used in games of Lincoln Shootout, Zuke grasped the keys with the fingers of his casted arm, took measure of the center of his red hood, and tossed them. Had the hood been a basket, Zuke would have hit nothing but net. The keys skated across the surface of the Chevette and right into The Dini's awaiting hands. "Go get them if you have to."

So desperate was Zuke to run fast, he felt as if he was caught in one of his dreams where he seemed to run on a super-fast treadmill, one which sped in the direction opposite of his intent. He stumbled, skidded and lurched up the hill, arriving at the railroad tracks in what seemed like ten minutes, even though it had been more like ten seconds. As he came up to where the ground leveled off, he saw Mulligan, or at least who he thought was Mulligan, down in the snow on his knees, bent forward, his hands out of sight near the ground. Mulligan clutched something—someone—just in front of the ten-foot high wrought iron fence that separated the cemetery from the land along the tracks.

Two thin arms rose up out of the sleeves of a loose-fitting coat, and whoever it was flailed helplessly against Mulligan's loggish arms and barrel torso.

As Zuke got closer, he could see the side of Wendy's face and that Mulligan was trying to pin her arms to the ground while at the same time he took swoops at Wendy's face and neck delivering something between a kiss and a lick. The two were both still fully dressed, and Mulligan was intent on burrowing his hips powerfully down as he tried to separate Wendy's legs. Zuke caught a glimpse of the side of Mulligan's face—it was unmistakably him—and his fellow resident of Chapman Hall looked only determined, lost in his struggle for Wendy. He was seemingly an animal out there in the storm, taking what he wanted. With only a hitch in Zuke's stride to take it all in, he bounded over one rail, then the other as he crossed the tracks and began the descent down to where Mulligan lay atop Wendy.

At first Mulligan didn't notice Zuke, who did the only thing he could think to do, which was to continue his sprint and try to punt Mulligan's head as if it were fourth and long, his team backed deep into the opponent's end zone. Whether it was because of the snow, which made everything as if Zuke were running on the surface of an ice rink, or that Mulligan caught a last-second glimpse of Zuke leaving him just enough time to flinch a little, Mulligan was able to get his head down and his forearm up for protection. Zuke's right dress shoe caught Mulligan in the cheek, a glancing, carpet-burn sort of contact, which caused Mulligan to bring both hands to his face.

Mulligan quickly regained himself and reached into the outside breast pocket of his black wool pea coat for the knife that he nearly always carried there, the same hunting knife which had contributed to his earlier probation and week-long suspension from Pison and the football team.

Zuke's errant kick had thrown him off balance, and so as he turned back toward Mulligan, it was natural for him to swing his left arm—the one with the cast—toward Mulligan's head. Zuke's arm contacted Mulligan's temple at the same time Mulligan's knife—so sharp that Zuke didn't even feel it—sliced through Zuke's coat and put a deep cut into the skin just above his bicep. Right then, with Zuke and Mulligan's faces close, Zuke thought he caught the strong scent of whiskey.

It wasn't the knife wound that lit up Zuke's head like liquid soap had been poured into his eyes, but the rattling of his broken scaphoid bone against Mulligan's head. Zuke's body and soul quaked at the pain.

During this brief and savage interaction, Wendy felt around in the snow closest to her, where there were plenty of the stones that lined both sides of the railroad tracks. Once she secured a firm grip on one, she only needed to roll over to reach Mulligan. Her body, still raging against the way Mulligan had been wallowing all over her and taking swipes at her face and neck with his wet mouth, was filled with the extra-strength power of adrenaline.

Lying next to Wendy, Mulligan was regaining his shaky consciousness and getting his fingers wrapped around his hunting knife when Wendy lifted what had become her rock, raggedly uneven and nearly the size of a baseball, and she smashed it down toward Mulligan's forehead as if she were intent on driving a railroad spike into one of the ties. Ever the nimble athlete, Mulligan got his head turned just a little, and so Wendy's strike glanced off his big forehead, not quite as deadly as it could have been. Still, the impact was nearly that of a head on collision during a football kickoff return, and the result was that Mulligan was knocked clean from consciousness.

It was just after 1:30 a.m. when The Dini, Wendy, and her father came walking into the curtained area where Zuke was in the emergency room. With twelve fresh stitches in his arm, Zuke had just received the results of his x-ray from a doctor, and he was now free to go.

"How are you?" Wendy asked. "I mean are you going to be okay?"

"I'm pretty good," Zuke said, surprised at the way Wendy looked. "Twelve stitches," he added, touching with his good arm the spot where he'd received them. Zuke had expected to see Wendy frazzled and on the edge of some sort of breakdown, probably in and out of sobbing tears. Perhaps, once again, Zuke had seen too many movies. Wendy only looked a little tired and mostly worried about Zuke's condition. The Dini, on the other hand, looked bad. All the life had gone out of his swoopy hair and his usual spray of personality had been twisted off. The dean, Wendy's father, hung back and Zuke couldn't gauge his demeanor. Zuke raised his casted arm. "My wrist is still broken of course but nothing moved out of place. They've got me on some pretty good stuff for the pain. How about you? You look better than expected."

"She's pretty pissed off," the dean said. Zuke was surprised to hear the dean use such a word. He hadn't previously imagined Mr. Parrot saying something as coarse as "piss."

"I'm fine," Wendy said. "I can't believe what an idiot I am." Zuke didn't even have to ask her what had happened. She just launched right into the story: "Mulligan and I both worked tonight. I practically didn't even see him. Turns out he brought a bottle of whiskey to the kitchen and took swigs of it off and on all night. We were real busy and there were three cooks working, all of them drinking too. You know, ever since I realized Mulligan went to school with us, I've sort of relaxed about him. Not that I like him—understand you—but you know, I sort of accepted him and quit worrying. I thought I'd overreacted."

"We saw he had his hood up," Zuke said. Over by the door The Dini nodded. He'd obviously already been over all this. "That's why you stopped?"

"Yeah, real genius huh? Outsmarted by a doofus like Mulligan."

The dean put his hand on Wendy's shoulder. "Honey," he said. "It was an honest mistake. You thought he needed help."

"When I saw him pulled over along the side of the road, I was thinking that I didn't like him but it would be pretty selfish of me just to leave him. It's not like we had to be buddies. I figured I'd just give him a lift back to campus, and he could call security. The really stupid thing I did was get out of the car. I thought maybe he just needed a jump."

"I insist that she keep jumper cables in the car," the dean said, shaking his head. Zuke could see the dean was feeling pretty guilty about the jumper cables, as if any father who insisted on such a thing was just asking for trouble.

"I smelled the booze right away," Wendy said.

"Drunk as a skunk is what he was," The Dini added disapprovingly.

"He came on real strong, grabbed my sleeve, and got right in my face. I yanked away from him and moved around to the other side of the car. As he came after me, I ran a few steps out into the snow but he was way too fast. He picked me up like I didn't weigh a thing and took me over to the other side of the railroad tracks. He kept telling me that he knew I wanted him. He'd seen me staring at him all the time at work." Wendy shivered now as if she were out in the cold again. "God knows what would have happened if you two hadn't shown up."

"You got a pretty good blow in yourself," Zuke said. "What's going on with Mulligan?"

The dean swallowed hard before he talked. He looked like he wanted to break something. "He's going to be charged with sexual assault and attempted rape."

"He's got a concussion," Wendy said, "and some abrasions on his face."

"He's going to jail as soon as he's healthy enough," the dean added. "I hope that's in an hour or two."

"Can we please get out of here?" The Dini asked. "The Dini doesn't like hospitals. The Dini needs some rest."

"Let's go," the dean agreed. When Zuke grabbed his things, and rose from his seat on the edge of a hospital gurney, the dean put his arm around him. "Thank you, son," he said. "Only the grace of God brought you and Phillip to the roadside, but you all still had to do something. I'm very grateful to you for your bravery."

"Same for your daughter," Zuke said. "I don't know what would have happened to me if Wendy hadn't knocked him a good one."

Wendy smiled at this and gave off a sort of growl as she raised her arm and made a muscle with her bicep.

"You're both heroes," The Dini said.

Wendy put her arms around Zuke and The Dini. "We're all a bunch of heroes," she said, sort of tugging everyone with her arms for the door. "Let's get the frip out of here." The four of them, with the dean hugging Wendy on one side and Zuke on the other, walked down the hall of the hospital emergency room, all of them in each other's arms.

CHAPTER SEVENTEEN

Tuesday, the morning after Mulligan's attack on Wendy, Zuke was very late to Expository Writing. The area above his bicep throbbed from where Mulligan had cut him, but it hurt far less than the time he'd slid over a rock playing touch football, shredded the skin on his shinbone, and played in a summer basketball tournament the next day. Besides, if Zuke had learned anything from his parents, it was that you went to work when you were able.

When Zuke entered Professor Moore's fourth-floor classroom in Burke Administration, he sat in the back of the room in one of the few empty seats next to Katie, the Duran Duran obsessive from the English Honor Society. She turned and looked at him as if she were his mother with some serious questions. The class was filled to capacity, twenty-five students, and as Zuke came in, Professor Moore nodded a greeting from where she sat off to the side on the window ledge. Jay Schweitzer stood behind the podium giving a talk, and on the chalkboard, he'd written the word *structure*. Underneath, he had a list going which included *line breaks, punctuation, syllabics, and rhyme scheme.*

Zuke's chair squeaked just a little when he sat down, a sound which caused Abby to turn from her seat from near the front. She waved to him, twisting back and forth the wrist of her left hand, a movement meant to emphasize her empty ring finger. Abby's expression was more ominous than excited, as if maybe the ring had been stolen rather than she'd called it off with Cheese. In response, Zuke mouthed the word, "Wow," and she shook her head, an action which Zuke read as *what a mess.*

As a result of what Mulligan had done, and especially of what he'd tried to do, *the mess* didn't seem so bad anymore to Zuke, as if Abby and Marie, who liked whom, and whom everyone would end up with—these were all just interesting matters that Zuke had a good enough life to be able to take the time to sort through. Thinking back to the hours he'd been in the hospital after Mulligan's attack, he could see that there had been a certain amount of exhilaration at the circumstances which could have been perceived as offering the opportunity to do a great thing. But Zuke knew it was just dumb luck (or dumb bad luck) that the situation had arrived at all, that he hadn't done any more than a lot of people would have done; in fact, Zuke was pretty sure he'd have taken a severe beating or worse if Wendy hadn't chipped in with her own rock thump to Mulligan's head.

Maybe, Zuke thought, he and Wendy had found greatness together. This made him smile, but then he thought of how silly it all was, this desire for greatness, over which at least in this case, he'd had no control. He was to some degree changed—not in the way he'd imagined he would be—but he did, at least for now, appreciate the day-to-day aspects of his life. There was also a pretty important lesson when it came to a person such as Mulligan: people can't be read absolutely and that to use the phrase "I can just tell" about a person is to choose a position of naïve ignorance.

It used to be that Zuke believed if only he was able to lead the Indiana Hoosiers to a national title in basketball, he would be considered great and the life that followed would naturally be the product of his greatness. There would be a great job, a great wife, and great prestige in his community. He had also connected happiness to his ability, or lack of ability, to gain the attention of a beautiful girl. How absurd. No matter who he was with or what he had done, life would often be muddled; the puzzle pieces would constantly have to be worked and reworked until it was over. Zuke had wanted the kiss at the end of the movie *Princess Bride*, or at the very least the one in the last scene of *Weird Science,* when the confrontation was over, the bad boyfriend had been set aside, and it was clear who ought to be with whom. Zuke wanted to arrive at the point in his life where it was obvious that only happiness lay ahead, but now he could see that his life was only as clear as he made it and only as clear as the choices those around him made. Plus, there were random events that were of no one's doing such as the ice storm that blew the transformer that changed the way Moon's night with Edie had gone. Abby had been engaged and now for some reason she wasn't. Today she may or may not want to begin a relationship with him. Marie had seemed every bit as compatible with Zuke as Abby had. Life is more complex than finding "that special someone." There was more to happiness than that.

"Notice in Frost's 'Woodpile,'" Jay continued, dressed as if he were already a Professor of English in a tweed jacket with elbow patches, "how regular the syllabics become in line eighteen." Earlier that morning, after what had amounted to a nap in his room, Zuke woke and felt that he ought to call his parents, at least tell them about Mulligan. The last his father had heard, Zuke had a date coming up, thought maybe he'd get some practice in even with the cast, and maybe even receive a medical red shirt for basketball. But what Zuke had wanted to do right as he woke up, was go straight to Coach Miller's office and tell him that he didn't want to be on the basketball team. He knew if he called home that he might lose his resolve or that his dad would say something to convince him to wait. Within this stretch of life where Zuke felt so much confusion, he knew himself well enough to know that when he got in the mood to confront his life, to face whatever it was that he'd kept pushing away to deal with another day, that when the feeling struck to do something, he needed to act right away because he knew the feeling wouldn't last long. And so he did it: quit the basketball team, one of the most decisive actions with regards to his future that Zuke had ever taken.

Coach Miller had been much more reasonable than Zuke thought possible. In fact, his response was such that Zuke began to wonder if he hadn't built up other obstacles in his mind to imaginary magnitudes. "Our locker room is always open to you," Coach had said. "If you ever feel like coming back, just come back." And so for the first time since Zuke was six years old, he wasn't on a basketball team.

From her seat next to Zuke in Moore's classroom, Katie nudged Zuke's arm with her elbow. Everyone was looking at him. He hadn't heard why. "Just please leave Mr. Zaucha alone on your way out," Professor Moore said, smiling just a little at Zuke's lack of awareness. She was back in front of the room, Jay was gathering his notes, and it was as if somehow Zuke had become the dreamy one while Professor Moore had transformed to the soul firmly rooted in reality. Zuke could see on the faces of his classmates that some of them already had heard about his night; others looked curious, wanting to know more, but most of them left without saying anything.

"I'm going to call Phillip," Jay said on his way out. The two of them were good friends. "I'm just sure he's ready to spill everything."

"He might even make some stuff up," Zuke said, although he didn't really believe it. The Dini was usually pretty silly and right in the middle of the Pison social buzz, but Mulligan's attack had hit him emotionally hard. Earlier in the morning, when Zuke had been coming from Coach Miller's office, he had seen The Dini at the Humble Prayer chapel, down on his knees at the altar. Zuke hoped against his better judgment that the church would be as faithful to The Dini as he had been to it.

"I guess that means me too," Professor Moore said, her arms full of a messy stack of papers and two Norton Anthologies. Her comment seemed to be a hint that Zuke could start talking, but instead he pulled "The Royal Castle" from his Trapper Keeper and handed it to her.

"Oh," she said. "I thought you might need a little extra time on this." Zuke smiled and Katie patted his cast softly as she got up and left. The floor creaked as Professor Moore followed her. "Toot-a-loo," Professor Moore said on her way out. Zuke, who had a nicotine-like habit of waiting for Glory, hadn't even realized he'd been doing it until it was just the two of them in the room.

Zuke tried to feel a happy ending, knew that he wanted one, but what would it be? Abby from Cheese right to Zuke, when only days before she'd accepted a marriage proposal? "Not engaged," Abby said, slipping into the chair that Katie had vacated. She wore a long gray sweater with a thick black belt around her waist, black tights, and high black boots. She had a theory which Zuke had adopted for himself: the worse she felt, the more care she put into her appearance. She looked beautiful to Zuke, if not a little thin.

"Did you do that for me?" Zuke asked about the ring.

"Did you want me to do it for you?" Abby ran her hand from her forehead through her red hair, tucking a strand of it behind her ear. Zuke thought he could watch her do that for the rest of his life. That was the movies talking again.

"I don't know," he said. "You're fantastic: good looking, athletic, a reader, funny, and you don't seem to mind my company." He laughed. "That last one is the big one." Zuke smiled and shrugged his shoulders. "You were engaged. You're not engaged. Now what?"

"I don't know. I've been thinking about it, and I guess I liked being the big basketball star's girlfriend." Abby sat up in her chair and leaned toward Zuke. "I liked how hard and for how long you pursued me." Outside in the hallway, two professors walked by and peeked in at them. It wasn't such an unusual sight to see Abby and Zuke in class talking. In fact, most of the English faculty probably rooted for the couple to happen. "That sounds vain I know," Abby continued, "but I mean it in an insecure way. Somehow you and Brett worked together to make me feel like I was worth somebody's time."

"Abby, of course…"

"I know, but still, why wouldn't I like all that attention? And you're one to talk. You don't give yourself enough credit." Zuke thought about that. What did he deserve credit for?

A ray of sunshine reflected on the desktop between Zuke and Abby. Outside in the hall, students began to file in for the next round of classes, and the peaceful silence that had permeated Burke Administration began to melt away. It looked so blue and bright outside the windows; it was as if Beau Fleuve had replaced its celestial light bulbs. "If you tell me you want us to give it a try right now, I'll do it," Abby said. Her eyes had a salty shine to them, and Zuke could see that she trusted him. It was a remarkable quality for him to see, something that caused Zuke to think maybe he could be (or already was) trustworthy. Abby continued: "But I think I ought to try and be good at being me for awhile, whatever that means, by myself. We've got a lot of time, me and you, to end up together."

Zuke nodded. If he and Abby chose to, they could take every class together for the rest of their undergraduate education. That is unless Zuke transferred. "That's a good phrase," Zuke said, always an admirer of the words Abby found to express herself. "Be good at being me. I think I'll try that too." Zuke thought that he'd spent at least the last five years obsessed with some girl thinking that if he could only date her then he'd be happy. Abby and Zuke sat in silence thinking and then, maybe just as a way of avoidance with regards to the status of his and Abby's relationship, Zuke said, "I quit the basketball team."

"It wasn't making you very happy." Zuke was surprised at how quickly Abby had responded to what he said. It was almost as if she was expecting it. "I never cared, you know, that you didn't play." Zuke remembered how excited she'd seemed when Cheese scored his record-breaking basket. But of course she liked Cheese; she nearly loved him, or she did love him, just not quite enough at the moment to promise to love him forever.

"Yeah, yeah," Zuke said, urging himself to get up before he gave in to what he was starting to feel, which was the desperate urge to take up Abby on what she said, that she'd date him right now if that's what he thought was best. "I just couldn't get my head right about it."

Abby got up from her chair, also looking none too sure of their decision, if they'd even made one. They were not, these two, confident relationship navigators. Abby opened her arms for a hug and as Zuke embraced her, he felt a twang in his arm and the stitches pull a little. It was a rather awkward moment after that, the two of them in the room with three floors of steps to traverse, plus a quarter-mile to the front of Chapman Hall where presumably Abby would say goodbye and continue on to Barrett. The two walked out into the hall and headed for the stairs, and Zuke kept thinking that although it felt like the end of a relationship, that he felt as if he were saying goodbye to a good friend whom he may never see again, he would in fact see Abby the very next day in American

Lit, and then the following day in linguistics, and that her presence would continue to be a part of his life for the rest of the semester, and then four days a week again for the entire spring. With all that time, Zuke figured, Abby was right. There was no need to hurry. Christmas break was ahead and they could both just think about what had just happened. No matter what Zuke wanted, he couldn't imagine a scenario where it was the right thing to do for Abby to jump from an engagement with Cheese to his steady girlfriend.

As the two made their way down the arch of steps that curled away from the outside of Burke, Zuke, without looking at Abby, reached for her free hand and took it, an action which she accepted and reciprocated by giving his fingers a firm squeeze. The two walked away toward the clock tower, then around it on the path which had been plowed clean by a blade attached to the front of a lawn mower tractor. All around them there were the many footprints in the snow that crisscrossed central campus, remnants of the snowball war from the night before. Hundreds of students walked to and from class, and no one paid any special attention to Zuke and Abby.

"I just wanted to see," Zuke said, releasing Abby's hand when they got to the steps leading up to Chapman Hall. He meant see what it would be like to hold her hand and walk across campus as if they were finally together.

"Me too," she responded and looked up at the sky as if a message might be written there. "It was nice."

"Tomorrow," Zuke said, "American Lit." He felt the moment tugging at him to just keep walking with Abby, to take her out, to take her for a drive, or to ask her—he didn't know—to go to Toys R Us and buy a sled. With no basketball obligations, Zuke realized it was now possible to take a more dramatic trip than that: they could drive up to O'Hare, run his credit card for two plane tickets, and end up anywhere.

"Tomorrow," Abby said, slowly turning away from Zuke and looking as if she might want him to stop her. Zuke watched her go until she disappeared around the Tree of Knowledge which glistened with the water that melted in the sun and trickled over what was left of the ice. An emotional wrench in Zuke's chest gave his heart a suffocating twist.

Just as Zuke entered the fourth floor hall of Chapman, he saw a police officer walking toward him, and Zuke assumed that he'd come as a follow up regarding Mulligan. "Good afternoon," Zuke said as a greeting, as an assumed beginning to the conversation they were about to have. But the officer nodded his head hello and continued past Zuke to the stairwell. Feeling confused, Zuke looked down to the far end just in time to see Barry Ruiz roll his wheelchair into the elevator accompanied by two more officers.

"Hey," Cowboy whispered, causing Zuke to jump. He'd been hiding behind the restroom door. "Are they gone?"

"The cops? And Barry?"

"Yeah. You won't believe it. It was Barry who's been causing the building to shake, doing something with high frequencies and his computer. That's why he had those giant speakers."

"He got arrested?"

"There was all that damage from the busted water pipes. I think they're saying he's somehow responsible. They found a whole bunch of notes on his computer for sabotaging stuff on campus. Remember Barry and all that Captain Midnight stuff?"

"What?"

"With the HBO signal?" Cowboy looked at his watch. "I'll tell you later. I'm going to lunch with Wendy and her dad."

While Cowboy hurried down the stairs, Zuke moved out into the hall feeling sort of spun, as if his world had been unraveled from a giant spool on a high powered sewing machine. With an attempted rape on Wendy, Barry apprehended by the police, no more basketball, and now possibly no more pursuit of Abby, many central features of Zuke's life had been smudged or erased.

Once in his room, Zuke took a deep breath, sat down at his desk, and once again looked to his *Say Anything* poster and the picture of Lloyd Dobler. Cusack looked so passively determined, dressed in his long trench coat and holding the boom box above his head as if he would happily make like a telephone pole and wait indefinitely for Diane to re-issue her love. Zuke had first seen the movie with Colleen Flannery, and they'd had a fight afterwards, a fight that rose up out of Zuke's belief that when the Diane Court character had given Dobler a pen as a break up gift, that character was treating Dobler as Colleen had often treated Zuke. He'd never been able to believe that Colleen really wanted to be with him; maybe she hadn't, but quite possibly it was Zuke's own insecurity that convinced Colleen she could do better. Zuke took notice of Abby's observation that he didn't give himself enough credit. He patted the boom box on his desk, the one he'd bought for the very reason that it looked just like the one on the movie poster. The cassette for the *Say Anything* soundtrack was right there in the player ready to roll on Peter Gabriel's "In Your Eyes." Briefly Zuke considered going over to Abby's dorm and playing the song outside her window, but that wasn't even needed. Hadn't she already said she'd date if he wanted to? Somehow Zuke felt that the offer might be one of those offers that was really just a tactful way of saying no.

Zuke placed his finger on the play button, ready to lean back, kick his feet up on his desk, and close his eyes to make an escape into the words of the song. He mashed the button halfway down but didn't engage it. His arms ached right along with Dobler's, who seemed to hold his boom box as Atlas had held the world, as a welcome romantic penance that could last for as long as Diane's eternity. Zuke, following the model of Cusack's character, had always believed that what he needed to do was get to know Abby, and that if he persevered along that line, she would eventually fall for him. But thoughts of Marie, and how he hadn't pursued her at all, those thoughts gave him pause.

Zuke took his finger off the play button and looked at his bookshelf full of movies. This wasn't the entirety of his collection from home, but it represented some of his favorites: *Weird Science*— two guys make a woman from a Barbie doll; *Sixteen Candles, The Karate Kid, The Pick-up Artist, Pretty in Pink;* they were nearly all the same movie, teens falling in love with happy endings. Kisses at the end. Zuke picked up *Weird Science* from the shelf, and suddenly he felt silly that he'd seen the movie so many times. *Glory,* he thought. *Bird.* These were people he knew and that he gave them all nicknames sort of objectified them, caused them to have more in common with Kelly LeBrock's Lisa in the foggy bathroom doorway than actual real people.

What Zuke and his friends really did, he realized, was sit around and make up fictional characters to *love.* He popped *Weird Science* hard against the edge of the desk and broke a fault line through the center of the case. He pulled on the edge of it, opened up the cassette, and used his fingers to splay out the tape before he threw it into the garbage. He repeated this process on six movies or so until he came to *Say Anything.* That one he didn't break, but instead held tightly in his good right hand, rubbing his thumbnail on some crusty tape that covered Cusack's head on the cardboard case. Zuke had watched at least parts of the movie once a week since he bought the video tape nearly a year ago. He'd watched it so much that several of the scenes had worn thin and were barely visible on the television. Zuke carried the tape over to the window, which he raised. It wasn't that he necessarily objected to the film, but he didn't need to put so much stock in it, use it as a foundation from which to live his life.

Awkwardly, with his right hand, Zuke coiled his arm as if he were going to throw a Frisbee, and he sent *Say Anything* into flight, high above the snow between Chapman and the Hughes Hall of Science. Airborne, the cover of the video separated from the tape and floated in the wind off to the right toward Burke before it landed in the snow. Zuke closed the window, thinking maybe he should go outside later and throw away the mess he'd made. His broken wrist ached a little, the cut on his arm had its own little heartbeat, and as Zuke went to his desk, he reached up for the poster which had hung near him for over a year, taking it down and rolling it up tightly before he pulled a rubber band from his desk drawer to secure it. He put the poster under his bed. On the corner of his desk, sat the tattered book *Illusions* that Marie had given him. He thought to call her. He thought to take the book down to the library or the coffee shop and see who he could meet there. But then he walked over to his door and locked it. He lay on his bed, took one of his pillows and propped it under his bad wrist to elevate it. The book was small and easy to hold and so with Zuke's good hand he began to read his present from Marie.

CHAPTER EIGHTEEN

Eight weeks passed after the night that Zuke bashed Mulligan's temple with his cast and Wendy delivered that nasty knockout blow. Under a dark January sky that threatened snow, Zuke walked across the campus of Pison College, several large business-sized envelopes tucked under his arm. Ice crunched under his boots. He was on the way to physical therapy, a last collaboration between him and the Pison athletic department, and Zuke wished Marie still lived on campus to look out the window at him.

Mulligan had recovered from his concussion and his trial was on the horizon. Cowboy and Wendy were firmly a couple, having even brought their families together for a New Year's Eve dinner. Abby had returned from Christmas break re-engaged to Cheese; she and Zuke had not talked about this nor did he have any intentions of raising the subject. The old Zuke would have created a dramatic scene—perhaps in the spirit of how Lloyd Dobler had told Diane Court to destroy the note he'd written her following their first sex— but this new Zuke couldn't see any point in demanding the locket back. What would he do, re-gift it? Sell it? Have it melted down into something else? Abby could keep the locket, or she could unload it however she saw fit. He had of course seen Abby nearly every weekday, and although the two remained friendly in their classes, they both seemed to make it a point to not sit by one another, to no longer carry on with passed notes and whispers in class. Whatever it was that had caused Abby and Zuke to want to be together had burned off like a fog in morning sunshine when they were free to do so. Those who knew Cheese said he was a changed man, humbled by the near loss of his girlfriend, and that he now showed regular appreciation for her. This, Zuke hoped, would last.

From the time he and Wendy had battled Mulligan in the snow by the railroad tracks, to the day classes had started for the spring semester, Zuke had tried to push everything—Abby, Marie, basketball, Mulligan—out of his mind so that he could focus on living the life before him: school, rehabilitation of his wrist, friends, and family. He'd written letters to his grandmother, his cousins in Utah, and his aunt in Hollywood, and he'd even begun his own workouts the best he could with the broken wrist. Zuke had told his father he was going to explore a transfer and this was something he did on his own, unlike after high school when his mother had completed most of the paperwork. Among the parcels tucked under Zuke's arms, were applications for Illinois, Indiana, and Purdue University. Also there was one for St. Joseph's College, just in case Zuke wanted to try and keep up with basketball at some other small school.

Zuke had made one exception from his plan to focus on being good at being himself, an exception which was now tucked under his arm. When he arrived at the blue mailbox just outside of McClain Gymnasium, the first snowflakes of what would be another big storm began to fall, and from under his arm he pulled a fifth manila envelope, this one addressed to Marie Barrett of Canterbury Lane, Beau Fleuve, Illinois. Zuke had not been able to push her completely from his thoughts and so on New Year's Day, after a night of television watching with his parents, and in place of a day of watching football games with his father, Zuke had read *Illusions* again, this time taking notes. It was a book that hypothesized a messiah that declined the role of dying for humanity, a book that supposed the physical limits of the world were an illusion, and a book which theorized a person was more in control of his or her own life than one might think. The letter to Marie was Zuke doing his part to make his life his own, as were the application materials to the various colleges and universities. A person controls some aspects of his or her life; other aspects are left to something else.

Zuke had read Marie's notes in the book too, and took a chance adding some of his own in the margins next to hers. *Illusions* was the first book Zuke had ever read twice. Already, he'd purchased a second copy for himself, along with four other books, all of which he'd bought for under ten dollars at a used book store. The act of stalking the shelves for unread treasures was like an identity sweater, an act Zuke had tried on to see how it fit, and he felt he'd arrived at the dawn of a new age for himself, one where books were going to matter as much or more than the movies.

A snowflake hit Marie's envelope right where the "B" in Beau Fleuve was and the ink ran a little on the page. Also in the package with the book was a twelve page double-spaced letter that Zuke had written to Marie in response to his reading. It was by far the longest piece that Zuke had ever written, and Zuke hoped the sheer volume of it would cause Marie to reconsider the notion she was finished with him. This was in part still some of the old Zuke, the kind of young man who thought if he did something as grand as hold a boom box over his head, then something dramatic was bound to happen.

When Zuke read *Illusions*, it had been as if Marie were sitting next to him, a strange sort of telepathy where the young woman she had been during her own reading flew across time and physical distance to sit next to Zuke in the form of her notes on the page. From his past experiences, Zuke knew that he risked an abnormal—out of this world—intensity in his desire to begin to know Marie, but this time he didn't feel overly responsible to temper that enthusiasm. This time Zuke felt confident that his connection had risen out of something more concrete than a fantasy erected from the bricks of the endless movies he had seen or from speculations built by him and his Brothers while they tossed pennies back and forth into plastic cups. This time his desire to connect was fueled by the real gift of a book Marie had given him on an actual date.

The experience of the reading and writing, the flow of energy that had been produced for writing by the reading, it had all caused Zuke, for the first time in his life, to feel as if he'd chosen the right major, even if the reasons for his doing so had initially been wrong. Zuke had become an English major for Abby, but he was going to stay one for books, for the conversations that could arise between people. Confident of his actions, Zuke pulled the handle of the mailbox down, and when he did, a scene from the movie *When Harry Met Sally* leapt into his mind—the one where Sally goes through an elaborate mailing routine: a letter in, close the flap to the mailbox, open it back up, check to see if the letter has gone down, and then on to the next letter where the process repeats itself. Since seeing Sally in the movie send out her mail in that fashion, Zuke had always emulated her idiosyncratic habit.

Now Zuke placed his own stack of packages into the nose of the mail chute, hesitating before he let them all plunge into the rectangular well of letters. He knew his applications, Marie's book, and his letter would reach their destinations. Marie might write him back. Zuke released the stack of packages, pulled his hand away, and let the metal door clang shut. Zuke's movies told him to make sure the packages hadn't somehow got caught in the door. But for once, he ignored the impulse. For once, Zuke walked away.

William J. Torgerson

William Torgerson is an assistant professor in the Institute For Writing Studies at St. John's University in Queens, New York. The son of two English teachers, Torgerson graduated in 1994 from Olivet Nazarene University, where he majored in English Education and spent a lot of time sitting on the bench of the school's basketball team. Over an eleven year span, Torgerson coached basketball and taught every grade six through twelve in the public schools of Indiana and North Carolina. He earned a masters degree in English Education at the University of North Carolina Charlotte and an M.F.A. degree in creative writing from Georgia College and State University. Currently, he lives in Connecticut with his wife and two daughters, and he can often be found listening to books or lectures on CD while making his regular commute into work.

Readers can reach him through his website:

WWW.WILLIAMTORGERSON.COM

About the Cover...

The *Love on the Big Screen* cover photo shows the Campus Theatre building at Georgia College & State University in Milledgeville, Georgia.

Constructed in 1935, the theatre operated a half-block from campus until it closed in 1983. After serving as downtown office space, the Campus Theatre was purchased by the university in 2008 and converted into space for its Department of Theatre, including a black box performance theatre, and the college bookstore, Box Office Books. Reopening in 2010, the front of the Campus Theatre looks the same as when it opened in 1935 and the inside retains some of the original brickwork and wood flooring.

Georgia College is the designated public liberal arts university for the state, providing the educational experience expected from an esteemed private college at the affordable price of a public university. Georgia College focuses on exceptional teaching in the classroom and experiential learning beyond the classroom.

Cover Photo by:
        Timothy L. Vacula
        University Communications
        Georgia College & State University

CPSIA information can be obtained at www.ICGtesting.com
Printed in the USA
BVOW071549050612

291711BV00003B/88/P